When Thiye ruled in Hjemur
Came strangers riding there,
And three were dark and one was gold,
And one like frost was fair.

Fair was she, and fatal as fair,
And cursed who gave her ear;
Now men are few and wolves are more,
And the Winter drawing near.

Vanye looked up between the pillars that crowned the conical hill called Morgaine's Tomb, and the declining sun shimmered there like a puddle of gold just disturbed by a plunging stone. In that shimmer appeared the head of a horse, and its forequarters, and a rider, and the whole animal; white rider on grey horse . . . The rider descended the snowy hill into shadows across his path—substantial . . . He knew that he should set spurs to the mare, yet he felt curiously numb, as though he had been awakened from one dream and plunged into the midst of another. He looked into the tanned woman's face within the fur hood . . . "I know you," he said then.

GATE OF IVREL

by
C. J. Cherryh

Introduction by
Andre Norton

DAW Books, Inc.
Donald A. Wollheim, Publisher
1633 Broadway, New York, N.Y. 10019

FIRST PRINTING, MARCH 1976

6   7   8   9   10   11   12

PRINTED IN U.S.A.

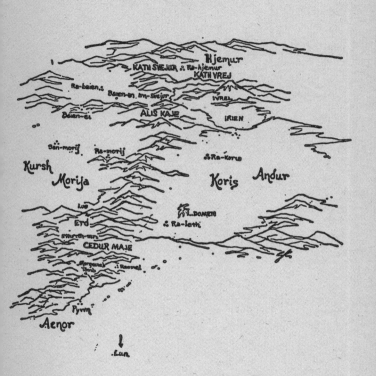

Hjemur
KATH SHEJUR   ⁂ Ra-hjemur
KATH VREJ
Ra-baien.⁂   IVREL
Baien-en   Irn-Svejar
Baien-ei   ALIS KAJE   IRIEN

San-morij   Ra-morij
⁂ Ra-Koris

Kursh   Koris   Andur
Morija

Lun
Erd   ⁂ Ra-leth
⁂DOMEN
Khursh-en
CEDUR MAJE
Morganel   .: Raswell
Tomb

Pyvvn
Aenor

.Lun

Introduction

by Andre Norton

There are those among us who are compulsive readers—who will even settle a wandering eye on a scrap of newspaper on the bus floor if nothing better offers. Books flow in and out of our lives in an unending stream. Some we remember briefly, others bring us sitting upright, tense with suspense, our attention enthralled until the last word on the last page is digested. Then we step regretfully from the world that author has created, and we know that volume will be chosen to stand on already too tightly packed shelves to be read again and again. In addition one is going to call other readers, wave this trophy bannerwise in the air—see what *I* have found!—proud to be the first among friends to have the great excitement of discovery.

This excitement does not come too often in a reader's lifetime of turning hundreds of pages. I have felt it perhaps only a dozen times in more than forty years of extensive reading. For me it was sparked by such books as *The Lord of the Rings,* the work of David Mason, a couple of A. Merritt's titles (which opened at the time a whole new world of speculation), plus some other favorites which I continue to reread with as much pleasure the second, fifth, tenth time as I did the first.

But never since reading *The Lord of the Rings* have I been so caught up in any tale as I have been in *Gate of Ivrel.* I do not know the author, but her talent is one I must envy. She has drawn an entirely believable hero on an alien and enchanting world, working in bits of customs, beliefs, and history so cleverly that it now certainly exists—somewhere. For such a creation does not remain only in the mind, it begins to take on life and breath, depth, to stand complete forever.

The usual flaw in any fantasy novel is that the hero is the typical super strongman so it needs frantic action and constant movement to preserve the illusion of life. Ms. Cherryh's dour Vanye is already alive from the moment he steps onto the stage she has set for him. Certainly he is no matchless hero of the Conan type, but he possesses a strong code of honor which holds him to a course of action he inwardly loathes and fears. The reader can *believe* fully in each of his doubts, understanding his wavering, and his constant fight against what he considers his weaknesses. One cheers when he pulls some small triumph from the shadow of defeat, even when he breaks the honor which is his last pathetic possession, because he sees there is something here greater than all conventional oaths and codes.

In *Gate of Ivrel* there are indeed no supermen or superwomen—rather there are very human beings, torn by many doubts and fears, who are driven by a sense of duty to march ahead into a dark they are sure holds death. Ancient evils hang like noisome cobwebs, the stubbornness of unbelievers wrecks again and again their quest. Wounded, nearly at the edge of their strength, shamefully foresworn in the eyes of all they could once call kin, they continue to push on to the last test of all.

Few books have produced such characters as to draw a reader with them, completely out of this mundane world. Here the careful evocation of a highly complex alien civilization is so skillfully managed that one accepts it all without any longer remembering that this is a creation of an imagination. It might be actual history—from another plane.

Reading *Gate of Ivrel* was an exciting experience for me, and I think I dare claim a wide background for knowing such books. My personal question rises:

"Why can't I write like this?"

I very much wish that I did.

Prologue

1

THE GATES WERE the ruin of the qhal. They were everywhere, on every world, had been a fact of life for millennia, and had linked the whole net of qhal civilizations—an empire of both Space and Time, for the Gates led into elsewhen as well as elsewhere . . . except at the end.

At first the temporal aspect of the Gates had not been a matter of great concern. The technology had been discovered in the ruins of a dead world in the qhal system—a discovery that, made in the first few decades in space, suddenly opened for them the way to the stars. Thereafter ships were used only for the initial transport of technicians and equipment over distances of light-years. But after each World Gate was built, travel to that world and on its surface became instantaneous.

And more than instantaneous. Time warped in the Gate-transfer. It was possible to step from point to point across light-years, unaged, different from the real time of ships. And it was possible to select not alone where one would exit, but when—even upon the same world, projecting forward to its existence at some different point along the course of worlds and suns.

By law, there was no return in time. It had been theorized ever since the temporal aspect of the Gates was discovered, that accidents forward in time would have no worse effect than accidents in the Now; but intervention in backtime could affect whole multiples of lives and actions.

So the qhal migrated through future time, gathering in greater and greater numbers in the most distant ages. They migrated in space too, and thrust themselves insolently into the affairs of other beings, ripping loose a segment of their

9

time also. They generally despised outworld life, even what was qhal-like and some few forms that could interbreed with qhal. If possible they hated these potential rivals most of all, and loathed the half-qhal equally, for it was not in their nature to bear with divergence. They simply used the lesser races as they were useful, and seeded the worlds they colonized with the gatherings of whatever compatible worlds they pleased. They could experiment with worlds, and jump ahead in time to see the result. They gleaned the wealth of other, non-qhal species, who plodded through the centuries at their own real-time rate, for use of the Gates was restricted to qhal. The qhal in the end had little need left, and little ambition but for luxury and novelty and the consuming lust for other, ever-farther Gates.

Until someone, somewhen, backtimed and tampered—perhaps ever so minutely.

The whole of reality warped and shredded. It began with little anomalies, accelerated massively toward time-wipe, reaching toward the ends of Gate-tampered time and Gate-spanned space.

Time rebounded, indulged in several settling ripples of distortion, and centered at some point before the overextended Now.

At least, so the theorists from the Science Bureau surmised, when the worlds that survived were discovered, along with their flotsam of qhal relics that had been cast back up out of time. And among the relics were the Gates.

2

The Gates exist. We can therefore assume that they exist in the future and in the past, but we cannot ascertain the extent of their existence until we use them. According to present qhal belief, which is without substantiation, world upon world has been disrupted; and upon such worlds elements are greatly muddled. Among these anomalies may be survivals taken from our own area, which might prove lethal to us if taken into backtime.

It is the Bureau's opinion that the Gates, once passed, must be sealed from the far side of space and time, or we continually risk the possibility of another such time-implosion as ruined the qhal. It is theorized by the qhal themselves that

*this area of space has witnessed one prior time-implosion of
undetermined magnitude, perhaps of a few years of span or
of millennia, which was occasioned by the first Gate and re-
ceptor discovered by the qhal, to the ruin first of the unknown
alien culture and subsequently of their own. There is therefore a constant risk so long as there will ever exist a single
Gate, that our own existence could be similarly affected upon
any instant. It is therefore the majority opinion of the Bureau
that utilization of the Gates should be permitted, but only for
the dispatch of a force to close them, or destroy them. A team
has been prepared. Return for them will of course be impossible; and the length of the mission will be of indeterminate
duration, so that, on the one hand, it may result in the immediate entrapment or destruction of the team, or, on the
other, it may prove to be a task of such temporal scope that
one or a dozen generations of the expeditionary force may
not be sufficient to reach the ultimate Gate.*

> *Journal, Union Science Bureau, Vol. XXX, p. 22*

3

*Upon the height of Ivrel standen Staines y-carven with sich
qujalish Runes, the which if man touche, given forth sich fires
of witcherie as taken soul and bodie withal. To all these Places
of Powers, grete forces move, the which qujalish sorceries yet
werken. Ye may knowe qujalish blude herewith, if childe be
born of gray eyen, in stature considerable, and if he flee gude
and seek after sich Places, for qujal lacken soules, and yet by
sorceries liven faire and younge more yeares than Men.*

> *—Book of Embry, Hait-an-Koris*

4

*In the year 1431 of the Common Reckoning, there arose
War between the princes of Aenor, Koris, Baien, and Koris-
sith, against the hold of Hjemur-beyond-Ivrel. In that year the
lord of Hjemur was the witch-lord Thiye son of Thiye, lord of
Ra-hjemur, lord of Ivrel of the Fires, which shadows Irien.*

*Now in this time there came to the exiled lord of Koris,
Chya Tiffwy son of Han, certain five Strangers whose like
was never before seen in the land. They gave that they had
come from the great Southe, and made themselves hearth-
welcome with Chya Tiffwy and the lord of Aenor, Ris Gyr*

*son of Leleolm. Now it was clearly observed that One of these
five strangers was surely of Qujalin blood, being a woman of
pale coloring and stature as great as most ordinary Men, while
Another of the partie was of golden coloring, yet withal not
unlike unto such as be born by Nature in Koris of Andur,
the others being dark and seeming men. Now surely the eyes
of both Gyr and Tiffwy were blinded by their great Desire,
they being sisters' sons, and Tiffwy's kingdom being held by
the lord from Ivrel of the Fires. Then persuaded they by great
Oaths and promises of rewardes the lords of Baien-an, the
chiefest among whom was also Cousin to them, this being lord
Seo, third brother's son of the great Andur-lord Rus. And of
Horse they gathered seven thousands and of Foot three thousands, and with the promises and Oath of the five, they set
forth their Standards against lord Thiye.*

*Now there standeth a Stone in the vale of Irien, Rune-
carven, which is like to the standing stones in Aenor and Sith
and much like to the great Span of the Witchfire in Ivrel, by
general report, and it was always avoided, howbeit no great
harm had come therefrom.*

*To this place the lords of Andur rallied behind Tiffwy
Han's-son and the Five, to make assault on Ivrel and Hjemur-
keep. Then it became full clear that Tiffwy had been deceived
by the Strangers, for ten thousands rode down Grioen's
Height into the vale of Irien at the foot of Ivrel, and of them
all perished, save one youth from Baien-an, hight Tem Reth,
whose mount fell in the course and so saved his life. When
he woke from his swoon there was nothing living upon the
field of Irien, neither man nor beast, and yet no Enemy had
possessed the field. Of the ten thousands there remained but
few Corpses, and upon them there was no Wounding found.
This Reth of Baien-an did quit the field alive, but much
grieving on this account did enter into the Monastery of
Baien-an, and spent his days at Prayers.*

*Having accomplished such Evil the Strangers vanished. It
was widely reported however by the folk in Aenor that the
Woman returned there, and fled in terror when they sought
arms against her. By them it is given that she perished upon
a hill of Stones, by them hight Morgaine's Tomb, for by this
name she was known in Aenor-Pyvvn, though it is reported
that she had many Names, and bore lord-right and titles. Here
it is said she sleeps, waiting until the great Curse be broken
and free her. Therefore each Yeare the folk of the village of*

Reomel bring Giftes and bind great Curses there also, lest perchance she wake and do them ill.

Of the Others, there was no trace found, neither at Irien nor in Aenor.

—Annals of Baien-an

CHAPTER I

TO BE BORN Kurshin or Andurin was a circumstance that mattered little in terms of pride. It only marked a man as a man, and not a savage, such as lay to the south of Andur-Kursh in Lun; nor tainted with witchery and *qujalin* blood, such as the folk of Hjemur and northward. Between Andur of the forests and Kursh of the mountains was little cause of rivalry; it was only to say that one was hunter or herder, but both were true men and godly men, and once—in the days of the High Kings of Koris—one nation.

To be born of a particular canton, like Morija or Baien or Aenor—this was a matter that deserved loyalty, a loyalty held in common with all Morijin or Baienen or Aenorin of whatever rank, and there was fierce love of home in the folk of Andur-Kursh.

But within each separate canton there were the clans, and the clans were the true focus of love and pride and loyalty. In most cantons several ruling clans rose and fell in continual cycles of rivalry and strivings for power; and there were the more numerous lesser clans, which were accustomed to obey. Morija was unique in that it had but one ruling clan and all five others were subject. Originally there had been the Yla and Nhi, but the Yla had perished to the last man at Irien a hundred years past, so now there remained only the Nhi.

Vanye was Nhi. This was to say that he was honorable to the point of obsession; he was a splendid and brilliant warrior, skilled with horses. He was however of a quicksilver disposition and had a recklessness that bordered on the suicidal. He was also stubborn and independent, a trait that kept the Nhi clan in a constant ferment of plottings and betrayals. Vanye did not doubt these truths about himself: this was after all the well-known character of the whole Nhi clan. It was expected of all who carried the blood, as each clan had its

attributed personality. A Nhi youth spent all his energies
either living up to expectations or living in defiance of his
less desirable traits.

His half-brothers possessed these attributes too, as of course
did lord Nhi Rijan, who was father to the lot of them. But
Vanye was Chya on his Korish mother's side; and Chya were
volatile and artistic, and pride often ruled their good sense.
His half-brothers were Myya, which was a Morij warrior-
clan, subject, but ambitious, and its folk were secretive and
cold and sometimes cruel. It was in Vanye's nature to be
reckless and outspoken as it was in the nature of his two
half-brothers to keep their own counsel. It was in his nature
to be rash, while it was in that of his brothers to be unfor-
giving. It was no one's fault, unless it was that of Nhi Rijan,
who had been reckless enough to beget a bastard Chya and
two legitimate Nhi-Myya and to house all three sons under
one roof.

And upon an autumn day in the twenty-third year of Nhi
Rijan in Ra-morij, a son of Rijan died.

Vanye would not go into the presence of Nhi Rijan his
father: it needed several of the Myya to force him into that
torchlit room, which reeked so strongly of fire and fear. Then
he would not look his father in the eyes, but fell on his face
on the floor, and touched his brow to the cold stone paving
and rested there unmoving while Rijan attended to his surviving heir. Nhi Erij was sorely hurt: the keen longsword had
nearly severed the fingers of his right hand, his swordhand,
and sweating priests and old San Romen labored with the
moaning prince, giving him drafts and poultices to ease his
agony while they tried to save the damaged members.

Nhi Kandrys had not been so fortunate. His body, brows
bound with the red cord to tie his soul within until the
funeral, rested between death-lights upon another bench in
the armory.

Erij stifled a scream at the touch and hiss of iron, and
Vanye flinched. There was a stench of burned flesh. Eventually Erij's moans grew softer as the drugged wine had effect.
Vanye lifted his head, fearing this brother dead also—some
died under the cautery, of the shock, and the drugged wine
together. But his half-brother yet breathed.

And Nhi Rijan struck with all the force of his arm, and
cast Vanye sprawling and dazed, his head still ringing as he
crawled to resume his kneeling posture, head down at his
father's feet.

"Chya murderer," his father said. "My curse, my curse on you." And his father wept. This hurt Vanye more than the blow. He looked up and saw a look of utter revulsion. He had never known Nhi Rijan could weep.

"If I had put an hour's thought into your begetting, bastard son, I would have gotten no sons on a Chya. Chya and Nhi are an unlucky mixing. I wish I had exercised more prudence."

"I defended myself," Vanye protested from bruised lips. "Kandrys meant to draw blood—see—" And he showed his side, where the light practice armor was rent, and blood flowed. But his father turned his face from that.

"Kandrys was my eldest," his father said, "and you were the merest night's amusement. I have paid dearly for that night. But I took you into the house. I owed your mother that, since she had the ill luck to die bearing you. You were death to her too. I should have realized that you are cursed that way. Kandrys dead, Erij maimed—all for the likes of you, bastard son. Did you hope to be heir to Nhi if they were both dead? Was that it?"

"Father," Vanye wept, "they meant to kill me."

"No. To put that arrogance of yours in its place—that, maybe. But not to kill you. No. You are the one who killed. You murdered. You turned edge on your brothers in practice, and Erij not even armed. The fact is that you are alive and my eldest son is not, and I would it were the other way around, Chya bastard. I should never have taken you in. Never."

. "Father," he cried, and the back of Nhi Rijan's hand smashed the word from his mouth and left him wiping blood from his lips. Vanye bowed down again and wept.

"What shall I do with you?" asked Rijan at last.

"I do not know," said Vanye.

"A man carries his own honor. He knows."

Vanye looked up, sick and shaking. He could not speak in answer to that. To fall upon his own blade and die—this, his father asked of him. Love and hate were so confounded in him that he felt rent in two, and tears blinded him, making him more ashamed.

"Will you use it?" asked Rijan.

It was Nhi honor. But the Chya blood was strong in him too, and the Chya loved life too well.

The silence weighed upon the air.

"Nhi cannot kill Nhi," said Rijan at last. "You will leave us, then."

"I had no wish to kill him."

"You are skilled. It is clear that your hand is more honest than your mouth. You struck to kill. Your brother is dead. You meant to kill both brothers, and Erij was not even armed. You can give me no other answer. You will become *ilin*. This I set on you."

"Yes, sir," said Vanye, touching brow to the floor, and there was the taste of ashes in his mouth. There was only short prospect for a masterless *ilin*, and such men often became mere bandits, and ended badly.

"You are skilled," said his father again. "It is most likely that you will find place in Aenor, since a Chya woman is wife to the Ris in Aenor-Pyvvn. But there is lord Gervaine's land to cross, among the Myya. If Myya Gervaine kills you, your brother will be avenged, and it will be without blood on Nhi hands or Nhi steel."

"Do you wish that?" asked Vanye.

"You have chosen to live," said his father. And from Vanye's own belt he took the Honor blade that was the peculiar distinction of the *uyin*, and he seized Vanye's long hair that was the mark of Nhi manhood, and sheared it off roughly in irregular lengths. The hair, Chya and fairer than was thought honest human blood among most clans, fell to the stone floor in its several braids; and when it was done, Nhi Rijan set his heel on the blade and broke it, casting the pieces into Vanye's lap.

"Mend that," said Nhi Rijan, "if you can."

The wind cold upon his shorn neck, Vanye found the strength to rise; and his numb fingers still held the halves of the shortsword. "Shall I have horse and arms?" he asked, by no means sure of that, but without them he would surely die.

"Take all that is yours," said the Nhi. "Clan Nhi wants to forget you. If you are caught within our borders you will die as a stranger and an enemy."

Vanye bowed, turned and left.

"Coward," his father's voice shouted after him, reminding him of the unsatisfied honor of the Nhi, which demanded his death; and now he wished earnestly to die, but it was no longer help for his personal dishonor. He was marked like a felon for hanging, like the lowest of criminals: exile had not demanded this further punishment—it was lord Nhi Rijan's own justice, for the Nhi had also a darker nature, which was implacable and excessive in revenge.

He put on his armor, hiding the shame of his head under a leather coif and a peaked helm, and bound about the helm the white scarf of the *ilin*, wandering warrior, to be claimed by whatever lord chose to grant him hearth-right.

Ilinin were often criminals, or clanless, or unclaimed bastards, and some religious men doing penance for some particular sin, bound in virtual slavery according to the soul-binding law of the *ilin* codes, to serve for a year at their Claiming.

Not a few turned mercenary, taking pay, losing *uyin* rank; or, in outright dishonor, became thieves; or, if honest and honorable, starved, or were robbed and murdered, either by outlaws or by hedge-lords that took their service and then laid claim to all that they had.

The Middle Realms were not at peace: they had not been at peace since Irien and the generation before; but neither were there great wars, such as could make an *ilin's* life profitable. There was only grinding poverty for midlands villages, and in Koris, the evil of Hjemur's minions—dark sorceries and outlaw lords much worse than the outlaws of the high mountains.

And there was lord Myya Gervaine's small land of Morij Erd which barred his way to Aenor and separated him from his only hope of safety.

It was the second winter, the cold of the high passes of the mountains, and a dead horse that finally drove him to the desperate step of trying to cross the lands of Gervaine.

A black Myya arrow had felled his gelding, poor Mai, that had been his mount since he first reached manhood; and Mai's gear now was on a bay mare he had of the Myya—the owner being beyond need of her.

They had harried him from Luo to Ethrith-mri, and only once had he turned to fight. Hill by hill they had forced him against the mountains of the south. He ran willingly now, though he was faint with hunger and there was scant grain left for his horse. Aenor was just across the next ridges. The Myya were no friends of the Ris in Aenor-Pyvvn, and would not risk his land.

It was late that he realized the nature of the road he had begun to travel, and that it was the old *qujalin* road and not the one he sought. Occasional paving rang under the bay

mare's hooves. Occasional stones thrust up by the roadside
and he began to fear indeed that it led to the dead places,
the cursed grounds. Snow fell for a time, whiting everything
out—stopping pursuit (he hoped that, at least). And he spent
the night in the saddle, daring only to sleep a time in the
early morning, after the movings in the brush were silenced
and he not longer feared wolves.

Then he rode the long day down from the Aenish side of
the pass, weak and sick with hunger.

He found himself entering a valley of standing stones.

There was no longer doubt that *qujalin* hands had reared
such monoliths. It was Morgaine's vale: he knew it now, of
the songs and of evil rumor. It was a place no man of Kursh
or Andur would have traveled with a light heart at noontide,
and the sun was sinking quickly toward dark, with another
bank of cloud rolling in off the ridge of the mountains at
his back.

He dared look up between the pillars that crowned the
conical hill called Morgaine's Tomb, and the declining sun
shimmered there like a butterfly caught in a web, all torn
and fluttering. It was the effect of Witchfires, like the great
Witchfire on Mount Ivrel where the Hjemur-lord ruled,
proving *qujalin* powers were not entirely faded there or here.

Vanye wrapped his tattered cloak about his mailed
shoulders and put the exhausted horse to a quicker pace, past
the tangle of unhallowed stones at the base of the hill. The
fair-haired witch had shaken all Andur-Kursh in war, cast
half the Middle Realms into the lap of Thiye Thiye's-son.
Here the air was still uneasy, whether with the power of the
Stones or with the memory of Morgaine, it was uncertain.

> When Thiye ruled in Hjemur
> came strangers riding there,
> and three were dark and one was gold,
> and one like frost was fair.

The mare's hooves upon the crusted snow echoed the old
verses in his mind, an ill song for the place and the hour.
For many years after the world had seen the welcome last of
Morgaine Frosthair, demented men claimed to have seen her,
while others said that she slept, waiting to draw a new generation of men to their ruin, as she had ruined Andur once
at Irien.

Fair was she, and fatal as fair,
and cursed who gave her ear;
now men are few and wolves are more,
and the Winter drawing near.

If in fact the mound did hold Morgaine's bones, it was
fitting burial for one of her old, inhuman blood. Even the
trees hereabouts grew crooked: so did they wherever there
were Stones of Power, as though even the nature of the
patient trees was warped by the near presence of the Stones;
like souls twisted and stunted by living in the continual
presence of evil. The top of the hill was barren: no trees
grew there at all.

He was glad when he had passed the narrow stream-
channel between the hills and left the vicinity of the Stones.
And suddenly he had before him as it were a sign that he had
run into better fortunes, and that heaven and the land of his
cousins of Aenor-Pyvvn promised him safety.

A small band of deer wandered belly-deep in the snows by
the little brook, hungrily stripping the red *howan* berries from
the thicket.

It was a land blessedly unlike that of the harsh Cedur Maje,
or Gervaine's Morij Erd, where even the wolves often went
hungry, for Aenor-Pyvvn lay far southward from Hjemur,
still untouched by the troubles that had so long lain over the
Middle Realms.

He feverishly unslung his bow and strung it, his hands
shaking with weakness, and he launched one of the gray-
feathered Nhi shafts at the nearest buck. But the mare chose
that moment to shift weight, and he cursed in frustration
and aching hunger: the shaft sped amiss and hit the buck in
the flank, scattered the others.

The wounded buck lunged and stumbled and began to run,
crazed with pain and splashing the white snow with great
gouts of blood. Vanye had no time for a second arrow. It
ran back into Morgaine's valley, and there he would not
follow it. He saw it climb—insane, as if the queerness in that
valley had taken its fear-hazed wits and driven it against
nature, killing itself in its exertions, driving it toward that
shimmering web which even insects and growing things
avoided.

It struck between the pillars and vanished.

So did the tracks and the blood.

The deer grazed, on the other side of the stream.

He gazed at the valley of the Stones, where there was no doubt that *qujalin* hands had reared such monoliths. It was Morgaine's vale: he knew it. The sight stirred something, a sense of *déjà-vu* so strong it dazed him for a moment, and he passed the back of his hand over his eyes, rubbing things into focus. The sun was sinking quickly toward dark, with another bank of cloud rolling in off the ridge of the mountains, shadowing most of the sky at his back.

He looked up between the pillars that crowned the conical hill called Morgaine's Tomb, and the declining sun shimmered there like a puddle of gold just disturbed by a plunging stone.

In that shimmer appeared the head of a horse, and its forequarters, and a rider, and the whole animal: white rider on a gray horse, and the whole was limned against the brilliant amber sun so that he blinked and rubbed his eyes.

The rider descended the snowy hill into the shadows across his path—substantial. A pelt of white *anomen* was the cloak, and the stranger's breath and that of the gray horse made puffs on the frosty air.

He knew that he should set spurs to the mare, yet he felt curiously numb, as though he had been wakened from one dream and plunged into the midst of another.

He looked into the tanned woman's face within the fur hood and met hair and brows like the winter sun at noon, and eyes as gray as the clouds in the east.

"Good day," she gave him, in a quaint and gentle accent, and he saw that beneath her knee upon the gray's saddle was a great blade with a golden hilt in the fashion of a dragon, and that it was Korish-work upon her horse's gear. He was sure then, for such details were in the songs they sang of her and in the book of Yla.

"My way lies north," she said in that low, accented voice. "Thee seems to go otherwise. But the sun is setting soon. I will ride with thee a ways."

"I know you," he said then.

The pale brows lifted. "Has thee come hunting me?"

"No," he said, and the ice crept downward from heart to belly so that he was no longer sure what words he answered, or why he answered at all.

"How is thee called?"

"Nhi Vanye, ep Morija."

"Vanye—no Morij name."

Old pride stung him. The name was Korish, mother's-clan, reminder of his illegitimacy. Then to speak or dispute with her at all seemed madness. What he had seen happen upon the hilltop refused to take shape in his memory, and he began to insist to himself that the hunger that had made him weak had begun to twist his senses as well, and that he had encountered some strange high-clan woman upon the forsaken road, and that his weakness stole his senses and made him forget how she had come.

Yet however she had come, she was at least half-*qujal*, eyes and hair bore witness to that: she was *qujal* and soulless and well at home in this blighted place of dead trees and snow.

"I know a place," she said, "where the wind does not reach. Come."

She turned the gray's head toward the south, as he had been headed, so that he did not know where else to go. He went as in a dream. Dusk was gathering, hurried on by the veil of cloud that was rolling across the sky. The wraithlike pallor of Morgaine drifted before him, but the gray's hooves cracked substantially into the crusted snow, leaving tracks.

They rounded the turning of the hill and startled a small band of deer that fed upon *howan* by the streamside. It was the first game he had seen in days. Despite his circumstance, he reached for his bow.

Before he could string it, a light blazed from Morgaine's outstretched hand and a buck fell dead. The others scattered.

Morgaine pointed to the hillside on their right. "There is a cave for shelter. I have used it before. Take what venison we need: the rest is due smaller hunters."

She rode away up the slope. He took his skinning-knife and prepared to do her bidding, though he liked it little. He found no wound upon the body, only a little blood from its nostrils to spot the snow, and all at once the red on the snow brought back the dream, and made him shiver. He had no stomach for a thing killed in such a way, and the wide-eyed horned head seemed as spellbound as he—unwilling dreamer too.

He glanced over his shoulder. Morgaine stood upon the shoulder of the hill holding the gray's reins, watching him. The first flakes of snow drifted across the wind.

He set his knife to the carcass and did not look it in the eye.

CHAPTER II

A FIRE blazed in the shallow cave's mouth, putting a wall of warmth between them and the driving snow. He did not want the meat, but he was many days weak with hunger, so that his joints ached and the least exertion put a tremor in his muscles. He must sit and smell it cooking, and when she had cooked and offered a bit to him, it looked no different than other meat, and smelled so achingly good that his empty belly ruled his other scruples. A man would not lose his soul for a little bit of venison, however the beast had been slain.

The night was beyond. Occasional snowflakes pelted past the barrier of the fire's heat, driven on a fierce gust. Outside, the horses, witch-horse and ordinary bay, stood together against the unfriendly wind; and when hot venison had taken the shaking from Vanye's limbs and put strength into him, he took a portion of what grain he had left and went outside, fed half to each. The gray—of that famous breed of Baien, so men sang—nuzzled his hands as eagerly and warmly as his own little mare. His heart was touched by the beauty of the gray stud. For the moment he forgot the evil and smoothed the pale mane and gazed into the great pale-lashed eyes and thought (for the Nhi were breeders of good horses) that he would much covet the get of that fine animal, in any herd: they were the breed of the lost High Kings of Andur, those great gray horses. But there were no more High Kings, only the lords of clans; and the breed had passed as the glories of Andur had passed.

Now of great kings there remained only the Hjemur-lord, far different than the brave bright kings of golden Koris-sith and Baien, that breed of men apart from clans, and greater. An older thing, a darker thing had stirred to life when the Hjemur-lord arose, and more than an army had gone down to die in Irien.

24

With that thought he shivered in the ice-edged wind and returned to the fire, to the center of all things unnatural in the night, where Morgaine sat wrapped in her snowy furs, beside her horse's gear and the dragon-blade glittering in its plain sheath. The silence between them had been as deep as that between old friends.

The wind whirled snow through the cave's mouth. It was a great storm. He reckoned for the first time that he would have died this night, unsheltered, weak from hunger. Had it not been for the meeting on the road, the deer, the offering of the cave, then he would have been in the open when the storm came down, and he much doubted that his failing strength could have endured an Aenish storm.

There was wood piled up by the door. How it had been cut he was loath to know, only that it gave them warmth. And when he came to put a little more upon the fire, to keep the barrier between them and the insistent wind, he saw Morgaine kneeling upon a place at the back of the cave and seeking for something beneath a pile of small stones.

I have used this place before, she had told him.

He looked in doubtful curiosity and saw that she drew forth a leather sack that was stiff and moldering, and when she poured into her hand it was only powder that came down. She snatched her hand from that as if she had touched something foul, and wiped her fingers on the earth. A bloody streak was upon her arm, parting the black leather of her sleeve where she had thrust the arm forth from the enveloping cloak, and her clean hand stole to that.

She sat there shivering, like one in the grip of some great fear. He sank down on his heels near her, puzzled, even pitying her, and wondering in the back of his mind how she had chanced to hurt herself in so short a time: no, it looked old; it was drying. She must have done it while he was busy at the deer's carcass.

"How long?" she asked him. "How long have I been away?"

"More than a hundred years," he said.

"I had thought—rather less." She moved her hand and looked down at the hurt, brushed at it, seemed to decide to ignore it, for it was not deep enough to be dangerous, only painful.

"Wait," he said, and obtained his own kit, and would gladly have tried to treat the wound for her: he thought he owed her that at least for this night's shelter. But she would have none of it, and insisted upon her own. He sat and watched uneasily while she drew out her own things, small metal containers, and other things he had no knowledge of. She treated her own injury, and did not bandage it, but a pinkish film covered it when she had done, and it did not bleed. *Qujalin* medicines, he judged; and perhaps she could not abide honest remedies, or feared they had been blessed, and might be harmful to her.

"How came you by that?" he asked, for it looked like an ax-stroke or sword-cut; but she had no tools, however the wood had been cut, and high on her arm as it was he could not judge how she could have chanced to do it.

"Aenorin," she said. "Lord Ris Heln Gyr's-son, he and his men."

Heln was nearly a hundred years in his own grave. Then he felt an uneasiness at his stomach and well understood the look Morgaine had had. She had ridden out of the Aenorin's chase and across his path—a hundred years in what by that wound had been the blink of an eye.

It was insane. He bowed down upon his face and then retreated, glad to leave her to her own thoughts.

And because he was saddle-weary and harried beyond any immediate concern of magics or fear of beasts, he wrapped himself in his thin cloak and leaned against the rock wall to sleep.

The crash of a new piece of wood into the fire awakened him, still unrested, and he saw Morgaine brush snow from her cloak and settle again in her accustomed place. Her eyes went to him, fixed unwelcomely upon his, so that he could not pretend he slept.

"Is thee rested?" she asked of him, and that curious Korish accent was of long ago, and chilled him more than the wind or the stone at his back.

"Somewhat," he said, and forced stiff muscles to set him upright. He had slept in armor many a night, and occasionally he had slept colder; but there had been too many days in the saddle lately, and too little rest between, and none at all the night before.

"Vanye," she said.

"Lady?"

"Come, near the fire. I have questions for thee."

He did so, not gladly, and settled wrapped in his threadbare cloak and cherished the heat. She sat wrapped in her furs, her face half in shadow, and gazed into his eyes.

"Heln found this place," she said. "A hunter I did not kill told him. Aenor-Pyvvn rose in arms then. They sent an army after me—" She laughed, the merest breath. "An army, to take this little cave. Of course I knew their coming. How not? They filled the southern field. I fled at once—yet it was close. But they even dared the valley of Stones; so I fled where they could not—would not—follow. And there I must wait until someone freed me. I am no older; I knew nothing of the years. But things have gone to dust, else the horses and we would fare better tonight. Thee fears me—"

It was so, it was clearly so: from a man his enemy he would have resented those words; Morgaine he feared and he was not ashamed. His heart beat painfully at each direct glance of those gray, unhuman eyes. If he did not know of a certainty that he would die, he would flee this little place and her company; but there was the storm. It howled outside with the fury of winter. He knew the mountains. Sometimes there was no break in the snow for days. Men unprotected died, turned up in spring all twisted and stiff in the melting snow, along with carcasses of horses and deer that the wolves had somehow missed.

"There is no harm in words between us," she said. She offered him wine of her own flask. He took it hesitantly, but the night was chill, and he had already shared food with her. He drank a little and gave it back. She wiped the mouth fastidiously and drank also, and stopped the flask again.

"I beg thee tell me the end of my tale," she said. "I was not able to know. What became of the men I knew? What was it I did?"

He stared into her eyes, this most cursed of all enemies of Andur-Kursh, the traitor guide that had sent ten thousand men to die and sunk half the Middle Kingdoms into ruin. And those words would not come to him. He would easily say them of her to someone else: but in that fair and unguarded face there was something that unfolded to him, that strangled the curse in his throat.

He found no words for her at all.

"I do not think then," she said, "that it has a pleasant ending, since thee does not want to say. But say it, Nhi Vanye."

"There is no more to tell," he said. "After Irien, after so great a defeat for Andur-Kursh, Hjemur took Koris, took all the lands from Alis Kaje east. You were not to be found, not after the chase the Aenorin gave you. You vanished. What allies you had left surrendered. All that followed you died. They say that there were prosperous villages and holds in south Koris in your day. There are none now. It is as desolate as these mountains. And Irien itself is cursed ground, and no one enters there, even of Hjemur's men. There is rumor," he added, "that the Thiye who rules now is the same that ruled then. I do not know if that is true. The Hjemur-lord has always been called Thiye Thiye's-son. But the country people say that it is the same man, kept young a hundred years."

"It could be done," she said in a low and joyless voice.

"That is the end of it," he said. "Everyone died." And he thrust from his mind what she said of Thiye, for it occurred to him that she was living proof that it could be done, that things could be done for which he wanted no explanation. He must share this place with her: he wanted to share nothing else.

She let him be then, asking no more questions, and he retreated to the other side of the fire and curled up again to sleep.

The morning came, miserable and still spitting snow. But soon there began to be a break in the clouds, which cheered Vanye's heart. He had feared one of those storms that stayed for days, that might seal him in this place with her unwelcome company, while the poor horses froze outside.

And she cooked strips of venison over the fire for their breakfast, and offered him a little of the wine too. He cut bits from the steaming venison with his knife against his thumb, and watched even with amusement as she, more delicate, cut hers most awkwardly into bits, and dusted each piece and inspected it, and only then cooked it further and prised it off the dagger tip for eating, tiny bites and manageable.

Then she wrapped up the rest in a square of leather that he had of his gear for the purpose.

"Will you not keep some," he asked, "or are you taking it all?"

"What means the white scarf?" she asked him.

He swallowed the last bit of venison as if it had turned to dust in his mouth. All at once the rest that he had eaten and drunk turned to sickness in his belly.

"I am *ilin*," he said.

"Thee has sheltered with me, taken food," she said. "And

the Chya of Koris gave me clan-welcome, and gave me lord-right, *ilin*."

He bowed his head to his hands upon the floor. She spoke the truth: alone of women, this was true of Morgaine, killer of armies. He raged at himself, even while his stomach knotted in fear; he had not even reckoned of it, for her being a woman; he had sheltered at her fire as he would have taken shelter at that of some Aenish farmwife. Such folk had no claim to make against an *ilin*.

Morgaine did.

"I beg exception," he said from that position. He was entitled to ask that, and he had no shame in asking. He dared look up at her. "I have kinsmen in Aenor-Pyvvn. I was going there. Lady, I am exiled in every province of Morija—I dare not go back there. I am little help to anyone." He took the helmet from his head—he had set it on again to go out into the cold—and, which he had not done, even for sleeping, he unlaced his coif at the throat and slipped it back from the shame of his shorn head, the fair brown hair falling free about his ears and across his brow. "I am outlawed in my clan: the Nhi and the Myya hunt me. So I became *ilin*. But I can find shelter only in Aenor-Pyvvn, and there you have said yourself you cannot go."

"For what was this done to thee?" she asked him, and he saw that he had succeeded in bringing shock even to the eyes of Morgaine.

"For murder, for brother-killing." He had told this to none, had avoided men and shelters even of country folk. The words came with difficulty to his lips. "It was a fight he forced, lady, but I killed my brother—my half-brother—and he was Myya. So there are two clans with blood-debt against me, and I am no help to you. I am grateful for the shelter— I thank you: but it is no use to you to make claim against me. Only name me some reasonable service and I will do that for you in payment. You cannot stay here, you are cursed in every hold in Andur-Kursh, and no one that hears your name or sees you will refrain from your life. Listen, for all that you are, you have been generous with me, and I am giving you good advice for it: the pass south of here leads through Aenor, and I am bound that way. I will somehow guide you through that land. I will bring you safely to the south of Aenor, where lands are warm, into Eriel, into the plains of Lun. They are savages that live there, but at least they have no bloodfeud with you and you can live there in safety. Listen to me and let me pay you with that thanks. That is the best that I can do for you, and I will do that honestly, grudging nothing."

"I refuse to grant exception," she said then, which was her right.

He swore, both foully and tearfully, and left her and went out and laid hands upon his horse's halter. He had time to think then, of the holy oath he had already made as *ilin,* and that oath-breaking was no light thing for his honor and least of all for his soul. He laid hand against the bay's rough cheek, and his head against its warm neck, and stayed there, shivering in the cold, but numb to it. Easy it would be if he could die there in the wind, robbed of warmth, to sink into the numbing snow and simply die, untouched by *qujalin* oaths.

New snow crunched beneath Morgaine's boots. She came and stood beside him, waiting for him to decide which he would, to yield up his soul by oath-breaking, or to risk it by serving the likes of her. For a man who was lost in either case, the only thing left was life: and life was sure to be longer by running now than by staying with Margaine Frosthair.

Then he thought of the deer, and already he felt a twitching at the back of his shoulders as if she sought his life. He would not be able to outrace that: other weapons, perhaps, but not the thing that had slain the deer and left no wound.

"It is lawful," she said, "what I ask."

"With you," he objected, "that year is likely to be the last of my life. And after that, I would be a marked man in Andur-Kursh."

"I will admit that is true. My own life is likely to be no longer. I have no pity to spare for thee."

She held out her hand for his. He yielded it, and she drew the ivory-hilted Honor blade from her belt and cut deeply, but not wide: the dark blood welled up slowly in the cold. She set her mouth to the wound, and then he did the same, the salt hot taste of his own blood knotting his stomach in revulsion. Then she went inside, and brought ash to stop it with, smearing it with the clan-glyph of the Chya, writ in his blood and her hearth-ash across his hand, the ancient custom of Claiming.

Then he bowed to his forehead in the burning snow, and the ice numbed the fire in his hand and made it cease throbbing. She had certain responsibilities for him now: to see that he did not starve, neither he nor his horse, though certain of the

hedge-lords were scant of that obligation, and kept the miser-
erable *ilinin* they claimed lean and hungry and their horses in
little better state when the *ilinin* were in hall.

Morgaine was of poorer estate: she had no hall to shelter
either of them, and the clan she signed him—his own birth-
clan—would as lief kill him as not. For his part, he must simply follow orders: no other law bound him now. He could
even be ordered against homeland or blood kin, though it was
no credit to the lord's honor if an *ilin* were so cruelly used. He
must fight her enemies, tend her hearth—whatever things she
required of him until a year had passed from the day of his
oath.

Or she might simply name him a task to accomplish, and he
would be bound to that task even beyond his year's time, until
it was done. And that also was exceedingly cruel, but it was according to the law.

"What service?" he asked of her. "Will you let me guide
you from here southward?"

"We go north," she said.

"Lady, it is suicide," he cried. "For you and for me."

"We go north," she said. "Come, I will bind up the hand."

"No," he said. He clutched snow in his fist, stopping the
bleeding, and held the injured hand against him. "I want no
medicines of yours. I will keep my oath. Let me tend to myself."

"I will not insist," she said.

Another thought, more terrible, occurred to him. He bowed
in request another time, delaying her return to the cave.

"What else?" she asked him.

"If I die you are supposed to give me honorable burial. I
do not want that."

"What—not to be buried?"

"Not by *qujalin* rites. No, I had rather the birds and the
wolves than that."

She shrugged, as if that did not at all offend her. "Birds and
wolves will likely care for both of us before all is done," she
said. "I am glad thee sees the matter that way. I probably
should have no time for amenities. Care for thyself and gather
thy gear and mine. We are leaving this place."

"Where are we bound?"

"Where I will to go."

He bowed acceptance with a heavy heart, knowing of increasing certainty that he could not reason with her. She meant

to die. It was cruel to have laid claim to an *ilin* under that circumstance, but that was the way of his oath. If a man survived
his year, he was purged of crimes and disgrace. Heaven would
have exacted due penance for his sins.

Many did not survive. It was presumed Heaven had exacted
punishment. They were counted honorable suicides.

He bound up his hand with the cleanly remedies that he
knew, though it hurt with dull persistence; and then he gathered up all their belongings, his and hers, and saddled both the
horses. The sky was beginning to clear. The sun shone down
on him as he worked, and glittered coldly off the golden hilt
of the blade he hung upon the gray's saddle. The dragon
leered at him, fringed mouth agape, clenching the blade in his
teeth; his spread legs made the guard; his back-winding tail
guarded the fingers.

He feared even to touch it. No Korish work, that, whatever
hand had made the plain sheath. It was alien and otherly, and
when he ventured in curiosity to ease the awful thing even a
little way from its sheath, he found strange letters on the
blade itself like a shard of glass—even touching it threatened
injury. No blade ever existed of such substance: and yet it
seemed more perilous than fragile.

He slipped it quickly back into its sheath, guilty as he heard
Morgaine's tread behind him.

"Let it be," she said harshly. And when he stared at her,
knowing of a surety he had done wrong, she said more gently:
"It is a gift of one of my companions—a vanity. It pleased
him. He had great skill. But if thee dislikes things *qujalin*, then
keep hands from it."

He bowed, avoiding her eyes, and began working at his own
gear, tying his few possessions into place at the back of the
saddle.

The blade's name was *Changeling*. He remembered it of the
songs, and wondered could a smith have given so unlucky a
name to a blade, even were he *qujal*. His own sword was of
humbler make, honest steel, well-tempered, nameless as befitted a common soldier or a lord's bastard son.

He hung it on his saddle, swung up to mount and waited upon Morgaine, who was hardly slower.

"Will you not listen to me?" He was willing to try reason a
last time. "There is no safety for you in the north. Let us go
south to Lun. There are tribes there that know nothing of you.
You would be able to make your way among them. I have

heard tell that there are cities far to the south. I would take you there. You could live. In the north, they will hunt you and kill you."

She did not even answer him, but guided the gray downhill.

CHAPTER III

THE WOLVES had been at the deer's carcass in the night, after the snow had ceased to fall so quickly. The area around the tattered bones were marked and patterned with the paws of wolves, and some of those tracks were wondrously large. Vanye looked down as their own trail crossed the trampled snow, and he saw the larger tracks he knew beyond doubt for beasts of Korish woods, more hound than wolf.

The carnage cast a further pall upon the morning, which was clearing to that ice-crystal brightness that blinded the senses, veiling all sins of ugliness into brilliance under a blue sky; but already the veil had been soiled for them, death with them, four-footed. Of natural wolves he had no great fear—they seldom bothered men, save in the most desperate winters. But Koris-beasts were another breed. They killed. They killed and never meant to eat—a perversion in nature.

Morgaine looked down at the tracks too, and seemed unperturbed; perhaps, he thought, she had never seen the like in her time, before Thiye learned to warp the rightness of nature into shapes he chose. Perhaps magics had grown more powerful than she remembered, and she did not know the dangers toward which they rode.

Or perhaps—it was the worse thought—he himself failed to realize with what he rode, knee to knee and peaceful on this bright morning. He feared her for her reputation: that was natural. And yet, he thought, perhaps he did not hold fear enough of her presence. She could kill without touching and without wound: he could not rid his mind of the deer's wide-eyed look, that ought by rights not to have been dead.

A gnawed bone lay athwart their path. His horse shied from it.

They rode back into the valley of the Stones, crossing the frozen stream, cracking the yet thin ice, and rode the winding trail beside the great gray rocks, under the shadow of the mound called Morgaine's Tomb. Despite the snow, the sky shimmered between the two carven pillars with the look of air above the heated rocks.

Morgaine looked up at it as they rode. There was upon her face a curious loathing. He began to understand that it had been far from Morgaine's will to have ridden into such a thing with Heln's men behind her.

"Who freed you?" he asked suddenly.

She looked back at him, puzzled.

"You said that someone must free you from this place. What is it? How were you held there? And who freed you?"

"It is a Gate," she said, and into his mind there flashed the nightmare image of white rider against the sun: it was hard to remember such madness. Like dreams, it tended to fade, for the sake of sanity.

"If it is a gate," he said, "then from where did you come?"

"I was *between* until something should disturb the field. That is the way with Gates that are not set. It is like a shallow pool of time, ever so shallow. I was washed up again, on this shore."

He gazed up at it, could not understand, and yet it was as good an explanation of what he had seen as any other.

"Who freed you?" he asked.

"I do not know," she said. "I rode in with men at my heels; a shadow passed me; I rode out again. It was like closing my eyes. No—not that either. It was just *between*. Only it was thicker than any *between* I have ever ridden. I think that thee was—thee says, *you*—were—the one that did free me. But I do not know how, and I doubt that you know."

"It is impossible," he said. "I never came near the Stones."

"I would not wager anything on that memory," she said.

She turned her head; he rode behind her here, for the path was narrow at the bottom of the hill. He had view of the gray's white swaying tail and Morgaine's white-cloaked and insolent back; and the presence of this structure she called a Gate cast a pall upon all his thoughts. He had leisure to repent his oath in this ill-omened place, and knew that in a year with Morgaine he was bound to see and hear many things an honest and once religious man would not find comfortable.

He had a sudden and uncomfortable vision as he saw her riding ahead of him upon that stretch of the old paved road up between the lesser monoliths: that here was another kind of anachronism, like a man visiting the nursery of his childhood, surrounded by sad toys. Morgaine was indeed out of the long-ago; and yet it was known that the *qujal* had been evil and wise and able to work things that men had happily forgotten. Not needing transport, not needing such things as mortal weapons, *qujal* only wished and practiced sorceries, and what they wished became substance—until they grew yet more evil, and ruined themselves.

And yet Morgaine rode, live and powerful, and carried under her knee a blade of forgotten arts, in the ruins of things she might well have known as they once had been.

It was said that Thiye Thiye's-son was immortal, renewing his youth by taking life from others, and that he would never die so long as he could find unfortunates on whom to practice this. He had tended to scoff at the rumor: all men died.

But Morgaine had not, not in more than a hundred years, and still was young. She found the hundred years acceptable. Perhaps she had known longer sleeps than this.

The higher passes were choked with snow. Gray and bay fought drifts, struggling with such effort that they made little time. They must often pause to rest the animals. Yet by afternoon they seemed to have made it through the worst places, and without meeting any of the Myya or seeing tracks of beasts.

It was good fortune. It was bound not to last.

"Lady," he said during one of their rests, "if we go on as we are we will be in the valley of Morij Erd; and if we enter there, chances are you will not find welcome for either of us. This horse of mine is out of that land; and Gervaine its lord is Myya and he has sworn a great oath to have my head on a pike and other parts of me similarily distributed. There is no good prospect for you or for me in this direction."

She smiled slightly. She had been in lighter humor since the morning, when they had quitted the valley of Stones and entered the more honest shade of pine woods and unhewn crags. "We bear east before then, toward Koris."

"Lady, you know your way well enough," he protested glumly. "Why was it needful to snare me for a guide?"

"How should I know otherwise that Gervaine is lord of Morij Erd?" she asked, still smiling. The eyes did not. "Besides, I did not say that you were to be a guide in these lands, *ilin*."

"What, then?"

But she did not answer. She had that habit when he asked what displeased her. More human folk might dispute, protest, argue. Morgaine was simply silent, and against that there was no argument, only deep frustration.

He climbed back into his saddle and saw thereafter that they bore more easterly, toward east Koris, toward that land that was most firmly in Thiye's hands.

Toward dusk they were in pine forest again. Gray-centered clouds sailed across the moon increasingly frequent as the night deepened, and yet they rode, fearful of more storms, fearful for the horses, for there was little grain remaining in both their saddlebags, and they wished to make what easy time they could, hopeful of coming to the lower country before the winter set a firm grip on the passes before them. The bright moon showed them the way.

But at last the clouds were thick and the trail became hardly passable, trees crowding close and obscuring the sky with their bristling shadow. A downed tree beside the road promised them at least a drier place to rest, and wood for fire. They stopped and Vanye hacked off smaller branches and heaped them into a proper form for a damp-wood fire.

How the fire came to be, Vanye did not see: he turned his back to fetch more wood, and turned again and it was started, a tiny tongue of fire within the damp branches. It smoked untidily: wet wood; but it remained, Morgaine leaning close to encourage it, and he gingerly fed it tinder.

"There is a certain danger in this," he advised Morgaine, looking at her closely over the little fire. "There may be men hereabouts to see the light or smell the smoke, and no men in these woods are friendly to any other. I do not care to meet what this may attract, and it is best we keep it small and not keep it the night long."

She opened her hand and in the dim light showed him a black and shiny thing, queer and ugly. It revolted him: he could not determine why, only that it would not be made by any hand he knew, and there was a foul unloveliness about the thing in her fair slim hand. "This is sufficient for brigands and for beasts," she said. "And I trust you are somewhat skilled with sword and with bow. *Ilinin* otherwise do not long survive."

He nodded silent acknowledgement.

"Fetch our gear," she bade him.

He did so, clearing snow from the great tree and resting all that could be harmed by damp upon that. She began to make a meal for them of the almost frozen meat, while he doled out a bit of the remaining grain to the poor horses. They nudged him in the ribs and coaxed pitiably, wanting the rest of it: but he steeled his heart against them, grieved and out of appetite for the good venison they had. Kurshin that he was, he could not eat with his animals in want. A man was to be judged by his horses and the fitness of them; and had it been grain they themselves were eating he would gladly have given them his share and gone hungry.

He went and settled glumly by the fire, working his stiffening hand, which was affected by the cold. "We must somehow get down from this height," he said, "by tomorrow, even if it takes us by some more dangerous road. We are out of grain but for one day. These horses cannot force drifts like these and go hungry too. We will kill them if we keep on."

She nodded quietly. "We are on a short road," she said.

"Lady, I do not know this way, and I have ridden the track from Morija to Koris's border to Erd several ways."

"It is a road I knew," she said, and looked up at the clouding sky, the pinetops black against the veiled moon. "It was less overgrown then."

He made a gesture against evil, unthought and reflexive. He thought then that it would anger her. Instead she glanced down briefly, as if avoiding reply.

"Where are we going?" he asked her. "Are we looking for something?"

"No," she said. "I know where it lies."

"Lady," he asked of her, for she seemed about to sink into another of her silences. He made a bow, earnestly; he could not bear another day of that. "Lady, where? Where are we going?"

"To Ivrel." And when in dread he opened his mouth to protest that madness: "I have not told you yet," she said, "what service I claim of thee."

"No," he agreed, "you have not."

"It is this, *ilin.* To kill the Hjemur-lord Thiye and to destroy his citadel if I die."

A laugh escaped him, became a sob. This was the thing she had promised the six lords she would do. Ten thousand men had died in that attempt, so that many surmised she had never been enemy to Thiye of Hjemur, but friend and servant-witch, set out to ruin the Middle Lands.

"Ah, I will go with thee," she said. " I do not ask you to do this thing alone; but if I am lost, that is your service to me."

"Why?" he asked abruptly. "For revenge? What wrong have I done you, lady?"

"I came to seal the Gates," she said, "and if I should be lost, that is the means to do it. I do not think I can teach you otherwise. But take my weapons and strike at the heart of Hjemur's hold: that would do it as well as I ever could."

"If you wish to ruin the Gates," he said bitterly, for he did not half believe her, "there was a beginning to be made at Aenor-Pyvvn's fires, and you rode past it."

"Pointless to meddle with it. They are all dangerous; but the master Gate is that you call the Witchfires: without it all the others must fade. They all once led to there: now they only exist, without depth or direction. They are the one thing that Thiye has not fully discovered how to manage. He cannot stop or use them singly. Thiye is no blood of mine, but he has had instruction. He plays with things he only half understands, although it may be," she added, "that a hundred years may have increased his wisdom."

"I understand nothing at all," he protested. "Set me free of this thing. It does no honor to you to ask such a thing of me. I will go with you, I swear this: I will do you *ilin*'s service until you have seen through what you will do, no matter how mean or how miserable things you ask of me. I swear that, even beyond my year, even to Ivrel, if that is where you are going. But do not ask me to do this thing and hang my oath as *ilin* on it."

"All these things," she said softly, "I have of the oath you have already given me." And then her voice became almost kindly: "Vanye, I am desperate. Five of us came here and four are dead, because we did not know clearly what we faced. Not all the old knowledge is dead here; Thiye has found teachers for himself, and perhaps he has indeed grown in knowledge: in some part I hope he has. His ignorance is as dangerous as his malice. But if I send you, I will not send you totally ignorant."

He bowed his head. "Do not tell me these things. If you need a right arm, I am there. No more than that."

"Well enough," she said, "well enough for now. I will not force any knowledge on thee that does not have to be."

And she applied knife to a twig and sharpened it to hold the strips of venison.

He slipped his helmet off, for it hurt his brow from long wearing, but he did not slip the coif: it was cold and shame still prevented him, even in her sight. He wrapped the cloak about him and undertook to cook his own food, and shared wine with her. He went over to the log after that, and stretched

himself upon the higher part of it, and she upon the lower a
time later. It was a peculiar sort of bed, but better by far than
the cold snow below them; and he tucked himself up like a
warrior on a bier, his longsword clasped upon his breast, for
he did not want to let it out of his grasp on this night, and in
this place. He did not even keep it in its sheath.

And late, when the fire had become very low, he became uneasy with the impression that there was something stirring besides the wind that cracked the icy branches, something large
and of weight; and he strained his eyes and hearing and held
his breath to see and listen to what it might be.

Suddenly he saw Morgaine's hand seek toward her belt beneath her cloak, and he knew that she was awake.

"I will put wood upon the fire," he said, this also for any
watcher. He rolled off the log into a crouch, almost expecting
a rush of something.

Brush cracked. Snow crunched, rapidly receding.

He looked at Morgaine.

"It was no wolf," she said. "Go feed the fire, and keep an
eye to the horses. If we ride out now we are perhaps no better
target than we are sitting here, but I fear this trail has changed
too much to chance it in the dark."

It was an uneasy night thereafter. The clouds grew thicker.
Toward morning there came the first siftings of snow.

Vanye swore, heartbreakingly, with feeling. He hated the
cold like death itself; it closed in about them until all the world
was white, and they drifted through the veiling wind as they
rode, like wraiths, nearly losing one another upon occasion,
until the lowering sky ceased to sift down on them and they
had an afternoon free of misery.

The trail ceased to be a trail at all, yet Morgaine still pro-
fessed to know the way: she had, she avowed, ridden it only
a few days ago, when trees were still young that now were
old, where others stood that now did not, and the path was
fair and well-ridden. Yet she insisted she would not mistake
their way.

And toward evening they did indeed come to what seemed
a proper road, or the remnant of one, and made a camp in a
pleasant place that was at least sheltered from the rising wind,
a hollow among rocks that looked out upon an open meadow
—rare in these hills. With the wind up and no dry bed for
their rest, he did what he could with pine boughs, and tried beneath the snow for grass for the horses, but it was too deep,
and iced. He fed the animals the last of the grain, wondering

what would become of them on the morrow, and then returned to the fire that Morgaine had made, there to sit
hunched in his cloak like a winter bird, miserable and deject-
ed. He slept early, taking what rest he could until Morgaine
nudged him with her foot. Thereafter she slept in the warm
place he had quitted, and he sat slumped against a rock and
wrapped his arms and legs about his longsword, trying against
his weariness to hold himself alert.

He nodded, unintended, jerked erect again. One of the horses snorted. He thought that he himself had startled it by his
sudden movement, but the uneasiness nagged at him.

Then he rose up with unsheathed sword in hand and walked
out to see the horses.

A weight hit his back, snarling and spitting and sounding
human. He cried out and spun, wrist shocked as the sword bit
bone; and something went loping off, hunched and shadowy
in the dark. There were others joining it in its retreat. He saw
a light flash, spun about to see Morgaine.

For an instant he cringed, fearing what she held no less than
he feared beasts out of Koris, and still trembling in every limb
from the attack.

She waited for him, and he came back to her, knelt down
on the mat of boughs and zealously cleaned his sword in snow
and rubbed it dry. He loathed the blood of Koris-things upon
the clean steel. His hurts were numb; he hoped that there had
not been any to break the skin. He did not think they had
pierced the mail shirt.

"These are not natural beasts," she said.

"No," he agreed. "They are far from natural. But they can
die by natural weapons."

"Is thee hurt?"

"No," he judged, surprised, even pleased that she had asked;
he nodded his head in a half-bow, tribute to courtesy which
liyo did not owe *ilin*. "No, I do not think so."

She settled again. "Will rest? I will wake a while."

"No," he said again. "I could not sleep."

She nodded, settled, and curled herself back to sleep.

The snows had passed by morning; the sun rose clear and
bright upon them, beginning even to melt a little of the snow,
and they took their way down the other side of the mountain
ridge, among pines and rocks and increasing openness of the
road.

Upon a height they suddenly had view of lower lands, of
white shading into green, where lesser altitudes had gained

less snow, and forest lay as far as the eye could see into lesser Koris and into the lower lands.

Far away beyond the haze lay the ominous cone of Ivrel, but it was much too far to see. There were only the hazy white caps of Alis Kaje, mother of eagles, and of Cedur Maje, which were the mountain walls of Morija, dividing Kursh from Andur, Thiye's realms from those of men.

They rode easily this day, found grass for the horses and stopped to rest a time, rode on farther and in lighter spirits. They came upon a fence, a low shepherd's fence of rough stones, the first indication that they had found of human habitation.

It was the first sight of anything human that Vanye had seen since the last brush of a Myya arrow, and he was glad to see the evidence of plain herder folk, and breathed easier. In the last few days and in such company as he now rode one could forget humanity, farms and sheep and normal folk.

Then there was a little house, a homely place with rough stone walls and a garden that had gone to weeds, snow-covered in patches. The shutters hung.

Morgaine shook her head, incredulity in her eyes.

"What was this place?" he asked her.

"A farm," said Morgaine, a fair and pleasant one." And then: "I spent the night here—hardly a month of my life ago. They were kindly folk who lived here."

He thought to himself that they must also have been fearless to have sheltered Morgaine after Irien; and he saw by leaning round in his saddle when they had passed to the far side of the house, that the back portion of the roof had fallen in.

Fire? he wondered. It was not a surprising vengeance taken on people that had sheltered the witch. Morgaine had an uncommon history of disasters where she passed, most often to the innocent.

She did not see. She rode ahead without looking back, and he let his bay—he called the beast Mai, as all his horses would be Mai—overtake the gray. They rode knee to knee, morose and silent. Morgaine was never joyous company. This sight made her melancholy indeed.

Then, upon a sudden winding of the trail, as the pines began to crowd close upon them and upon the little fence, there sat two ragged children.

Male and female they seemed to be, raggle-taggle, shag-haired little waifs of enormous dark eyes and pinched cheeks, sitting on the fence itself despite the snow. They scrambled up, eyes pools of distress, stretching out bony hands.

"Food, food," they cried, "for charity."

The gray, Siptah, reared up, lashing with his hooves; and Morgaine reined him aside, narrowly missing the boy. She had hard shift to hold the animal, who shied, wide-nostrilled and round-eyed until his haunches brought up against the wall up-on the other side, and Vanye curbed his Mai with a hard hand, cursing at the reckless children. Such waifs were not an un-common sight in Koris. They begged, stole shamelessly.

There but for Rijan, Vanye thought occasionally: lord's bas-tards sometimes came to other fates than he had known before his exile. The poor were frequent in the hills of Andur, clan-less and destitute, and poor girls' fatherless children generally came to ill ends. If they survived childhood they grew up as bandits in earnest.

And the girl perhaps would spawn more of her own kind, misery breeding misery.

They could not be more than twelve, the pair of them, and they seemed to be brother and sister—perhaps twins. They had the same wolf-look in their eyes, the same pointed lean-ness to their faces as they huddled together away from the dangerous hooves.

"Food," they still pleaded, holding out each a hand.

"We have enough to spare." Vanye directed his words to Morgaine, a request, for their saddlebags were still heavy with the frozen venison of days before. He pitied such as these chil-dren, loathsome as they were, always gave them charity when he could—for luck, remembering what he was.

And when Morgaine consented with a nod he leaned across and lifted the saddlebag from Siptah's gray back and was about to open it when the girl, venturing close to Mai, snatched his saddleroll off the rear of the saddle, slashing one of its bindings.

He cursed volubly, wiser than to drop their food and give chase to one while the boy lingered: he tossed the leather-wrapped packet at Morgaine, flung his leg over the horn. The boy fled too, vaulting the wall. Vanye went close after him.

"Have a care," Morgaine wished him.

But the fleeing urchins dropped his belongings. Content with that, he paused to gather things up, annoyed that they re-turned to jeer at him like the naughty children they were, dancing about him.

He snatched as the boy darted too close to him, meaning no

more than to cuff him and shake him to sober sense; the boy twisted in his grip and gave forth a stream of curses, and the girl with a shriek rushed at him and clawed at his hand upon the boy—a bodkin in her hand. It pierced deep, enough that he snatched back his hand.

They shrieked and ran, leaving him with the spoils, and vanished among the trees. He was still cursing under his breath when he returned to Morgaine, sucking at the painful wound the little minx had dealt his hand.

"Children of imps," he muttered. "Thieves. Misgotten brigands." He had lost face before his *liyo*, his lady-lord, and swung up into Mai's saddle with sullen grace, having tied his gear behind. Until this time he had felt unworthily used, taken in treachery and unworthily on *her* part: it was the first time he had to feel that he had fallen short in his obligation, and that made him doubly debted, disgracing both himself and his *liyo*.

And then he began to feel strangely, like a man having drunk too much wine, his head humming and his whole person strangely at variance with all that was about him.

He gazed at Morgaine in alarm, reluctant to plead for help, but suddenly he felt he needed it. He could not understand what was the matter with his senses. It was like the onset of fever. He swayed in the saddle.

Morgaine's slim arm stayed him. She put Siptah close to him, holding him. He heard her voice speaking sharply to him and sternly ordering him to hold himself up.

He centered his weight and slumped, wit enough to do that, at least, distributing his failing body over Mai's neck. The saddlehorn was painful; the bending cut off his wind. He could not even summon the strength in his arms to deal with that.

Morgaine was afoot. She had his injured hand. He felt pain in it, distantly, felt her warm mouth touch it. She dealt with it like snakebite, spitting out the poison, cursing at him or at her own fell spirits in a tongue he could not understand, which frightened him.

He tried to help her. He could not think of anything for a time, and was surprised to find that she had moved again, and was upon Siptah, leading his horse by the reins, and that they were riding again upon the snowy road. She had on his own plain cloak: the furs were warming him.

He clung to the saddle until his numb body finally told him that she had bound him so that he could not fall. He let himself go then, and yielded to the horse's motion. Thirst plagued him. He could not summon the will to ask for anything. He was dimly aware of interludes of travel, interspersed with darkness.

And the darkness was growing in the sky.

He was dying. He became sure of it. It began to trouble him that he might die and she forget her promise and send him into the hereafter with alien rites. He was terrified at the thought: for that terror alone he refused to die. He fought every lapse into unconsciousness. At times he almost gained will and wit enough to speak to her, but all his words came out twisted, and she generally ignored him, assuming him fevered, or not caring.

Then he knew that there were riders about them. He saw the crest upon him that led them, that of wolf with a deer within its jaws, and he knew the mark and tried desperately to warn her.

Still even they took his words for raving. Morgaine fell in with them, and they were escorted down into the vale of Koris, toward Ra-leth.

CHAPTER IV

THERE WAS A tattered look about the hall, full of cobwebs in the corners, the mortar crumbling here and there, making hollow gaps between the big irregular stones so that spiders had abundant hiding places. The wooden frame did not quite meet the stone about the door. The bracket for the burning torch hung most precariously by a single one of its four bolts.

The bed itself sagged uncomfortably. Vanye searched about with his left hand to discover the limits of it: his right hand was sorely swollen, puffed with venom. He could not clearly remember what had been done, save that he lay here while things came clear again, and there was a person who hovered about him from time to time, fending others away.

He realized finally that the person was Morgaine, Morgaine without her cloak, black-clad and slim in men's clothing, and yet with the most incongrous *tgihio*—overrobe—of silver and black: she had a barbaric bent yet unsuspected; and the blade *Changeling* was hung over her chair, and her other gear propping her feet—most unwomanly.

He gazed at her trying to bring his mind to clarity and remember how they had come there, and still could not. She saw him and smiled tautly.

"Well," she said, "thee will not lose the arm."

He moved the sore hand and tried to flex the fingers. They were too swollen. What she had said still frightened him, for the arm was affected up to the elbow, and that hurt to bend.

"Flis!" Morgaine called.

A girl appeared, backing into the room, for she had hands full of linens and a basin of steaming water.

The girl made shift to bow obeisance to Morgaine, and Morgaine scowled at her and jerked her head in the direction of Vanye.

The hot water pained him. He set his teeth and endured the compresses of hot towels, and directed his attention instead to

46

his attendant. Flis was dark-haired and sloe-eyed, intensely, hotly female. The low peasant bodice gaped a bit as she bent; she smiled at him and touched his face. Her bearing, her manner, was that of many a girl in hall that was low-clan or no clan, who hoped to get of some lord a child to lift her to honorable estate. No seed of his could ennoble anyone, but she surely plied her arts with him because he was safe at the moment and he was a stranger.

She soothed his fever with her hands and gave him well-watered wine to drink, and talked to him in little sweet words which made no particular sense. When her hands touched his brow he realized that she made no objection of his shorn hair, which would have warned any sensible woman of his character and his station and sent her indignantly hence.

Then he remembered that he was surely in the hall of clan Leth, where outcasts and outlaws were welcome so long as they bore the whims of lord Kasedre and were not particular what orders they obeyed. Here such a man as he was no novelty, perhaps of no less honor than the rest.

Then he saw Morgaine on her feet, looking at him over the shoulder of the girl Flis, and Morgaine gave him a faintly disgusted look, judgment of the awkwardly predatory maid. She turned and paced to the window, out of convenient view.

He closed his eyes then, content to have the pain of his arm attended, required to do nothing. He had lost all the face a man could lose, being rescued by his *liyo*, a woman, and given over to servants such as this.

Leth tolerated Morgaine's presence, even paid her honor, to judge by the splendor of the guest-robe they offered her, and indulged her lord-right, treating her as equal.

Flis's hand strayed. He moved it, indignant at such treatment in his *liyo*'s presence, and her a woman. Flis giggled.

Brocade rustled. Morgaine paced back again, scowled and nodded curtly to the girl. Flis grew quickly sober, gathered up her basin and her towels with graceless haste.

"Leave them," Morgaine ordered.

Flis abandoned them on the table beside the door and bowed her way out.

Morgaine walked over to the bed, lifted the compress on Vanye's injured hand, shook her head. Then she went over to the door and slid the chair over in such fashion that no one outside could easily open the door.

"Are we threatened?" Vanye asked, disturbed by such precautions.

Morgaine busied herself with her own gear, extracting some of her own unguents from the kit. "I imagine we are," she said. "But that is not why I barred the door. We are not provided with a lock and I grow weary of that minx spying on my business."

He watched uneasily as she set her medicines out on the table beside him. "I do not want—"

"Objections denied." She opened a jar and smeared a little medication into the wound, which was wider and more painful than before, since the compress. The medication stung and made it throb, but numbed the wound thereafter. She mixed something into water for him to drink, and insisted and ordered him to drink it.

Thereafter he was sleepy again, and began to perceive that Morgaine was the agent of it this time.

She was sitting by him still when he awoke, polishing his much-battered helm, tending his armor, he supposed, from boredom. She tilted her head to one side and considered him.

"How fare you now?"

"Better," he said, for he seemed free of fever.

"Can you rise?"

He tried. It was not easy. He realized in his blindness and his concern with the effort itself, that he was not clothed, and snatched at the sheet, nearly falling in the act: Kurshin were a modest folk. But it mattered little to Morgaine. She estimated him with an analytical eye that was in itself more embarrassing than the blush she did not own.

"You will not ride with any great endurance," she said, "which is an inconvenience. I have no liking for this place. I do not trust our host at all, and I may wish to quit this hall suddenly."

He sank down again, reached for his clothing and tried to dress, one-handed as he was.

"Our host," he said, "is Kasedre, lord of Leth. And you are right. He is mad."

He omitted to mention that Kasedre was reputed to have *qujalin* blood in his veins, and that that heredity was given as reason for his madness; Morgaine, though unnerving in her oddness, was at least sane.

"Rest," she bade him when he had dressed, for the effort had taxed him greatly. "You may need your strength. They have our horses in stables downstairs near the front entry, down this hall outside to the left, three turns down the stairs and left to the first door. Mark that. Listen, I will show you what I have observed of this place, in the case we must take our leave separately."

And sitting on the bed beside him she traced among the bedclothes the pattern of the halls and the location of doors and rooms, so that he had a fair estimation of where things lay without having laid eye upon them. She had a good faculty for such things: he was pleased to learn his *liyo* was sensible and experienced in matters of defense. He began to be more optimistic of their chances in this place.

"Are we prisoners," he asked, "or are we guests?"

"I am a guest in name, at least," she said, "but this is not a happy place for guesting."

There was a knock at the door. Someone tried it. When it did not yield, the visitor padded off down the hall.

"Do you have any wish to linger here?" he asked.

"I feel," she said, "rather like a mouse passing a cat: probably there is no harm and the beast looks well-fed and lazy; but it would be a mistake to scurry."

"If the cat is truly hungry," he said, "we delude ourselves." She nodded.

This time there was a deliberate knock at the door.

Vanye scrambled for his longsword, hooked it to his belt, convenient to the left hand. Morgaine moved the chair and opened the door.

It was Flis again. The girl smiled uncertainly and bowed. Vanye saw her in clearer light this time, without the haze of fever. She was not as young as he had thought. It was paint that blushed her cheek and her dress was not country and innocence: it was blowsy. She simpered and smiled past Morgaine at Vanye.

"You are wanted," she said.

"Where?" asked Morgaine.

Flis did not want to look up into Morgaine's eyes: addressed, she had no choice. She did so and visibly cringed: her head only reached Morgaine's shoulders, and her halo of frizzled brown seemed dull next to Morgaine's black and silver. "To hall, lady." She cast a second wishing look back at Vanye, back again. "Only you, lady. They did not ask the man."

He is *ilin* to me," she said. "What is the occasion?"

"To meet my lord," said Flis. "It is all right," she insisted. "I can take care for him."

"Never mind," said Morgaine. "He will do very well without, Flis. That will be all."

Flis blinked: she did not seem particularly intelligent. Then she backed off and bowed and went away, beginning to run.

Morgaine turned about and looked at Vanye. "My apologies," she said dryly. "Are you fit to go down to hall?"

He bowed assent, thoroughly embarrassed by Morgaine, and wondering whether he should be outraged. He did not want Flis. Protesting it was graceless too. He ignored her gibe and avowed that he was fit. He was not steady on his feet. He thought that it would pass.

She nodded to him and led the way out of the room.

Everything outside was much the same as she had described to him. The hall was in general disrepair, like some long abandoned fortress suddenly occupied and not yet quite liveable. There was a mustiness about the air, a queasy feeling of dirt, and effluvium of last night's feasting, of grease and age and untended cracks, and earth and damp.

"Let us simply walk for the door," Vanye suggested when they reached that lower floor and he knew that the lefthand way led to the outside, and their horses, and a wild, quick ride out of this place of madmen. "*Liyo,* let us not stay here. Let us take nothing from this place, let us go, now, quickly."

"Thee is not fit for a chase," she said. "Or I would, gladly. Be still. Do not offend our hosts."

They walked unescorted down the long corridors, where sometimes were servants that looked like beggars that sometimes appeared at hold gates, asking their three days of lawful charity. It was shame to a lord to keep folk of his hall in such a state. And the hold of Leth was huge. Its stones were older than Morgaine's ride to Irien, older by far in all its parts, and in its day it had been a grand hall, most fabled in its beauty. If she had seen it then, it was sadly otherwise now, with the tapestries in greasy rags and bare stone showing through the tattered and dirty carpets on the floors. There were corridors which they did not take, great open halls that breathed with damp and decay, closed doors that looked to have remained undisturbed for years. Rats scurried sullenly out of their path, seeking the large cracks in the masonry, staring out at them with small glittering eyes.

"How much of this place have you seen?" he asked of her.

"Enough," she said, "to know that there is much amiss here. Nhi Vanye, whatever bloodfeuds you have with Leth, you are *ilin* to me. Remember it."

"I have none with Leth," he said. "Sensible men avoid them altogether. Madness is like yeast in this whole loaf. It breeds and rises. Guard what you say, *liyo*, even if you are offended."

And of a sudden he saw the lean face of the boy leering out at them from a cross-corridor, the sister beside him, rat-eyed and smiling. Vanye blinked. They were not there. He could not be sure whether he had seen them or not.

The door to the main hall gaped ahead of them. He hastened to overtake Morgaine. There were any number of bizarre personages about, a clutch of men that looked more fit to surround some hillside campfire as bandits—they lounged at the rear of the hall; and a few high-clan *uyin* that he took for Leth, who lounged about the high tables in the hall. These latter were also lean and hungry and out-at-the-elbows, their *tgihin* gaudy, but frayed at hems: to do justice to their charity and hospitality to Morgaine, they were indeed less elegant than what they had lent to her.

And there was a man that could only have been Leth Kasedre, who sat in the chair of honor at center, youngish to look upon—he could surely have been no more than thirty, and yet his babyish face was sallow, beneath a fringe of dark hair that wanted trimming: no warrior's braid for this one, and much else that went to make up a man seemed likely wanting too. His hair hung in twining ringlets. His eyes were hunted, darting from this to that; his mouth was like that of a sick man, loose, moist at the edges. He exuded heat and chill at once, like fever.

And his clothing was splendor itself, cloth-of-gold, his narrow chest adorned with brooches and clasps and chains of gold. A jeweled Honor blade was at his belt, and a jeweled longsword, which added decoration useless and pathetic. The air about him was thick with the reek of perfumes that masked decay. As they came near him there was no doubt. It was a sickroom smell.

Kasedre arose, extended a thin hand to offer place to Morgaine, who tucked up her feet and settled on the low bench courtiers had vacated for her, a place of honor; she wore *Changeling* high at her back and released the hook that secured the shoulderstrap at her waist, letting strap and blade slide to her hip for comfort, sitting. She bowed gracefully; Kasedre returned the courtesy.

Vanye must perforce kneel at the Leth's feet and touch brow to floor, respect which the Leth hardly deigned to acknowledge, intent as he was on Morgaine. Vanye crept aside to his place behind her. It was bitter: he was a warrior—had been, at least; he had been proud, though bastard, and certain-

ly Nhi Rijan's bastard ranked higher than this most notorious
of hedge-lords. But he had seen *ilinin* at Ra-morij forced to
such humiliation, refused Claiming, forgotten, ignored, no one
reckoning what the man might have been before he became
ilin and nameless. It was not worth protest now: the Leth was
supremely dangerous.

"I am intrigued to have the likes of you among us," said
Leth Kasedre. "Are you truly that Morgaine of Irien?"

"I never claimed to be," said Morgaine.

The Leth blinked, leaned back a little, licked the corners
of his mouth in perplexity. "But you are, truly," he said.
"There was never the like of you in this world."

Morgaine's lips suddenly acquired a smile as feral as
Kasedre's could be. "I am Morgaine," she said. "You are
right."

Kasedre let his breath go in a long sigh. He performed
another obeisance that had to be answered, rare honor for a
guest in hall. "How are you among us? Do you come back—
to ride to other wars?"

He sounded eager, even delighted at the prospect.

"I am seeing what there is to be seen," said Morgaine. "I
am interested in Leth. You seem an interesting beginning to
my travels. And," a modest lowering of eyes, "you have been
most charitable in the matter of my *ilin*—if it were not for
the twins."

Kasedre licked his lips and looked suddenly nervous.
"Twins? Ah, wicked, wicked, those children. They will be
disciplined."

"Indeed they should be," said Morgaine.

"Will you share dinner with us this evening?"

Morgaine's precise and delighted smile did not vary. "Most
gladly, most honored, Leth Kasedre. My *ilin* and I will
attend."

"Ah, but ill as he is—"

"My *ilin* will attend," she said. Her tone was delicate ice,
still smiling. Kasedre flinched from that and smiled also,
chanced in the same moment to look toward Vanye, who
glared back, sullen and well sure of the murder resident in
Kasedre's heart: hate not directed at Morgaine—he was in
awe of her—but of the sight of a man who was not his to
order.

Of a sudden, wildly, he feared Morgaine's own capabilities.
She slipped so easily into mad Kasedre's vein, well able to
play the games he played and tread the maze of his insanities.

Vanye reckoned again his worth to his *liyo*, and wondered whether she would yield him up to Kasedre if need be to escape this mad hall, a bit of human coin strewn along her way and forgotten.

But so far she defended her rights with authoritative persistence, whether for his sake or in her own simple arrogance.

"Have you been dead?" asked Kasedre.

"Hardly," she said. "I took a shortcut. I was only here a month ago. Edjnel was ruling then."

Kasedre's mad eyes glittered and blinked when she casually named a lord his ancestor, dead a hundred years. He looked angry, as if he suspected some humor at his expense.

"A shortcut," she said, unruffled, "across the years you folk have lived, from yesterday to now, straightwise. The world went wide, around the bending of the path. I went through. I am here now, all the same. You look a great deal like Edjnel."

Kasedre's face underwent a rapid series of expressions, ending in delight as he was compared to his famous ancestor. He puffed and swelled so far as his narrow chest permitted, then seemed again to return to the perplexities of the things she posed.

"How?" he asked. "How did you do it?"

"By the fires of Aenor above Pyvvn. It is not hard to use the fires to this purpose—but one must be very brave. It is a fearful journey."

It was too much for Kasedre. He drew a series of deep breaths like a man about to faint, and leaned back, resting his hands upon that great sword, staring about at his gape-mouthed *uyin*, half of whom looked puzzled and the other part too muddled to do anything.

"You will tell us more of this," said Kasedre.

"Gladly, at dinner," she said.

"Ah, sit, stay, have wine with us," begged Kasedre.

Morgaine gave forth that chill smile again, dazzling and false. "By your leave, lord Kasedre, we are still weary from our travels and we will need a time to rest or I fear we shall not last a late banquet. We will go to our room and rest a time, and then come down at whatever hour you send for us."

Kasedre pouted. In such as he the moment was dangerous, but Morgaine continued to smile, bright and deadly, and full of promises. Kasedre bowed. Morgaine rose and bowed.

Vanye inclined himself again at Kasedre's feet, had a

moment to see the look that Kasedre cast at Morgaine's back.

It was, he was glad to see, still awestruck.

Vanye was shaking with exhaustion when they reached the security of their upstairs room. He himself moved the chair before the door again, and sat down on the bed. Morgaine's cold hand touched his brow, seeking fever.

"Are you well?" she asked.

"Well enough. Lady, you are mad to sample anything of his at table tonight."

"It is not a pleasant prospect, I grant you that." She took off the dragon sword and set it against the wall.

"You are playing with him," said Vanye, "and he is mad."

"He is accustomed to having his way," said Morgaine. "The novelty of this experience may intrigue him utterly."

And she sat down in the other plain chair and folded her arms. "Rest," she said. "I think we may both need it."

He eased back on the bed, leaning his shoulder against the wall, and brooded over matters. "I am glad," he said out of those thoughts, "that you did not ride on and leave me here senseless with fever as I was. I am grateful, *liyo*."

She looked at him, gray eyes catwise and comfortable. "Then thee admits," she said, "that there are some places worse to be *ilin* than in my service?"

The thought chilled him. "I do admit it," he said. "This place being chief among them."

She propped her feet upon her belongings: he lay down and shut his eyes and tried to rest. The hand throbbed. It was still slightly swollen. He would have gladly gone outside and packed snow about it, reckoning that of more value than Flis's poultices and compresses or Morgaine's *qujalin* treatments.

"The imp's knife was plague-ridden," he said.

Then, remembering: "Did you see them?"

"Who?"

"The boy—the girl—"

"Here?"

"In the downstairs corridor after you passed."

"I am not at all surprised."

"Why do you endure this?" he asked. "Why did you not resist them bringing us here? You could have dealt with my injury yourself—and probably with them too."

"You perhaps have an exaggerated idea of my capacities. I am not able to lift a sick man about, and argument did not seem profitable at the moment. When it does, I shall consider doing something. But you are charged with my safety, Nhi Vanye, and with protecting me. I do expect you to fulfill that obligation."

He lifted his swollen hand. "That—is not within my capacity at the moment, if it comes to fighting our way out of here."

"Ah. So you have answered your own first question." That was Morgaine at her most irritating. She settled again to waiting, then began instead to pace. She was very like a wild thing caged. She needed something for her hands, and there was nothing left. She went to the barred window and looked out and returned again.

She did that by turns for a very long time, sitting a while, pacing a while, driving him to frenzy, in which if he had not been in pain, he might also have risen and paced the room in sheer frustration. Had the woman ever been still, he wondered, or did she ever cease from what drove her? It was not simple restlessness at their confinement. It was the same thing that burned in her during their time on the road, as if they were well enough while moving, but any untoward delay fretted her beyond bearing.

It was as if death and the Witchfires were an appointment she were zealous to keep, and she resented every petty human interference in her mission.

The sunlight in the room decreased. Things became dim. When the furniture itself grew unclear, there came a rap on the door. Morgaine answered it. It was Flis.

"Master says come," said Flis.

"We are coming," said Morgaine. The girl delayed in the doorway, twisting her hands.

Then she fled.

"That one is no less addled than the rest," Morgaine. "But she is more pitiable." She gathered up her sword, her other gear too, and concealed certain of her equipment within her robes. "Lest," she said, "someone examine things while we are gone."

"There is still the chance of running for the door," he said. "*Liyo*, take it. I am stronger. There is no reason I cannot somehow ride."

"Patience," she urged him. "Besides, this man Kasedre is interesting."

"He is also," he said, "ruthless and a murderer."

"There are Witchfires in Leth," she said. "Living next to the Witchfires as the Witchfires seem to have become since I left—is not healthful. I should not care to stay here very long."

"Do you mean that the evil of the thing—of the fires—has made them what they are?"

"There are emanations," she said, "which are not healthful. I do not myself know all that can be the result of them. I only know that I do not like the waste I saw about me when I rode out at Aenor-Pyvvn, and I like even less what I see in Leth. The men are more twisted than the trees."

"You cannot warn these folk," he protested. "They would as lief cut our throats as not if we cross them. And if you mean something else with them, some—"

"Have a care," she said. "There is someone in the hall."

Steps had paused. They moved on again, increasing in speed. Vanye swore softly. "This place is full of listeners."

"We are surely the most interesting listening in the place," she said. "Come, and let us go down to the hall. Or do you feel able? If truly not, I shall plead indisposition myself—it is a woman's privilege—and delay the business."

In truth he faced the possibility of a long evening with the mad Leth with dread, not alone of the Leth, but because of the fever that still burned in his veins. He would rather try to ride now, now, while he had the strength. If trouble arose in the hall, he was not sure that he could help Morgaine or even himself.

In truth, he reckoned that among her weapons she had the means to help herself: it was her left-handed *ilin* that might not make it out.

"I could stay here," he said.

"With *his* servants to attend you?" she asked. "You could not gracefully bar the door against them yourself, but no one thinks odd the things I do. Say that you are not fit and I will stay here and bar the door myself."

"No," he said. "I am fit enough. And you are probably right about the servants." He thought of Flis, who, if she entertained everyone in this loathsome hall with the same graces she plied with him, would probably be fevered herself, or carry some more ugly sickness. And he recalled the twins, who had slipped into the dark like a pair of the palace rats: for some reason they and their little knives inspired him with more terror than Myya archers had ever done. He could not strike at them as they deserved; that they were children still stayed his hand; and yet they had no scruples, and their daggers were razor-sharp—like rats, he thought again, like rats, whose sharp teeth made them fearsome despite their size. He dreaded even for Morgaine with the like of them skittering about the halls and conniving together in the shadows.

She left. He walked at his proper distance half a pace behind Morgaine, equally for the sake of formality and for safety's sake. He had discovered one saw things that way, things that happened just after Morgaine had glanced away. He was only *ilin*. No one paid attention to a servant. And Kasedre's servants feared her. It was in their eyes. That was, in this hall, great tribute.

And even the bandits as they entered the hall watched her with caution in their hot eyes, a touch of ice, a cold wind over them. It was curious: there was more respect in the afterwave of her passing than the nonchalance they showed to her face.

A greater killer than any of them, he thought unworthily; they respected her for that.

But the Leth, the *uyin* that gathered at the high tables, watched her through polite smiles, and there was lust there too, no less than in the bandits' eyes, but cold and tempered with fear. Morgaine was supremely beautiful. Vanye kept that thought at a distance within himself—he was tempted to few liberties with the *qujal*, and that one last of all. But when he saw her in that hall, her pale head like a blaze of sun in that darkness, her slim form elegant in *tgihio* and bearing the dragon blade with the grace of one who could truly use it, an odd vision came to him: he saw like a fever-dream a nest of corruption with one gliding serpent among the scuttling lesser creatures—more evil than they, more deadly, and infinitely beautiful, reared up among them and hypnotizing with basilisk eyes, death dreaming death and smiling.

He shuddered at the vision and saw her bow to Kasedre, and performed his own obeisance without looking into the mad, pale face: he retreated to his place, and when they were served, he examined carefully and sniffed at the wine they were offered.

Morgaine drank; he wondered could her arts make her proof against drugs and poisons, or save him, who was not. For his part he drank sparingly, and waited long between drafts, toying with it merely, waiting for the least dizziness to follow: none did. If they were being poisoned, it was to be more subtle.

The dishes were various: they both ate the simple ones,

and slowly. There was an endless flow of wine, of which they both drank sparingly; and at last, at long last, Morgaine and Kasedre still smiling at each other, the last dish was carried out and servants pressed yet more wine on them.

"Lady Morgaine," begged Kasedre then, "you gave us a puzzle and promised us answers tonight."

"Of Witchfires?"

Kasedre bustled about the table to sit near her, and waved an energetic hand at the harried, patch-robed scribe who had hovered constantly at his elbow this evening. "Write, write," he said to the scribe, for in every hall of note there was an archivist who kept records properly and made an account of hall business.

"How interesting your Book would be to me," murmured Morgaine, "with all the time I have missed of the affairs of men. Do give me this grace, my lord Kasedre—to borrow your Book for a moment."

Oh mercy, Vanye thought, *are we doomed to stay here a time more?* He had hoped that they could retreat, and he looked at the thickness of the book and at all the bored lordlings sitting about them flushed with wine, looking like beasts thirsting for the kill, and reckoned uneasily how long their patience would last.

"We would be honored," replied Kasedre. It was probably the first time in years that anyone had bothered with the musty tome of Leth, replete as it must be with murderings and incest. The rumors were dark enough, though little news came out of Leth.

"Here," said Morgaine, and took into her lap the moldering book of the scribe, while the poor old scholar—a most wretched old man and reeking of drink—sat at her brocaded knee and looked up at her, wrinkle browed and squinting. His eyes and nose ran. He blotted at both with his sleeve. She cracked the book, disturbing pages moldered together, handling the old pages reverently, separating them with her nail, folding them down properly as she sought the years she wanted.

Somewhere at the back of the hall some of the less erudite members of the banquet were engaged in riotous conversation. It sounded as if a gambling game were in progress. She ignored it entirely, although Kasedre seemed irritated by it; the lord Leth himself squatted down to hear her, hanging upon her long silence in awe. Her forefinger traced words. Vanye's view over her shoulder showed yellowed parchment and ink that had turned red-brown and faint. It was a wonder that one who lisped the language as uncertainly as she did could manage that ancient scrawl, but her lips moved as she thought the words.

"My dear old friend Edjnel," she said softly. "Here is his death—what, murdered?" Kasedre craned his neck to see the word. "And his daughter—ah, little Linna—drowned upon the lakeshore. This is sad news. But Tohme did rule, surely—"

"My father," interjected Kasedre, "was Tohme's son." His eyes kept darting to her face anxiously, as if he found fear of her condemnation.

"When I remember Tohme," she said, "he was playing at his mother's knee: the lady Aromwel, a most gracious, most lovely person. She was Chya. I rode to this hall upon a night . . ." She eased the fragile pages backward. "Yes, here, you see:

". . . *came She even to Halle, bearing sad Tidings from the Road. Lorde Aralde . . .*—brother to Edjnel and to my friend Lrie, who went with me to Irien, and died there—*Lorde Aralde had met with Mischance upon his faring in her Companie that attempted the Saving of Leth against the Darke, which advanceth out of . . .* Well, well, this was another sad business, that of lord Arald. He was a good man. Unlucky. An arrow out of the forest had him; and the wolves were on my trail by then. . . . *herein she feared the Border were lost, that there would none rallye to the Saving of the Middle Realms, save only Chya and Leth, and they strippt of Men and sorely hurt. So gave she Farewell to Leth and left the Halle, much mourned . . .* Well, that is neither here nor there. It touches me to think that I am missed at least in Leth." Her fingers sought further pages. "Ah, here is news. My old friend Zri—he was counselor to Tiffwy, you know. Or do you not? Well. . . . *Chya Zri has come to Leth, he being friend to the Kings of Koris.*" A feral grin was on her face, as if that mightily amused her. "Friend—she laughed softly—"aye, friend to Tiffwy's wife, and thereon hung a tale."

Kasedre twisted with both hands at his sleeve, his poor fevered eyes shifting nervously from her to the book and back again. "Zri was highly honored here," he said. "But he died."

"Zri was a fox," said Morgaine. "Ah, clever, that man. It was surely like him *not* to have been at Irien after all, although he rode out with us. Zri had an ear to the ground

constantly: he could smell disaster, Tiffwy always said. And
Edjnel never trusted him. But unfortunately Tiffwy did. And
I wonder indeed that Edjnel took him in when he appeared
at the gates of Leth. . . . *he has honored us by his Presence,
tutor . . . to the younge Prince Leth Tohme . . . to guide in
all divers manner of Statecraft and Publick Affaires, being
Guardian also of the Lady Chya Aromwel and her daughter
Linna, at the lamented Decease of Leth Edjnel . . .*"

"Zri taught my grandfather," said Kasedre when Morgaine
remained sunk in thought. He prattled on, nervous, eager to
please. "And my father for a time too. He was old, but he
had many children—"

One of the *uyin* tittered behind his hand. It was injudicious.
Leth Kasedre turned and glared, and that *uyo* bowed himself
to his face and begged pardon quickly, claiming some action
in the back of the hall as the source of his amusement.

"What sort was Tohme?" asked Morgaine.

"I do not know," said Kasedre. "He drowned. Like aunt
Linna."

"Who was your father?"

"Leth Hes." Kasedre puffed a bit with pride, insisted to
turn the pages of the book himself, to show her. "He was a
great lord."

"Tutored by Zri."

"And he had a great deal of gold." Kasedre refused to be
distracted. But then his face fell. "But I never saw him. He
died. He drowned too."

"Most unfortunate. I should stay clear of water, my lord
Leth. Where did it happen? The lake?"

"They think—" Kasedre lowered his voice— "that my
father was a suicide. He was always morose. He brooded
about the lake. Especially after Zri was gone. Zri—"

"—drowned?"

"No. He rode out and never came back. It was a bad night.
He was an old man anyway." His face assumed a pout. "I
have answered every one of your questions, and you promised
my answer and you have not answered it. Where were you,
all these years? What became of you, if you did not die?"

"If a man," she said, continuing to read while she answered
him, "rode into the Witchfires of Aenor-Pyvvn, then he would
know. It is possible for anyone. However, it has certain—
costs."

"The Witchfires of Leth," he said, licking moisture from
the corners of his mouth. "Would they suffice?"

"Most probably," she said. "However, it is chancy. The fires have certain potential for harm. I know the safety of Aenor-Pyvvn. It could do no bodily harm. But I should not chance Leth's fires unless I had seen them. They are by the lake, which seems to take so much toll of Leth. I should rather other aid than that, lord Leth. Seek Aenor-Pyvvn." She still gave him only a part of her attention, continuing to push the great moldering pages back one after another. Then her eyes darted to the aged scholar. "Thee looks almost old enough to remember me."

The poor old man, trembling, tried the major obeisance at being directly noticed by Morgaine, and could not make it gracefully. "Lady, I was not yet born."

She looked at him curiously, and then laughed softly. "Ah, then I have no friends left in Leth at all. There are none so old." She thumbed more pages, more and more rapidly. ". . . *This sad day was funeral for Leth Tohme, aged seventeen yeares, and his Consort . . . lady Leth Jeme . . .* Indeed, indeed—at one burying."

"My grandmother hanged herself for grief," said Kasedre.

"Ah, then your father must have become the Leth when he was very young. And Zri must have had much power."

"Zri. Zri. Zri. Tutors are boring."

"Had you one?"

"Liell. Chya Liell. He is my counselor now."

"I have not met Liell," she said.

Kasedre bit at his lips. "He would not come tonight. He said he was indisposed. "I"—he lowered his voice—"have never known Liell indisposed before."

". . . *Liell of the Chya . . . has given splendid entertainments . . . on the occasion of the birthday of the Leth, Kasedre, most honorable of lords . . . two maidens of the . . .* Indeed." Morgaine blinked, scanned the page. "Most unique. And I have seen a great many entertainments."

"Liell is very clever," said Kasedre. "He devises ways to amuse us. He would not come tonight. That is why things are so quiet. He will think of something for tomorrow."

Morgaine continued to scan the pages. "This is interesting," she assured Kasedre. "I must apologize. I am surely wearying you and interfering with your scribe's recording of my visit, but this does intrigue me. I shall try to repay your hospitality and your patience."

Kasedre bowed very low, thoughtlessly necessitating obeisance by all at the immediate table. "We have kept in every detail the records of your dealings with us in this visit. It is a great honor to our hall."

"Leth has always been very kind to me."

Kasedre reached out his hand, altogether against propriety —it was the action of a child fascinated by glitter—and his trembling fingers touched the arm of Morgaine, and the hilt of *Changeling*.

She ceased to move, every muscle frozen for an instant; then gently she moved her arm and removed his fingers from the dragon blade's hilt.

Vanye's muscles were rock-hard, his left hand already feeling after the release of his nameless sword. They could perhaps reach the midpoint of the hall before fifty swords cut them down.

And he must guard her back.

Kasedre drew back his hand. "Draw the blade," he urged her. "Draw it. I want to see it."

"No," she said. "Not in a friendly hall."

"It was forged here in Leth," said Kasedre, his dark eyes glittering. "They say that the magic of the Witchfires themselves went into its forging. A Leth smith aided in the making of its hilt. I want to see it."

"I never part with it," said Morgaine softly. "I treasure it greatly. It was made by Chan, who was the dearest of my own companions, and by Leth Omry, as you say. Chan carried it a time, but he gave it to me before he died in Irien. It never leaves me, but I think kindly of friends in Leth when I remember its making."

"Let us see it," he said.

"It brings disaster wherever it is drawn," she said, "and I do not draw it."

"We *ask* this."

"I would not—" the painted smile resumed, adamant— "chance any misfortune to the house of Leth. Do believe me."

A pout was on Leth Kasedre's features, a flush upon his sweating cheeks. His breathing grew quick and there was a sudden hush in the hall.

"We *ask* this," he repeated.

"No," said Morgaine. "This I will not."

He snatched at it, and when she avoided his grasp, he spitefully snatched the book instead, whirled to his feet and cast it into the hearth, scattering embers.

The old scholar scuttled crabwise and sobbing after the book, spilling ink that dyed his robes. He rescued it and sat there brushing the little charring fire from its edges. His old lips moved as if he were speaking to it.

And Kasedre shrieked, railing upon his guests until the froth gathered at the corners of his mouth and he turned a most alarming purple. Ingratitude seemed the main burden of his accusations. He wept. He cursed.

"*Qujalin* witch," he began to cry then. "Witch! Witch! Witch!"

Vanye was on his feet, not yet drawing, but sure he must.

Morgaine took a final sip of wine and gathered herself up also. Kasedre was still shouting. He raised his hand to her, trembled as if he did not quite have the courage to strike. Morgaine did not flinch; and Vanye began to ease his blade from the sheath.

Tumult had risen in the hall again: it died a sudden death, beginning at the door. There had appeared there a tall, thin man of great dignity, perhaps forty, fifty years in age. The silence spread. Kasedre began instead to whimper, to utter his complaints under his breath and petulantly.

And incredibly this apparition, this new authority, walked forward to kneel and do Kasedre proper reverence.

"Liell," said Kasedre in a trembling voice.

"Clear the hall," said Liell. His voice was sane and still and terrible.

There was no noise at all, even from the bandits at the rear; the *uyin* began to slink away. Kasedre managed to put up an act of defiance for a moment. Liell stared at him. Then Kasedre turned and fled, running, into the shadows behind the curtains.

Liell bowed a formal and slight courtesy to them both.

"The well-renowned Morgaine of the Chya," he said softly. Here was sanity. Vanye breathed a soft sigh of relief and let his sword slip back. "You are not the most welcome visitor ever to come to this hall," Liell was saying, "but I will warn you all the same, Morgaine: whatever brought you back will send you hence again if you bait Kasedre. He is a child, but he commands others."

"I believe we share clan," she said, cold rebuff to his discourtesy. "I am adopted, kri Chya; but of one clan, you and I."

He bowed again, seemed then to offer true respect. "Your pardon. You are a surprise to me. When the rumor came to me, I did not believe it. I thought perhaps it was some charlatan with a game to play. But you are quite the real thing, I see that. And who is this, this fellow?"

"It is all family," Vanye said, a touch of insolence, that Liell had not been courteous with Morgaine. "I am Chya on my mother's side."

Liell bowed to him. For a moment those strangely frank eyes rested directly upon him, draining him of anger. "Your name, sir?"

"Vanye," he said, shaken by that sudden attention.

"Vanye," said Liell softly. "Vanye. Aye, that is a Chya name. But I have little to do with clan Chya here. I have other work. . . . Lady Morgaine, let me see you to your rooms. You have stirred up quite a nest of troubles. I heard the shouting. I descended—to your rescue, if you will pardon me."

Morgaine nodded him thanks and began to walk with him. Vanye, ignored now, fell in a few paces behind them and kept watch on the doors and corridors.

"I truly did not believe it at first," said Liell. "I thought Kasedre's humors were at work again, or that someone was taking advantage of him. His fantasies are elaborate. May I ask why—?"

Morgaine used that dazzling and false smile on Liell. "No," she said, "I discuss my business with no one I chance to leave behind me. I will be on my way soon. I wish no help. Therefore what I do is of no moment here."

"Are you bound for the territory of Chya?"

"I am clan-welcome there," she said, "but I doubt it would be the same warmth of welcome I knew if I were to go there now. Tell me of yourself, Chya Liell. How does Leth fare these days?"

Liell waved an elegant hand at their surroundings. He was a graceful man, handsome and silver-haired; his dress was modest, night-blue. His shoulders lifted in a sigh. "You see how things are, lady, I am well sure. I manage to keep Leth whole, against the tide of events. As long as Kasedre keeps to his entertainments, Leth thrives. But its thin blood will not breed another generation. The sons and grandsons of Chya Zri—who, I know, found no favor in your eyes—still are the bulwark of Leth in its old age. They serve me well. That in hall—that is the get of Leth, such as remains."

Morgaine refrained from comment. They began to mount the stairs. A pinched little face peered at them from the turning, withdrew quickly.

"The twins," said Vanye.

"Ah," said Liell. "Hshi and Tlin. Nasty characters, those."

"Clever with their hands," said Vanye sourly.

"They are Leth. Hshi is the harpist in hall. Tlin sings. They also steal. Do not let them in your rooms. I suspect it was Tlin who is responsible for your being here. The report was very like her misbehaviors."

"Hardly necessary that she trouble herself," said Morgaine. "My path necessarily led to Ra-leth. I had the mood to come this way. The girl could prove a noisome pest."

"Please," said Liell. "Leave the twins to me. They will not trouble you. . . . What set Kasedre off tonight?"

"He became overexcited," said Morgaine. "I take it that he does not often meet outsiders."

"Not of quality, and not under these circumstances."

They wound up the remaining stairs and came into the hall where their apartments were. The servants were busy at their tasks, lighting the lamps. They made great bows as Liell and Morgaine swept past them.

"Did you eat well?" Liell asked.

"We had sufficient," she said.

"Sleep soundly, lady. Nothing will trouble you." He made a formal bow as Morgaine went inside her own door, but as Vanye would have followed her, Liell prevented him with an outthrust arm.

Vanye stopped, hand upon hilt, but Liell's purpose seemed speech, not violence. He leaned close, set a hand upon Vanye's shoulder, a familiarity a man might use with a servant, talking to him quickly in whispers.

"She is in great danger," said Liell. "Only I fear what she may do. She must leave here, and tonight. Earnestly I tell you this." He leaned closed until Vanye's back was against the wall, and the hand gripped his shoulder with great intensity. "Do not trust Flis and do not trust the twins above all else, and beware of any of Kasedre's people."

"Which you are not?"

"I have no interest in seeing this hall ruined—which could happen if Morgaine takes offense. Please. I know what she is seeking. Come with me and I will show you."

Vanye considered it, gazed into the dark, sober eyes of the man. There was peculiar sadness in them, a magnetism that compelled trust. The strong fingers pressed into the flesh of his shoulder, at once intimate and compelling.

"No," he said. It was hard to force the words. "I am *ilin*. I take her orders. I do not arrange her business for her."

And he tore himself from Liell's fingers and sought the door, trembling so that he missed the latch, opened it and thrust it closed, securely, behind him. Morgaine looked at him questioningly, even offering concern. He said nothing to her. He felt sick inside, still fearing that he should have trusted Liell, and yet glad that he had not.

"We must get out of this place," he urged her. "Now."

"There are things yet to learn," she said. "I only found the beginnings of answers. I would have the rest. I can have, if we remain."

There was no disputing Morgaine. He curled up near their own little hearth, a small and smoky fireplace that heated the room from a common duct, warming himself on the stones. He left her the bed, did she choose to use it.

She did not. She paced. Eventually the restlessness assumed a kind of rhythm, and ceased to be maddening. Just when he had grown used to that, she settled. He saw her by the window, staring out into the dark, through a crack in the shutters, an opening that let a further draft into their chill room.

"Folk never seem to sleep in Leth-hall," she commented to him finally, when he had changed his posture to keep his joints from going stiff. "There are torches about in the snow."

He muttered an answer and sighed, glanced away uncomfortably as she turned from the window then and began to turn down the bed. She slipped off the overrobe and laid it across the foot, laid aside her other gear, hung upon the endpost, and cloth tunic and the fine, light mail, itself the worth of many kings of the present age, boots and the warmth of her leather undertunic, stretched in the luxury of freedom from the weight of armor, slim and womanly, in riding breeches and a thin lawn shirt. He averted his eyes a second time toward nothing in particular, heard her ease within the bed, make herself comfortable.

"Thee does not have to be overnice," she murmured when he looked back. "Thee is welcome to thy half."

"It is warm here," he answered, miserable on the hard stone and wishing that he had not seen her as he had seen her. She meant the letter of her offer, no more; he knew it firmly, and did not blame her. He sat by the fire, *ilin* and trying to remind himself so, his arms locked together until his muscles ached. Servant to this. Walking behind her. To lie unarmored next to her was harmless only so long as she meant to keep it so.

Qujal. He clenched that thought within his mind and cooled his blood with that remembrance. *Qujal,* and deadly. A man of honest human birth had no business to think otherwise.

He remembered Liell's urging. The sanity in the man's eyes attracted him, promised, assured him that there did exist reason somewhere. He regretted more and more that he had not listened to him. There was no longer the excuse of his well-being that kept them in Ra-leth. His fever was less. He examined his hand that her medications had treated, found it scabbed over and was only a little red about the wound, the swelling abated. He was weak in the joints but he could ride. There was no further excuse for her staying, but that she wanted something of Kasedre and his mad crew, something important enough to risk both their lives.

It was intolerable. He felt sympathy for Liell, a sane man condemned to live in this nightmare. He understood that such a man might yearn for something other, would be concerned to watch another man of sense fall into the web.

"Lady." He came and knelt by the bed, disturbing her sleep. "Lady, let us be out of here."

"Go to sleep," she bade him. "There is nothing to be done tonight. The place is astir like a broken hive."

He returned to his misery by the fire, and after a time began to nod.

There was a scratching at the door. Minute as it was, it became sinister in all that silence. It would not cease. He started to wake Morgaine, but he had disturbed her once; he did not venture her patience again. He sought his sword, both frightened and self-embarrassed at his fear: it was likely only the rats.

Then he saw, slowly, the latch lift. The door began to open. It stopped against the chair. He rose to his feet, and Morgaine waked and reached for her own weapon.

"Lady," came a whisper, "it is Liell. Let me in. Quickly."

Morgaine nodded. Vanye eased the chair aside, and Liell entered as softly as possible, eased the door shut again. He was dressed in a cloak as if for traveling.

"I have provisions for you and a clear way to the stables," he said. "Come. You must come. You may not have another chance."

Vanye looked at Morgaine, shaped the beginning of a plea

with his lips. She frowned and suddenly nodded. "What effect on you, Chya Liell, for this treason?"

"Loss of my head if I am caught. And loss of a hall to live in if Kasedre's clan attacks you, as I fear they will, with or without his wishing it. Come, lady, come. I will guide you from here. They are all quiet, even the guards. I put *melorne* in Kasedre's wine at bedside. He will not wake, and the others are not suspecting. Come."

There was no one stirring in the hall outside. They trod the stairs carefully, down and down the several turns that led them to main level. A sentry sat in a chair by the door, head sunk upon his breast. Something about the pose jarred the senses: the right hand hung at the man's side in a way that looked uncomfortable for anyone sober.

Drugged too, Vanye thought. They walked carefully past the man nonetheless, up to the very door.

Then Vanye saw the wet dark stain that dyed the whole front of the man's robe, less conspicuous on the dark fabric. Suspicion leaped up. It chilled him, that a man was killed so casually.

"Your work?" he whispered at Liell, in Morgaine's hearing. He did not know whom he warned: he only feared, and thought it well that whoever was innocent mark it now and be advised.

"Hurry," said Liell, easing open the great door. They were out in the front courtyard, where one great evergreen shaded them into darkness. "This way lies the stables. Everything is ready."

They kept to the shadows and ran. More dead men lay at the stable door. It suddenly occured to Vanye that Liell had an easy defense against any charge of murder: that they themselves would be called the killers.

And if they refused to come, Liell would have been in difficulty. He had risked greatly, unless murder were only trivial in this hall, among madmen.

He stifled in such dread thoughts. He yearned to break free of Leth's walls. The quick thrust of a familiar velvet nose in the dark, the pungency of hay and leather and horse purged his lungs of the cloying decay of Leth-hall. He had his own bay mare in hand, swung up to her back; and Morgaine thrust the dragon blade into its accustomed place on her saddle and mounted Siptah.

Then he saw Liell lead another horse out of the shadows, likewise saddled.

"I will see you safely to the end of Leth's territories," he said. "No one here questions my authority to come and go. I am here and I am not, and at the moment, I think it best I am not."

But a shadow scurried from their path as they rode at a quiet walk through the yard, a shadow double-bodied and small. A patter of feet hurried to the stones of the walk.

Liell swore. It was the twins.

"Ride now," he said. "There is no hiding it longer."

They put their heels to the horses and reached the gate. Here too were dead men, three of them. Liell sharply ordered Vanye to see to the gate, and Vanye sprang down and heaved the bar up and the gate open, throwing himself out of the way as the black horse of Liell and gray Siptah hurtled past him, bearing the two into the night.

He hurled himself to the back of the bay mare—poor pony, not the equal of those two beasts—and urged her after them with the sudden terror that death itself was stirring and waking behind them.

CHAPTER V

THE LAKE OF Domen was ill-famed in more than the
Book of Leth. The old road ran along its shore and by the
bare-limbed trees that writhed against the night sky. It did
not snow here: snow was rare in Korish lands, low as they
were, although the forests nearest the mountains went wintry
and dead. The lake reflected the stars, sluggish and mirrorlike
—still, because, men said, parts of it were very deep.

They rode at a walk now. The horses' overheated breath
blew puffs of steam in the dark, and the hooves made a lonely
sound on the occasional stretch of stones over which the
trail ran.

And about them was the forest. It had a familiar look. Of
a sudden Vanye realized it for the semblance of the vale of
Aenor-Pyvvn.

The presence of Stones of Power: that accounted for the
twisting, the unusual barrenness in a place so rife with trees
as Koriswood. It was the Gate of Koris-leth that they were
nearing. The air had a peculiar oppression, like the air before
a storm.

And soon as they passed along the winding shore of the
lake they saw a great pillar thrusting up out of the black
waters. In the dim moonlight there seemed some engraving
on it. Soon other stumps of pillars were visible as they rode
farther, marking old and *qujalin* ruins sunk beneath the
waters of the lake.

And two pillars greater than the others crowned a bald hill
on the opposite shore.

Morgaine reined in, gazing at the strange and somber view
of sunken city and pillars silhouetted against the stars. Even
at night the air shimmered about the pillars and the brightest
stars that the shimmer could not dim gleamed through that
Gate as through a film of troubled water.

"We are safe from pursuit," said Liell. "Kasedre's clan fears this lakeshore."

"They seem prone to drowning," Morgaine observed. She dismounted, rubbed Siptah's cheek and dried her hand on the edge of his blanket.

Vanye slid down as they did, and caught his breath, reached for Siptah's reins and those of Liell's black horse. The two beasts would not abide each other. Exhausted, out of patience, he walked Siptah and his own bay mare to cool them and spread his own cloak over Liell's ill-tempered black in the meantime. The air was chill. They had ridden such a pace that the two greater horses were spent and his own little Mai had nearly burst her heart keeping up with them. Long after the two blooded horses were cooled and fit he was still tending to Mai, rubbing her to keep her from chill, until at last he dared let her drink the icy water and have a little grain from their stores. He was well content afterward to curl up on his cloak which he had recovered from the black, and try to sleep, shivering himself in what he feared was a recurrence of fever. He heard Liell's soft voice and that of Morgaine, discussing the business of Leth, discussing old murders or old accidents that had happened on this lakeshore.

Then Morgaine disturbed his rest, for she never parted from *Changeling,* and wanted it from her gear. She slipped the dragon blade's Korish-work strap over her head and hung it from her shoulder to her hip, and walked the shore a time with Liell's black figure beside hers.

Then, in the great stillness, Vanye heard the coming of distant riders. Of that impulse he sprang up, flung saddle upon Siptah first: *she* was his first duty; and by this time Morgaine and Liell seemed to have heard, for they were coming back. Vanye pulled Siptah's girth to its proper tension and secured it, then furiously began to saddle poor Mai. The mare would die. If they were harried much farther, the little beast would go down under him. He hurt for her: the Nhi blood in him loved horses too well to use them so, though Nhi could be cruel in other ways.

Liell flung saddle to the black himself. "I still much doubt," he said, "that they will come to this shore."

"I trust distance more than luck," said Morgaine. "Do as you will, Chya Liell."

And she swung up to Siptah's back, having settled *Changeling* in its accustomed place at the saddle, and laid heels to the gray.

Vanye attempted to mount and follow after. Liell's hand caught his arm, pulled him off balance, so that he staggered and looked at the man in outrage.

"Do not follow her," hissed Liell. "Listen to me. She will have the soul from you before she is done, Chya. Listen to me."

"I am *ilin*," he protested. "I have no choice."

"What is an oath?" Liell whispered urgently, all the while Siptah's hooves grew faint upon the shingle. "She seeks the power to ruin the middle lands. You do not know how great an evil you are aiding. She lies, Chya Vanye. She has lied before, to the ruin of Koris, of Baien, of the best of the clans and the death of Morij-Yla. Will you help her? Will you turn on your own? *Ilin*-oath says betray family, betray hearth, but not the *liyo*; but does it say betray your own kind? Come with me, come with me, Chya Vanye."

For an aging man, Liell had surprising power in his hand: it numbed the blood from Vanye's hand by its grip upon his elbow. The eyes were hard and glittering, close to him in the dark. The sound of pursuit was nearer.

"No," Vanye cried, ripping loose, and started to mount. Pain exploded across the base of his skull. The world turned in his vision and he had momentary view of Mai's belly passing over him as the mare bolted. She jumped him, managing to avoid him with her hooves; he scrambled up against the earthen bank, half-blind, seeking to draw his sword.

Liell was upon him then, wresting his hand from the hilt, close to overpowering him, dazed as he was; but the thought of being taken by Leth animated him to frenzy. He twisted, not even trying to defend himself, only to tear free, to reach Morgaine's side and keep his oath for his soul's sake. Mai was out of reach; the black was at hand. He sprang for that saddle and laid heels to him before he was even sure of the reins, gathering them up and settling low in the saddle from his precarious balance. Black legs flashed long in the dark, muscles reached and gathered, bounding obstacles, splashing over inlets of the lake, surging up rises of the shore.

The black at last had run all he chose to run, beyond the shore and far upon the trail: Vanye laid heel to him again. merciless in his fear. The animal gathered himself and plunged forward again.

Morgaine's pale form was ahead. At last she looked around, seeming to hear him; she whipped up Siptah, and he cried out to her in despair, urging the black to further effort.

And she held back, pulling up, weapon in hand until he had come closer.

"Vanye," she exclaimed softly as he drew alongside. "Is thee thief too? What came of Liell?"

He reached behind his head, felt a tenderness at the back of his head despite the leather coif. Dizziness assailed him, whether of the blow or of the fever, he did not know.

"Liell is no friend of yours," he said.

"Did you kill him?"

"No," he breathed, and was content to hang over the saddlebow a moment until his sight cleared. Then he urged the black into a gentle pace, Siptah keeping with him: no horses that had run all the distance from Ra-leth could overtake them now.

"Is thee much hurt?" she asked.

"No."

"What did he? Did he lift weapon against you?"

"Tried to hold me—tried to persuade me to break oath."

And the other thing he would not tell her, the urging and then the vile feeling he had had of the look in Liell's eyes, a feverish anxiousness that had wanted something of him, a touch that had twice sunk cruelly into his arm, an avarice matching the hunger in his eyes.

It was not a thing he could tell anyone: he did not know what to name it, or why he had provoked it, or what it aimed at, only that he would die before he fell into the hands of Leth, and most especially those of Liell.

His back had been turned: the man could easily have cut him across the backs of the knees, quickest way to disable a man elsewhere armored, slain him out of hand; instead he had fetched him a crack across the skull, had risked greatly taking him hand to hand when he could have killed him safely: he had wanted him alive.

He could not remember it without shuddering. He wanted nothing of the man. It filled him with loathing to possess the gear and the horse that he had stolen: the black beast with its ill temper was a creature more splendid and less honest than his little Mai, and leaving his little mare in those hands grieved him.

Deep forest closed about them, straight and proper trees now, and they walked the horses until there was no sky overhead, only the interlacing branches. The horses were spent and they themselves were blind with weariness.

"This is no place to stop," he protested when Morgaine

reined in. "Lady, let us sleep in the saddle tonight, walk the
horses while they may. This is Koriswood, and it may have
been different in your day, but this is the thick of it. Please."

She sighed in misery, but for once she looked at him and
listened, and consented with a nod of her head. He dismounted and took the reins of both horses, both too weary
to contest each other, and led them.

She rested a time, then leaned down and bade him stop,
offered to take the reins and walk and lead the horses; he
looked at her, tired as he was, and had not wit to argue with
her. He only turned his back and kept walking, to which she
consented by silence.

And eventually she slept, Kurshin-wise, in the saddle.

He walked so far as he could, long hours, until he was
stumbling with exhaustion. He stopped then and put his hand
on Siptah's neck.

"Lady," he said softly, not to break the hush of the listening wood. "Lady, now you must wake because I must sleep.
Things are quiet."

"Well enough," she agreed, and slid down. "I know the
road, although this land was tamer then."

"I must tell you," he continued hoarsely, "I think Chya
Liell will follow when he can gather the forces. I think he
lied to us in much, *liyo*."

"What was it happened back there, Vanye?"

He sought to tell her. He gathered the words, still could not.
"He is a strange man," he said, "and he was anxious that I
desert you. He attempted twice to persuade me—this last time
in plain words."

She frowned at him. "Indeed. What form did this proposal
take?"

"That I should forget my oath and go with him."

"To what?"

"I do not know." The remembering made his voice shake;
he thought that she might detect the tremor, and quickly
gathered up the black's reins and flung himself into the
saddle. "The first time—I almost went. The second—somehow I preferred your company."

Her odd pale face stared up at him in the starlight. "Many
of the house of Leth have drowned in that lake. Or have at
least vanished there. I did not know that you were in difficulty. I would not gladly have left you. I did judge that there
was some connivance between you and Liell: so when you did

not follow—I dared not delay there between two who might be enemies."

"I was reared Nhi," he said. "We do not oath-break. We do not oath-break, *liyo*."

"I beg pardon," she said, which *liyo* was never obliged to say to *ilin*, no matter how aggrieved. "I failed to understand."

And of that moment the horses shied, exhausted as they were, heads back and nostrils flaring, whites of the eyes showing in the dim light. Something reptilian slithered on four legs, whipping serpentwise into the thicker brush. It had been large and pale, leprous in color. They could still hear it skittering away.

Vanye swore, his stomach still threatening him, his hands managing without his mind, to calm the panicked horse.

"Idiocy," Morgaine exclaimed softly. "Thiye does not know what he is doing. Are there many such abroad?"

"The woods are full of beasts of his making," Vanye said. "Some are shy and harm no one. Others are terrible things, beyond belief. They say the Koris-wolves were made, that they were never so fierce and never man-killers before—" He had almost said, before Irien, but did not, in respect of her. "That is why we must not sleep here, lady. They are made things, and hard to kill."

"They are not made," she said, "but brought through. But you are right that this is no good place to rest. These beasts—some will die, like infants thrust prematurely into too chill or too warm a place: some will be harmless; but some will thrive and breed. Ivrel must be sweeping a wide field. Ah, Vanye, Thiye is an ignorant man. He is loosing things—he knows not what. Either that or he enjoys the wasteland he is creating."

"Where do they come from, such things as that?"

"From places where such things are natural. From other *tonights*, and other Gates, and places where *that* was fair and proper. And there will be no native beasts to survive this onslaught if it is not checked. It is not man that such an attack wars on—it is nature. The whole of Andur-Kursh will find such things straying into its meadows. Come. Come."

But he had lost his inclination to sleep, and kept the reins in his own hand. He closed his eyes as Morgaine set them on their way again, still saw the pale lizard form, large as a man, running across the open space. That was one of the witless nonsensitites in Koriswood, more ugly than dangerous. Report told of worse. Sometimes, legend said, carcasses were found near Irien, things impossible, abortions of Thiye's art, some almost formless and baneful to the touch, and others of forms so fantastical that none would imagine what aspect the living beast had had.

His only comfort in this place was that Morgaine herself was horrified; she had that much at least of human senses in her. Then he remembered her coming to him, out of the place she called *between*, washed up, she said, *on this shore*.

He began to have dim suspicion what she was, although he could not say it in words: that Morgaine and the pale horror had reached Andur-Kursh in the same way, only she had come by no accident, had come with purpose.

Aimed at Gates, at Thiye's power.

Aimed at dislocating all that lay on this shore, as these unnatural things had come. Standing where the Hjemur-lord stood, she would be no less perilous. She shared nothing with Andur-Kursh, not even birth, if his fears were true, and owed them nothing. *This* he served.

And Liell had said she lied. One of the twain lied: that was certain. He wondered in an agony of mind how it should be if he learned of a certainty that it was Morgaine.

Something else fluttered in the dark—honest owl, or something sinister; it passed close overhead. He tautened his grip upon his nerves and patted the nervous black's neck.

It was long until the morning, until in a clear place upon the trail they dared stop and let sleep take them by turns. Morgaine's was the first sleep, and he paced to keep himself awake, or chose an uncomfortable place to sit, when he must sit, and at last fell to meddling with the black horse's gear, that the horse still bore, for in such place they dared not unsaddle, only loosened the girths. It shamed him, to have stolen a second time; and he felt the keeping of more than he needed of the theft was not honorable, but all the same it was not sense to cast things away. He searched the saddlebags and kit to learn what he had possessed and, it was in the back of his thoughts, to learn something of the man Liell.

He found an object which answered the question, such that set his stomach over.

It was a medal, gold, set in the hilt of a saddle knife, the sort many a man bore beneath the skirt of his saddle; and on it was a symbol of the blockish, ugly look he had seen graven on the Stones. It was *qujalin*. Whenever any strange and long-ago things were found, folk called them *qujalin* and avoided them, or burned them, or cast them into deeps and tried to

lose them. Most such were likely only forgotten oddities,
Kurshin and harmless. Somehow he did not think this was
such as that.

He showed it to Morgaine when she wakened to take her
turn at watch.

"It is an *irrhn*," she said to him. "A luck-piece. It has no
other significance." But she turned it over and over in her
hands, examining it.

"It is no luck," said Vanye, "to a human man."

"There is *qujalin* blood mixed in Leth," she said, "and Liell
is its tutor. Tutors have ruled there nigh a hundred years.
Each of the heirs of Leth has produced a son and drowned
within the year. If Kasedre is capable of siring a son, he will
most probably join his ancestors, and Liell will still be tutor
to the son," she added irrelevantly, looking at the blade,
"who sired Hshi and Tlin."

"And on what," Vanye muttered sourly. "Keep the blade,
liyo. I do not want to carry it, and perhaps it may bring luck
to you."

"I am not *qujal*," she said.

That assertion, he reflected, might have filled him with
either doubt or relief some days ago, at their meeting; now it
fitted uncomfortably well with the thing he had begun to suspect of her.

"Whatever you are," he said, "spare me the knowing of it."

She nodded, accepting his attitude without apparent offense.
She slipped the knife within her belt and rose.

A green-feathered arrow hit the ground between her feet.

She reached to her back, hand to weapon, quick as the
arrow itself. And as quick, Vanye seized her and pushed her,
heedless of hurting: Chya warning, that arrow. If she fired,
they would both be green-feathered in an instant.

"Do not," he appealed to her, and turned, both arms wide,
toward their unseen observers. "Hai, Chya! Chya! will you
put kin-slaying on your souls? We are clan-welcome with you,
cousins."

Brush rustled. He watched the fair, tall men of his own
mother's kindred slip out of the shadows, where surely a few
more kept arrows trained upon their hearts; and he set himself deliberately between them and Morgaine's own arrogance,
which was like a Myya's for persistence, and likely to be the
death of her.

They did not even ask names of them, but stood there
waiting for them to speak and identify themselves. Looking

at the living person of one who had been minutely described in ballads a century ago, wondering perhaps if they were not mad—he could estimate what passed in their minds. They only stared at Morgaine, and she at them, furiously, in her hand a weapon that could deal death faster than their arrows.

They would kill her of course, if she could die; but she would have done considerable damage: and her *ilin* who was her shield would be quite dead. He had heard of a certain Myya who strayed the border and was found with three Chya arrows lodged in his heart, all touching. Clan Chya lived in a hard land. They were impressed by few threats. It was typical of them that they had not yielded and begged shelter from the encroaching beasts, as had other folk; or died, as had two others. They used Hjemur's vile beasts for game, and harried the border of Hjemur and kept Thiye contained out of sheer Chya effrontery.

Vanye placed hands on thighs and made a respectful bow, which Morgaine did not: she did not move, and it was possible that the Chya did not know that they were in danger.

"I am Nhi Vanye, i Chya," he said, "*ilin* to this lady, who is clan-welcome with Chya."

The leader, a smallish man with the simple braid of a second-*uyo*, cousin-kin to the main clan, grounded his long-bow and set both hands upon it, eyes upon him. "Nhi Vanye, cousin to Chya Roh. You are i Chya, that is true, but I thought it was understood that you are not clan-welcome here."

"She is," he said, which was the proper answer: an *ilin* was not held to his own law when he served his *liyo*: he could trespass, as safe or as threatened as she was. "She is Morgaine kri Chya, who has a clan-welcome that was never withdrawn."

They were frightened. They had the look of men watching a dream and trying not to become enmeshed in it. But they looked from her to the gray horse Siptah and back again, and swords stayed sheathed and bows lowered.

"We will take you to Ra-koris," said the little man. "I am Taomen, *tan-uyo*."

Then Morgaine gave him a bow of courtesy, and Vanye kept his silence hereafter, as befitted a servant whose *liyo* had finally deigned to take matters into her own hands.

The Chya were not happy at the meeting, it was clear. Clan-welcome had not been formally withdrawn because surely it had seemed a pointless vengeance on the dead. And the young lord of Chya, Chya Roh, his own cousin, whom he had never seen, still pursued bloodfeud with Nhi for the sake of his mother's dishonor at the hands of Rijan. Roh would as soon put an arrow through him as would Myya Gervaine, he was sure, and probably with greater accuracy.

There was a vast clearing in the Koriswood, that the noon sun blessed with a pleasant glow; the whole of it was full of sprawling huts of brush and logs—Chya, the only clan without a hall of stone. Once there had been the old Ra-koris, a splendid hall, home of the High Kings; its ruin lay some distance from this, and it was alleged to be haunted by angry ghosts of its proud defenders, that had held last and hardest against the advance of Hjemur. The grandsons and great-grandsons of the warriors of Morgaine's age kept only this wooden hall, their possessions few and their treasures gone, only their bows and their skill and the gain of their hunting between them and starvation. Yet none of them looked sickly, and the women and children watching them as they rode in were straight and tall, though plain: there was beauty in this people, much different from the blighted look of clan Leth.

Boys raced ahead of them, yet all was strangely silent, as though they maintained hunter's discipline even in their home. At the great arch of the main hut the greatest number of people had gathered, and here they dismounted, escorted still by Taomen and his men. They retained their weapons, and all was courtesy, men yielding back for them in haste.

Ra-koris was a smoky, earth-floored hall of rough logs, yet it had a certain splendor: it had two levels and many halls opening off the main room. Tasseled and wrought hides were the hangings, antlers and strange horns adorned its posts. It was lit by torches even at noontime, and by a hearth larger than many halls of stone could boast, its only masonry, that great hearth and its venting.

"Here you will be lodged until Roh can be called," said Taomen.

Morgaine chose to settle at the main hearth, and by the timorous charity of the hall women, they were served a plain meal of waybread and venison and Chya mead, which they found good indeed after the suspect fare of Leth.

But folk avoided them, and watched them from the shadows of the wooden hall, whispering together.

Morgaine ignored them all and rested. Vanye nursed his sore hand and finally, troubled by the heat in the hall, at last gave up his pride and removed helm and coif, probing the soreness of the base of his skull, where Liell had struck him. A youth of the Chya laughed: a youth who did not yet even wear the braid; and Vanye looked at him angrily, then bowed his head and ignored the matter. He was not in such a position that he could complain of their treatment of him. Morgaine must be his chief concern, and she theirs.

And late in the day, when the bit of sky visible through the little windows of the high arch had gone from sun to shadow, there was a stir at the door and hunters came, men in brown leather, armed with bows and swords.

And among them was one that Vanye knew would be close kin of his, even before the youth came forward and met them as lord of the hall: for he had seen high-clan Chya before; when he was a child, and this was the image of all of them— of himself as well. The young lord looked more like a brother than his own brothers did.

"I am Chya Roh," he said, stepping to the center of the *rhowa,* the earthen platform at the head of the hall. His lean, tanned features were set with anger at their presence, boding no good for them. "Morgaine kri Chya is dead," he said, "a hundred years ago. What proof do you bear that you are she?"

Morgaine unfolded upward from her cross-legged posture with rare grace, smooth and silken, and without a bow of courtesy offered an object into Vanye's hand. He arose with less grace, paused to look at the object before he passed it into Roh's hand: it was the antlered insignia of the old High Kings of Koris, and when he saw that he knew it for a great treasure, and one that might have formed part of the lost crown treasury.

"It was Tiffwy's," she said. "His pledge of hospitality— should I need it, he said, to command of his men what I would."

Roh's face was pale. He looked at the amulet, and clenched it in his fist, and his manner was suddenly subdued. "Chya gave you what you asked a hundred years ago," he said, "and not a man of the four thousand returned. You have much blood on your hands, Morgaine kri Chya; and yet I must honor my ancestor's word—this once. What do you seek here?"

"Brief shelter. Silence. And whatever knowledge you have of Thiye and Hjemur."

"All three you may have," he said.

"Did Chya's record survive?"

"The Ra-koris you know is ruin now. Wolves and other beasts have it to themselves. If Chya's Book survives, that is where it lies. We have no means nor leisure for books here, lady."

She bowed in courtesy. "I have a warning to give you: Leth is roused. We left them in some little stir. Guard your borders."

Roh's lips were thin. "You are gifted with the raising of storms, lady. We will set men to watch your trail. It may be Leth will come this far, but only if they are desperate. We have taught Leth manners before."

"They are mightily irritated. Vanye's horse is Leth-bred, and we quit their hospitality suddenly, in a dispute with lord Kasedre and his counselor Chya Liell."

"Liell," said Roh softly. "*That* black wolf. I commend the quality of your enemies, lady. How much welcome do you ask?"

"The night only."

"Are you bound north?"

"Yes," she said.

Roh bit his lip. "That old quarrel? They say Thiye lives. It has never been in our imagination that you could survive too. But we are through giving you men, lady. That is done. We have none left to spare you."

"I ask none."

"You take *this?*" It was Roh's one acknowledgment that Vanye lived; his proud young eyes shifted aside and back again. "You could do better, lady."

But then he went and bade his women make place for Morgaine in the upper levels of the hall, and separate place for Vanye by the hearth. This Morgaine allowed, for Chya was a proper hall, and they were indeed under its peace as they had not been in Leth. And after that Morgaine and Roh talked together some little time, asking and answering, until she finally took her leave and passed upstairs.

Then Vanye gratefully put off his armor, down to his shirt and his leather breeches, and prepared the blankets they had given him by the warm hearthside.

Taomen came, spoke to him softly and bade him come to Roh; it was a thing he could not refuse. Roh sat cross-legged on the *rhowa*, with other men about him.

Of a sudden Vanye's feeling of ease left him. There was merry noise elsewhere in the hall, busy chatter of women and of children; it continued, masking softer words, and there were men ringed about so that no one outside the circle could see what was done there.

He did not kneel, not until they made it clear he must; then all the *uyin* of the Chya sank down on their haunches about him and about Roh, swords laid before them, as when clan judgment was passed.

He thought of crying aloud to Morgaine, warning her of treachery; but he did not truly fear for her, and his own pride kept him silent. These were his kin: to trouble an *ilin* for a family matter violated honor, violated the very concepts of honor under the *ilin*-codes, but Roh's offense was a powerful one. He did not know this cousin of his: his hope of Roh's honor was scant, but it kept him from utter panic.

"Now," said Roh, "and truthfully, Nhi Vanye, account for her and for your business with her."

"Nothing she told you was a lie and nothing less than the truth. She is Morgaine, and I am an *ilin* to her."

Roh looked him over, long and harshly. "So Rijan threw you out. You robbed him of one of his Myya wife's precious nestlings and he banished you. But you are due no kinship from us. My aunt did not choose your begetting. I only blame her because she did not leave Morija and come back to us. She was no captive by then, great with child as she was."

"To what should she come back—to your welcome?" Temper overcame sense, for Roh's words stung. "I honor her, Chya. And Chya's honor would not have taken her back as she had been, not after Rijan had had her, whether or not she were willing. She gave me life and died doing it, and I know the misery she had of Rijan better than you folk, that had not the stomach for coming into Morija to get her back, after Rijan rode into Chya lands to take her from you. Where is your honor, men of Chya?"

The stillness was absolute. Suddenly the hall was deserted but for them. The fire crackled. A log fell, showering embers.

"What became of her?" asked Roh at last, tilting the balance toward life and reason. "Was it death in childbirth, as they said?"

"Yes."

Roh let go his breath slowly. "Better had Rijan drowned you. Perhaps he regretted that he did not. But you are here. So live. Nhi Vanye, Rijan's bastard. Now what shall we do with you?"

"Do as she asked and let us pass from this hall tomorrow."

"Do you serve her willingly?"

"Yes," he said, "it was fair Claiming. I was in need. Now I am in her debt and I must pay it."

"Where is she going?"

"She is my lady," he said, "and it is not right for me to say anything of her business. Look to your own. You will have Leth at your borders for her sake."

"Where is she going, Nhi Vanye?"

"Ask her, I say."

Roh snapped his fingers. Men reached for the blades laid before them. They unsheathed them so that the points formed a ring about him. Somewhere in hall a dish fell. A woman ran cat-footed into the corridor beyond, drew the curtain and was gone.

"Ask Morgaine," Vanye said again; and when his breathing space grew less and an edge rested familiarly on his shoulder, he maintained his composure and did not flinch, though his heart was beating fit to burst. "If you continue, Chya Roh, I shall decide there is no honor at all in Chya. And I shall be ashamed for that."

Roh considered him in silence. Vanye went sick inside: his nerves were strung, waiting, the least pressure from them likely to send from his lips a shout to raise the hall and Morgaine from sleep. He was not brave. He had long ago discovered in himself that he had no courage for enduring pain or threat. His brothers had discovered that in him before he had. It was the same feeling that churned in him now, the same that he had known when they, out of old San Romen's protective witness, had bullied him to his knees and brought tears to his eyes. That one fatal time he had seized arms against Kandrys's tormenting of him, one time only: his hands had killed, not his mind, which was blank and terrified, and had his hands not been filled with a weapon they would have found him as always, as he was now.

But Roh snapped his fingers a second time and they let him alone. "Get to your place," said Roh, *"ilin."*

He rose then, and bowed, and walked—it was incredible that he could walk steadily—to the place he had left at the hearth. There he lay down again, and wrapped himself in his cloak and clenched his teeth and let the fire warm the tremors from his muscles.

He wanted to kill. For every affront ever paid him, for all the terror ever set into him, he wanted to kill; and he squeezed the tears from his eyes and began to reckon that perhaps his father had been right, that his hand had been more honest than he knew. He feared a great many things: he feared death; he feared Morgaine and he feared Liell and the madness of

Kasedre; but there never was fear such as there was in being alone among kinsmen, among whom he was always bastard and outcast.

Once, when he was a child, Kandrys and Erji had lured him into the storage basements of Ra-morij, and there overpowered him and hung him from a beam in the deep cellars, alone in the dark and with the rats. They had only come after him after the blood had left his hands and he could not find the strength to scream any longer. Then they had come with lights, and cut him down, hovering over him white-faced and terrified for fear that they had killed him. Afterward they had threatened worse if he showed the cruel marks the ropes had made.

He had not complained to anyone. He had learned the conditions of his welcome in Nhi even then, had learned to clutch his scraps of honor to himself in silence, had practiced, had bit his lip and kept his own counsel, until he had fairly won the honor of the warrior's braid, and until the demands of *uyin* honor must keep Kandrys and Erji from their more petty tormentings of him.

But the looks were there, the subtle, hating looks and secret contempt that became evident when he committed any error that cost him honor.

Even the Chya tried him, in the same way—scented fear and went for it, like wolves to a deer.

Yet something there was in him that yearned to like the lord of Chya, this man so like himself, that showed kindred blood in his face and in his bearing. Roh was legitimate: Roh's father had virtually abandoned the lady Ilel to her fate, captive and bearing Rijan's bastard, that must in nowise return to confound the purity of Chya—to contest with his son Roh.

And Chya both feared him, and scented fear, and would have gone for his throat if not for their debt to Morgaine.

Late, late into the long night, his not-quite-rest was disturbed by a booted foot crunching a cinder not far from his head, and he came up on his arm as Roh dropped to his haunches looking down at him. In panic he reached for the sword beside him; Roh clamped his hand down on the hilt, preventing him.

"You came from Leth," said Roh softly. "Where did you meet her?"

"At Aenor-Pyvvn." He sat up, tucked his feet under him, tossed the loose hair from his eyes. "And I still say, ask Morgaine her business, not her servant."

Roh nodded slowly. "I can guess some things. That she still purposes what she always did, whatever it was. She will be the death of you, Nhi Vanye i Chya. But you know that already. Take her hence as quickly as you can in the morning. We have Leth breathing at our borders this night. Reports of it have come in. Men have died. Liell will stop her if he can. And there is a limit to what service we will pay this time in Chya lives."

Vanye stared into the brown eyes of his cousin and found there a grudging acceptance of him: for the first time the man was talking to him, as if he still had the dignity of an *uyo* of the high clan. It was as if he had not acquitted himself so poorly after all, as if Roh acknowledged some kinship between them. He drew a deep breath and let it go again.

"What do you know of Liell?" he asked of Roh. "Is he Chya?"

"There was a Chya Liell," said Roh. "And our Liell was a good man, before he became counselor in Leth." Roh looked down at the stones and up again, his face drawn in loathing. I do not know. There are rumors it is the same man. There are rumors he in Leth is *qujal*. That he—like Thiye of Hjemur —is *old*. What I can tell you is that he is the power in Leth, but if you have come from Leth, you know that. At times he is a quiet enemy, and when the worst beasts have come into Koriswood, the worst sendings of Thiye, Liell's folk have been no less zealous than we to rid Koris of the plague: we observe hunter's peace on occasion, for our mutual good. But our harboring Morgaine will not better relations between Leth and Chya."

"I believe your rumors," said Vanye at last. Coldness rested in his belly, when he thought back to the lakeshore.

"I did not," said Roh, "until this night, that *she* came into hall."

"We will go in the morning," said Vanye.

Roh stared into his face yet a moment more. "There is Chya in you," he said. "Cousin, I pity you, your fate. How long have you to go of your service with her?"

"My year," he said, "has only begun."

And there passed between them the silent communication that that year would be his last, accepted with a sorrowful shake of Roh's head.

"If so happen," said Roh, "if so happen you find yourself free—return to Chya."

And before Vanye could answer anything, Roh had walked

off, retiring to a distant corridor of the rambling hall that led
to other huts, warrenlike.

He was shaken then by the thing that he had never dreamed
to receive: Chya would take him in.

In a way it was only cruelty. He would die before his year
was out. Morgaine was death-prone, and he would follow; and
in it he had no choice. A moment ago he had had no particular hope.

Only now there was. He looked about at the hall, surely one
of the strangest of all holds in Andur-Kursh. Here was refuge,
and welcome, and a life.

A woman. Children. Honor.

These were not his, and would not be. He turned and
clasped his arms about his knees, staring desolately into the
fire. Even should she die, which was probably the thought in
Roh's mind, he had his further bond, to ruin Hjemur.

If so happen you find yourself free.

In all the history of man, Hjemur had never fallen.

CHAPTER VI

THE WHOLE OF Chya seemed to have turned out in the morning to see them leave, as silent at their going as they had been at their arrival; and yet there seemed no ill feeling about them now that Roh attended them to their horses, and himself held the stirrup for Morgaine to mount.

Roh bowed most courteously when Morgaine was in the saddle, and spoke loudly enough in wishing her well that the whole of Chya could hear. "We will watch your backtrail at least," he said, "so that I do not think you will have anyone following you through Chya territories very quickly. Be mindful of our safety too, lady."

Morgaine bowed from the saddle. "We are grateful, Chya Roh, to you and all your people. Neither of us has slept secure until we slept under your roof. Peace on your house, Chya Roh."

And with that she turned and rode away, Vanye after her, amid a great murmuring of the people. And as at their coming, so at their going, the children of Chya were their escort, running along beside the horses, heedless of the proprieties of their elders. There was wild excitement in their eyes to see the old days come to life, that they had heard in songs and ballads. They did not at all seem to fear or hate her, and with the delightedness of childhood took this great wonder as primarily for their benefit.

It was, Vanye thought, that she was so fair, that it was hard for them to think ill of her. She shone in sunlight, like sun on ice.

"Morgaine!" they called at her, softly, as Chya always spoke, "Morgaine!"

And at last even her heart was touched, and she waved at them, and smiled, briefly.

Then she laid heels to Siptah, and they left the pleasant hall behind, with all the warmth of Chya in the sunlight. The forest closed in again, chilling their hearts with its shadow, and for a very long time they both were silent.

He did not even speak to her the wish of his heart, that they turn and go back to Chya, where there was at least the hope of welcome. There was none for her. Perhaps it was that, he thought, that made her face so downcast throughout the morning.

As the day went on, he knew of certainty that it was not the darkness of the woods that bore upon her heart. Once they heard a strange wild cry through the branches, and she looked up, such an expresson on her face as one might have who had been distracted from some deep and private grief, bewildered, as if she had forgotten where she was.

That night they camped in the thick of the wood. Morgaine gathered the wood for the fire herself, making it small, for these were woods where it was not well to draw visitors. And she laughed sometimes and spoke with him, a banality he was not accustomed to in her: the laughter had no true ring, and at times she would look at him in such a way that he knew he lay near the center of her thoughts.

It filled him with unease. He could not laugh in turn; and he stared at her finally, and then suddenly bowed himself to the earth, like one asking grace.

She did not speak, only stared back at him when he had risen up, and had the look of one unmasked, looking truth back, if he could know how to read it.

Questions trembled on his lips. He could not sort out one that he dared ask, that he did not think would meet some cold rebuff or what was more likely, silence.

"Go to sleep," she bade him then.

He bowed his head and retreated to his place, and did so, until his watch.

Her mood had passed by the morning. She smiled, lightly enough, talked with him over breakfast about old friends— hers: of the King. Tiffwy, how his son had been, the lady who was his wife. It was that kind of thing one might hear from old people, talk of folk long dead, not shared with the young; the worse thing was that she seemed to know it, and her gray eyes grew wistful, and searched his, seeking understanding, some small appreciation of the only things she knew how to say with him.

"Tiffwy," he said, "must have been a great man. I would like to have known him."

"Immortality," she said, "would be unbearable except among immortals." And she smiled, but he saw through it.

She was silent thereafter, and seemed downcast, even while they rode. She thought much. He still did not know how to enter those moods. She was locked within herself.

It was as if he had snapped whatever thin cord bound them by that word: *I would like to have known him.* She had detected the pity. She would not have it of him.

By evening they could see the hills, as the forest gave way to scattered meadows. In the west rose the great mass of Alis Kaje, its peaks white with snow: Alis Kaje, the barrier behind which lay Morija. Vanye looked at it as a stranger to this side of the mountain wall, and found all the view unfamiliar to him, save great Mount Proeth, but it was a view of home.

And thereafter the land opened more to the north and they stood still upon a hillside looking out upon the great northern range.

Ivrel.

The mountain was not so tall as Proeth, but it was fair to the eye and perfect, a tapering cone equal to left and to right. Beyond it rose other mountains, the Kath Vrej and Kath Svejur, fading away into distance, the ramparts of frosty Hjemur. But Ivrel was unique among all mountains. The little snow there was atop it capped merely the summit: most of its slopes were dark, or green with forests.

And at its base, unseen in the distance that made Ivrel itself seemed to drift at the edge of the sky, lay Irien.

Morgaine touched heels to Siptah, startled the horse into motion, and they rode on, downslope and up again, and she spoke never a word. She gave no sign of stopping even while stars brightened in the sky and the moon came up.

Ivrel loomed nearer. Its white cone shone in the moonlight like a vision.

"Lady." Vanye leaned from his saddle at last, caught the reins of the gray. *"Liyo,* forbear. Irien is no place to ride at night. Let us stop."

She yielded then. It surprised him. She chose a place and dismounted, and took her gear from Siptah. Then she sank down and wrapped herself in her cloak, caring for nothing else. Vanye hurried about trying to make a comfortable camp for her. These things he was anxious to do: her dejection weighed upon his own soul, and he could not be comfortable with her.

It was of no avail. She warmed herself at the fire, and

stared into the embers, without appetite for the meal he
cooked for her, but she picked at it dutifully, and finished it.

He looked up at the mountain that hung over them, and felt
its menace himself. This was cursed ground. There was no
sane man of Andur-Kursh would camp where they had
camped, so near to Irien and to Ivrel.

"Vanye," she said suddenly, "do you fear this place?"

"I do not like it," he answered. "—Yes, I fear it."

"I laid on you at Claiming to ruin Hjemur if I cannot. Have
you any knowledge where Hjemur's hold lies?"

He lifted a hand, vaguely toward the notch at Ivrel's base.
"There, through that pass."

"There is a road there, that would lead you there. There is
no other, at least there was not."

"Do you plan," he asked, "that I shall have to do this
thing?"

"No," she said. "But that may well be."

Thereafter she gathered up her cloak and settled herself for
the first watch, and Vanye sought his own rest.

It seemed only a moment until she leaned over him, touching his shoulder, quietly bidding him take his turn: he had
been tired, and had slept soundly. The stars had turned about
in their nightly course.

"There have been small prowlers," she said, "some of unpleasant aspect, but no real harm. I have let the fire die, of
purpose."

He indicated his understanding, and saw with relief that she
sought her furs again like one who was glad to sleep. He put
himself by the dying fire, knees drawn up and arms propped
on his sheathed sword, dreaming into the embers and listening
to the peaceful sounds of the horses, whose sense made them
better sentinels than men.

And eventually, lulled by the steady snap of the cooling embers, the whisper of wind through the trees at their side, and
the slow moving of the horses, he began to struggle against his
own urge to sleep.

She screamed.

He came up with sword in hand, saw Morgaine struggling
up to her side, and his first thought was that she had been bit-
ten by something. He bent by her, seized her up and held her
by the arms and held her, she trembling. But she thrust him
back, and walked away from him, arms folded as against a
chill wind; so she stood for a time.

"Liyo?" he questioned her.

"Go back to sleep," she said. "It was a dream, an old one."

"*Liyo*—"

"Thee has a place, *ilin*. Go to it."

He knew better than to be wounded by the tone: it came from some deep hurt of her own; but it stung, all the same. He returned to the fireside and wrapped himself again in his cloak. It was a long time before she had gained control of herself again, and turned and sought the place she had left. He lowered his eyes to the fire, so that he need not look at her; but she would have it otherwise: she paused by him, looking down.

"Vanye," she said, "I am sorry."

"I am sorry too, *liyo*."

"Go to sleep. I will stay awake a while."

"I am full awake, *liyo*. There is no need."

"I said a thing to you I did not mean."

He made a half-bow, still not looking at her. "I am *ilin*, and it is true I have a place, with the ashes of your fire, *liyo*, but usually I enjoy more honor than that, and I am content."

"Vanye." She sank down to sit by the fire too, shivering in the wind, without her cloak. "I need you. This road would be intolerable without you."

He was sorry for her then. There were tears in her voice; of a sudden he did not want to see the result of them. He bowed, as low as convenience would let him, and stayed so until he thought she would have caught her breath. Then he ventured to look her in the eyes.

"What can I do for you?" he asked.

"I have named that," she said. It was again the Morgaine he knew, well armored, gray eyes steady.

"You will not trust me."

"Vanye, do not meddle with me. I would kill you too if it were necessary to set me at Ivrel."

"I know it," he said. "*Liyo*, I would that you had listened to me. I know you would kill yourself to reach Ivrel, and probably you will kill us both. I do not like this place. But there is no reasoning with you. I have known that from the beginning. I swear that if you would listen to me, if you would let me, I would take you safely out of Andur-Kursh, to—"

"You have already said it. There is no reasoning with me."

"Why?" he asked of her. "Lady, this is madness, this war of yours. It was lost once. I do not want to die."

"Neither did they," she said, and her lips were a thin, hard line. "I heard the things they said of me in Baien, before I passed from that time to this. And I think that is the way I will be remembered. But I will go there, all the same, and that is my business. Your oath does not say that you have to agree with what I do."

"No," he acknowledged. But he did not think she heard him: she gazed off into the dark, toward Ivrel, toward Irien. A question weighed upon him. He did not want to hurt her, asking it; but he could not go nearer Irien without it growing heavier in him.

"What became of them?" he asked. "Why were there so few found after Irien?"

"It was the wind," she said.

"Liyo?" Her answer chilled him, like sudden madness. But she pressed her lips together and then looked at him.

"It was the wind," she said again. "There was a gate-field there—warping down from Ivrel—and the mist there was that morning whipped into it like smoke up a chimney, a wind . . . a wind the like of which you do not imagine. That was what passed at Irien. Ten thousand men—sent through. Into nothing. *We* knew, my friends and I, we five: we knew, and I do not know whether it was more terrible for us knowing what was about to happen to us than for those that did not understand at all. There was only starry dark there. Only void in the mists. . . . But I lived of course. I was the only one far back enough: it was my task to circle Irien, Lrie and the men of Leth and I—and when we were on the height, it began. I could not hold my men; they thought that they could aid those below, with their king, and they rode down; they would not listen to me, you see, because I am a woman. They thought that I was afraid, and because they were men and must not be, they went. I could not make them understand, and I could not follow them." Her voice faltered; she steadied it. "I was too wise to go, you see. I am civilized; I knew better. And while I was being wise—it was too late. The wind came over us. For a moment one could not breathe. There was no air. And then it passed, and I coaxed poor Siptah to his feet, and I do not clearly remember what I did after, except that I rode toward Ivrel. There was a Hjemurn force in my way. I fell back and back then, and there was only the south left open. Koris held a time. Then I lost that shelter; and I retreated to Leth and sheltered there a time before I retreated again toward Aenor-Pyvvn. I meant to raise an army there; but they would not hear me. When they came to kill me, I cast myself into the

Gate: I had not other refuge left. I did not know it would be so long a wait."

"Lady," he said, "this—this thing that was done at Irien, killing men without a blow being struck . . . when we go there, could not Thiye send this wind down on us too?"

"If he knew the moment of our coming, yes. The wind—the wind was the very air rushing into that open Gate, a field cast to the Standing Stone in Irien. It opened some gulf between the stars. To maintain it extended more than a moment as it was would have been disaster to Hjemur. Even he could not be that reckless."

"Then, at Irien—he knew."

"Yes, he knew." Morgaine's face grew hard again. "There was one man who began to go with us, who never stood with us at Irien—he that wanted Tiffwy's power, that betrayed Tiffwy with Tiffwy's wife—that later stood tutor of Edjnel's son, after killing Edjnel."

"Chya Zri."

"Aye, Zri, and to the end of my days I will believe it, though if it was so he was sadly paid by Hjemur. He aimed at a kingdom, and the one he had of it was not the one he planned."

"Liell." Vanye uttered the name almost without thinking it, and felt the sudden impact of her eyes upon his.

"What makes you think of him?"

"Roh said that there was question about the man. That Liell is . . . that he is old, *liyo*, that he is old as Thiye is old."

Morgaine's look grew intensely troubled. "Zri and Liell. Singularly without originality, to have drowned all the heirs of Leth—if drowned they were."

He remembered the Gate shimmering above the lake, and knew what she meant. Doubts assailed him. He ventured a question he fully hated to ask. "Could you—live by this means, if you wished?"

"Yes," she answered him.

"Have you?"

"No," she said. And, as if she read the thing in his mind: "It is by means of the Gates that it is done, and it is no light thing to take another body. I am not sure myself quite how it is done, although I think that I know. It is ugly: the body must come from someone, you see. And Liell, if that is true, is growing old."

He shivered, remembering the touch of Liell's fingers upon his arm, the hunger—he read it for hunger even then—within his eyes. *Come with me and I will show you*, he had said. *She*

will have the soul from you before she is done. Come with me,
Chya Vanye. She lies. She has lied before.
  Come with me.
He breathed an oath, a prayer, something, and stumbled to
his feet, to stand apart a moment, sick with horror, sensitive
for the first time to his youth, his trained strength, as something that had been the object of covetousness.

He felt unclean.

"Vanye," she said, concern in her voice.

"They say," he managed then, turning to look at her, "that
Thiye is aging too—that he has the look of an old man."

"If," she said levelly, "I am dead or lost and you go against
Hjemur alone—do not consider being taken prisoner there. I
would not by any means, Vanye."

"Oh Heaven," he murmured. Bile rose in his throat. Of a
sudden he began to comprehend the stakes in these wars of
qujal and men, and the prize there was for losing. He stared at
her—he knew, like the veriest innocent, and met a lack of all
proper horror.

"Would you do this?" he asked.

"I think that one day," she said, "to do what I must do, I
would have to consider it."

He swore. For a very little he would have left her in that
moment. She began at last to show concern of it, the smallest
impulse of humanity, and it was that which held him.

"Sit down," she said. He did so.

"Vanye," she said then. "I have no leisure to be virtuous. I
try, I try, with what of me there is left. But there is very little.
What would you do, if you were dying, and you had only to
reach out and kill—not for an extended old age, with pain,
and sickness, but for another youth? For the *qujal* there is
nothing after, no immortality, only to die. They have lost their
gods, or lost whatever belief they ever had. That is all there is
for them—to live, to enjoy pleasure—to enjoy power."

"Did you lie to me? Are you of their blood?"

"I have not. I am not *qujal*. But I know them. Zri . . . if you
are right, Vanye, it explains much. Not for ambition, but of
desperation: to live. To save the Gates, on which he depends.
I had not looked for that in him. What did he say to you,
when he spoke with you?"

"Only that I should leave you and come with him."

"Well that you had better sense. Otherwise—"

And then her eyes grew guarded, and she took the black
weapon from her belt: he thought in the first heartbeat that

she had perceived some intruder; and then to his shock he saw the thing directed at him. He froze, mind blank, save of the thought that she had suddenly gone mad.

"Otherwise," she continued, "I should have had such a companion on my ride to Ivrel that would assure I did not live, such a companion as would wait until the nearness of the Gate lent him the means to deal with me—alive. I left you upon a bay mare, Chya Vanye, and you chose Liell's horse thereafter. That was who I thought it was when first I saw you riding after me, and I was not anxious for Liell's company alone. I was surprised to realize that it was you, instead."

"Lady," he exclaimed, holding forth his hands to show them empty of threat. "I have sworn to you . . . lady, I have not deceived you. Surely—it could not happen, it could not happen and I not know it. I would know, would I not?"

She arose, still watching him, constantly watching him, and drew back to the place where rested her cloak and her sword.

"Saddle my horse," she bade him.

He went carefully, and did as she ordered him, knowing her at his back with that weapon. When he was done, he gave back for her, and she watched him carefully, even to the moment that she swung up into the saddle.

Then she reined about and toward the black horse. All at once he read her thoughts, to kill the beast and leave him afoot, since she would not kill him, *ilin.*

He hurled himself between, looked up with outraged horror; it was not honor to do such a thing, to abuse the *ilin*-oath, to kill a man's horse and leave him stranded. And for one moment there was such a look of wildness on her face that he feared she would use the weapon on him and the beast.

Suddenly she jerked Siptah's head about to the north and spurred off, leaving him behind.

He stared after her a moment, dazed, knowing her mad.

And himself likewise.

He cursed and heaved up his gear, flung saddle on the black, secured the girth, hauled himself into the saddle and went—the beast knowing full well he belonged with the gray by now. The horse needed no touch of the heel to extend himself, but ran, downhill and around a turning, across a stream and up again, overtaking the loping gray.

He half expected a bolt that would take him from the saddle or tumble his horse dead instead; Morgaine turned in the saddle and saw him come. But she allowed it, began to rein in.

"Thee is an idiot," she said when he had come alongside.

And she looked then as if she could give way to tears, but she did not. She thrust the black weapon into the back of her belt, under the cloak, and looked at him and shook her head. "And thee is Kurshin. Nothing else could be so honorably stupid. Zri would surely have run, unless Zri is braver than he once was. We are not brave, we that play this game with Gates; there is too much we can lose, to have the luxury to be virtuous, and to be brave. I envy you, Kurshin, I do envy anyone who can afford such gestures."

He pressed his lips tightly. He felt simple, and shamed, realizing now she had tried to frighten him; none of it made sense with him—her moods, her distrust of him. His voice turned brittle. "I am easy to deceive, *liyo,* much more than you could be; any of your simplest tricks can amaze me, and no few of them frighten me."

She had no answer for him.

At times she looked at him in a way he did not like. The air between them had gone poisonous. *Go away,* the look said. *Go away, I will not stop you.*

He would not have left her hurt and needing him; there was oath-breaking and there was oath-breaking, and to break *ilin-*bond when she was able to care for herself was a heavy matter, but there was that in her manner which convinced him that she was far from reasoning.

The light grew in the sky, into a cold, dreary morning, with clouds rolling in from the north.

And early in that morning the land fell away below them and the hills opened up into the slope of Irien.

It was a broad valley, pleasant to the eye. As they stopped upon the verge of that great bowl, Vanye was not sure that this was the place. But then he saw that its other side was Ivrel, and that there was a barrenness in its center, far below. They were too far to see so fine a detail as a single Standing Stone, but he reckoned that for the center of that place.

Morgaine slid down from Siptah's back and troubled to unhook *Changeling* from its place, by which he knew she meant some long delay. He dismounted too; but when she turned and walked some distance away along the slope he did not estimate that she meant him to follow. He sat down upon a large rock and waited, gazing into the distances of the valley. In his mind he imagined the thousands that had ridden into it, upon one of those gray spring mornings that cloaked the valleys with mist, where men and horses moved like ghosts in the fog—of darkness swallowing up everything, the winds, as she had said, drawing the mist like smoke up a chimney.

But upon this morning there were the low-hanging clouds and a winter sun, and grass and trees below. A hundred years had repaired whatever scars there had been left, until one could not have reckoned what had happened there.

Morgaine did not return. He waited long past the time that he had begun to grow anxious about her; and at last he gathered up his resolve and rose and walked the way that she had gone, about the curve of he hill. He was relieved when he found her, only standing and gazing into the valley. For a moment he almost dared not go to her; and then he thought that he should, for she was not herself, and there were beasts and men in these hills that made Irien no place to be alone.

"Liyo," he called to her as he came. And she turned and came to him, and walked back with him to the place where they had left the horses. There she hung the sword where it belonged, and took up the reins of Siptah, and paused again, looking over the valley, "Vanye," she said, "Vanye, I am tired."

"Lady?" he asked of her, thinking at first she meant that they would stop here a time, and he did not like the thought of that. Then she looked at him, and he knew then it was a different tiredness she spoke of.

"I am afraid," she admitted to him, "and I am alone, Vanye. And I have no more honor and no more lives to spend. Here"—she stretched out her hand, pointing down the slope— "here I left them, and rode round this rim, and from over there—" she pointed far off across the valley, where there was a rock and many trees upon the rim. "From that point I watched the army lost. We were a hundred strong, my comrades and I; and over the years we have grown fewer and fewer, and now there is only myself. I begin to understand the *qujal.* I begin to pity them. When it is so necessary to survive, then one cannot be brave anymore."

He began then to understand the terror in her, the same intense terror there was in Liell, he thought, who also wished something of him. He wished no more truth of her: it was the kind that wrought nightmares, that held no peace, that asked him to forgive things that were unthinkable.

Spare us this, he wanted to say to her. *I have honored you. Do not make this impossible.*

He held his tongue.

"I might have killed you," she said, "in panic. I frighten

easily, you see, I am not reasonable. I have ceased to take
risks at all. It is unconscionable—that I should take risks with
the burden I carry. I tell myself the only immorality I have
committed is in trusting you after aiming at your life. Do you
see, I have no luxury left, for virtues."

"I do not understand," he said.

"I hope that you do not."

"What do you want of me?"

"Hold to your oath." She swung up to Siptah's back, waited
for him to mount, then headed them not across the vale of
Irien, but around the rim of the valley, that trail which she
had followed the day of the battle.

She was in a mood that hovered on the brink of madness,
not reasoning clearly. He became certain of it. She feared him
as if he were death itself making itself friendly and comfortable with her, feared any reason that told her otherwise.

And forebore to kill, forbore to violate honor.

There was that small, precious difference between what he
served and what pursued them. He clung to that, though Morgaine's foreboding seeped into his thoughts, that it was that
which would one day kill her.

The ride around the rim was long, and they must stop several times to rest. The sun went down the other part of the
sky and the clouds began to gather thickly over Ivrel's cone,
portending storm, a northern storm of the sort that sometimes
whirled snow down on such valleys as this, north of Chya, but
more often meant tree-cracking ice, and misery of men and
beasts.

The storm hovered, sifting small amounts of sleet. The day
grew dimmer. They paused for one last rest before moving onto the side of Ivrel.

And chaos burst upon them—their only warning a breath
from Siptah, a shying of both their horses. Another moment
and they would have been afoot. Half-lighting, Vanye
sprang back to the saddle, whipped out his longsword and laid
about him in the twilight at the forms that hurled at them
from the woods and from the rocks, men of Hjemur, fur-clad
men afoot at first, and then men on ponies. Five laced the
dark, Morgaine's little weapon taking toll of men and horses
without mercy.

They spurred through, reached the down-turning of the
trail. The slope was alive with them. They clambered up on
foot, dark figures in the twilight, and not all of them looked
human.

Knives flashed as the horde closed with them, threatening the vulnerable legs and bellies of the horses, and they fought and spurred the horses, turning them for whatever least resistance they could find for escape. Morgaine cried out, kicked a man in the face and rode him down. Vanye drove his heels into the black's flanks and sent the horse flying in Siptah's wake.

There was no hope in fighting. His *liyo* was doing the most sensible thing, laying quirt to the laboring gray, putting the big horse to the limit, even if it drove them off their chosen way; and Vanye did the same, his heart in his throat no less for the way they rode than for the pursuit behind them—skidding down a rocky slope, threading the blind shadows along unknown trail and through a narrow defile in the rocks to reach the flat to Irien's west.

There, weary as their horses were, they had the advantage over the Hjemurn ponies that followed them, for the horses' long legs devoured the ground, and at last pursuit seemed failing.

Then out of the west, riders appeared ahead of them, coming from the narrow crease of hills, an arc of riders that swept to enclose them, thrusting them back.

Morgaine turned yet again, charging them at their outer edge, trying to slip that arc before it cut them off from the north, refusing to be thrust back into the ambush at Irien. Siptah could hardly run now. He faltered. They were not going to make it. And here she reined in, weapon in hand, and Vanye drew the winded black in beside her, sword drawn, to guard her left.

The riders ringed them about on all sides now, and began to close inward.

"The horses are done," Vanye said. "Lady, I think we shall die here."

"I have no intention of doing so," she said. "Stay clear of me, *ilin*. Do not cross in front of me or even ride even with me."

And then he knew the spotted pony of one that was at the head of the others, ordering his riders to come inward; and near him there was the blaze-faced bay that he expected to see.

They were Morij riders, that ran the border by Alis Kaje, and sometimes harried even into this land when Hjemur's forces or Chya's grew restive.

He snatched at Morgaine's arm, received at once an angry look, quick suspicion. Terror.

C. J. Cherryh

"They are Morij," he pleaded with her. "My clan. Nhi. *Liyo,* take none of their lives. My father—he is their lord, and he is not a forgiving man, but he is honorable. *Ilin*'s law says my crimes cannot taint you: and whatever you have done, Morija has no bloodfeud with you. Please, lady. Do not take these men's lives."

She considered; but it was sense that he argued with her, and she must know it. The horses were likely to die under them if they must go on running. There would likely be more Hjemurn forces to the north even if they should break clear now. Here was refuge, if no welcome. She lowered her weapon.

"On your soul," she hissed at him. "On your soul, if you lie to me in this."

"That is the condition of my oath," he said, shaken, "and you have known that as long as I have been with you. I would not betray you. On my soul, *liyo.*"

The weapon went back into its place. "Speak to them," she said then. "And if you have not a dozen arrows in you—I will be willing to go with them on your word."

He put up his sword and lifted his hands wide, prodding the exhausted black a little forward, until he was within hailing distance of the advancing riders, whose circle had never ceased to narrow.

"I am *ilin,*" he cried to them, for it was no honor to kill *ilin* without reckoning of his lord. "I am Nhi Vanye. Nhi Paren, Paren, Lellen's-son—you know my voice."

"Whose service, *ilin* Nhi Vanye?" came back Paren's voice, gruff and familiar and blessedly welcome.

"Nhi Paren—these hills are full of Hjemur-folk tonight, and Leth too, most likely. In Heaven's mercy, take us into your protection and we will make our appeal at Ra-morij."

"Then you serve some enemy of ours," observed Nhi Paren, "or you would give us an honest name."

"That is so," said Vanye, "but none that threatens you now. We ask shelter, Nhi Paren, and that is the Nhi's right to grant or refuse, not yours, so you must send to Ra-morij."

There was a silence. Then: "Take them both," came across the distance. The riders closed together. For a moment as they were closely surrounded, Vanye had the overwhelming fear that Morgaine might suddenly panic and bring death on both of them, the more so as Paren demanded the surrender of their weapons.

And then Paren had his first clear sight of Morgaine in the

darkness, and exclaimed the beginning of an invocation to Heaven. The men about him made signs against evil.

"I do not think that it will be comfortable for you to handle my weapons, being that your religion forbids," said Morgaine then. "Lend me a cloak and I will wrap them, so that you may know that I will not use them, but I will continue to carry them. I think that we were well out of this area. Vanye spoke the truth about Hjemur."

"We will go back to Alis Kaje," Paren said. And he looked at her as if he thought long about the matter of the weapons. Then he bade Vanye give her his cloak, and watched carefully while she wrapped all her gear within the cloak and laid it across her saddlebow. "Form-up," he bade his men then, and though they were surrounded by riders, he put no restraint on them.

They rode knee to knee, he and Morgaine, with men all about them; and before they had ridden far, Morgaine made to pass the cloak-wrapped arms to him. He feared to take it, knowing how the Nhi would see it; and it was instant: weapons crowded them. A man of clan San, more reckless than the others, took them from him, and Vanye looked at Morgaine in distress, knowing how she would bear that.

But she was bowed over, looking hardly able to stay in the saddle. Her hand was pressed to her leg. Threads of blood leaked through her pale fingers.

"Bargain us a refuge," she said to him, "however you can, *ilin.* There is neither hearth-right nor bloodfeud I have with clan Nhi. And have them stop when it is safe. I have need to tend this."

He looked on her pale, tense face, and knew that she was frightened. He measured her strength against the jolting ride they would have up the road into Alis Kaje, and left her, forced his way through other riders to reach Nhi Paren.

"No," said Paren, when he had pleaded with him. It was firm. It was unshakable. He could not blame the man, in the lands where they were. "We will stop at Alis Kaje."

He rode back to her. Somehow she did keep the saddle, white-lipped and miserable. The sleet-edged wind made her flinch at times; the horse's motion in the long climb and descent wrung now and then a sound from her: but she held, waiting even as they found their place to halt, until he had dismounted and reached up to help her down.

He made a place for her, and begged her medicines of the one who had her belongings. Then he looked round at the grim band of men, and at Paren, who had the decency to bid them back a distance.

He treated the wound, which was deep, as best he could manage with her medicines: his soul abhorred even to touch them, but he reasoned that her substance, whatever it was, would respond best to her own methods. She tried to tell him things: he could make little sense of them. He made a bandage of linen from the kit, and at least had slowed the bleeding, making her as comfortable as he could.

When he arose, Nhi Paren came to him, looked down at her and walked back among his men, bidding them prepare to ride.

"Nhi Paren." Vanye cursed and went after him, stood among them in the dark with men on all sides already mounting. "Nhi Paren, can you not delay at least until the morning? Is there such need to hurry now, with the mountains between us?"

"You are trouble yourselves, Nhi Vanye," said Paren. "You and this woman. There is Hjemur under arms. No. There will be no stopping. We are going through to Ra-morij."

"Send a messenger. There is no need to kill her in your haste."

"We are going through, said Paren.

Vanye swore blackly, choked with anger. There was no cruelty in Nhi Paren, only Nhi obdurate stubbornness. He changed his own saddleroll to the front of his saddle, lashing it to pad it. Anger still seethed in him.

He turned to lead the horse back to Morgaine. "Bid a man help me up with her then," he said to Paren through his teeth. "And be sure that I will recite the whole of it to Nhi Rijan. There is justice in him, at least; his honor will make him sorry for this senseless stubbornness of yours, Nhi Paren."

"Your father is dead," said Paren.

He stopped, aware of the horse pushing at his back, the reins in his hand. His hands moved without his mind, stopping the animal. All these things he knew, before he had to take account of Paren, before he had to believe the man.

"Who is the Nhi?" he asked.

"It is your brother," said Paren. "Erij. We have standing orders, should you ever set foot within Morija, to take you at once to Ra-morij. And that is what we must do. It is not," Paren said in a softer tone, " to my taste, Nhi Vanye, but that is what we will do."

He understood then, numb as he was. He bowed slightly, acknowledged reality; which gesture Nhi Paren received like a gentleman, and looked embarrassed and distressed, and bade men help him take Morgaine up so that he could carry her.

Morij-keep, Ra-morij, was alleged to be impregnable. It sat high upon a hillside, tiered into it, with all of a mountain at its back and its walls and gates made double before it. It had never fallen in war. It had been sometimes the possession of Yla and lately of Nhi, but that had been by marriages and by family intrigue and lastly by the ill-luck of Irien, but never by siege against the fortress itself. Rich herds of horses and of cattle grazed the lands before it; in the valley its villages nestled in relative security, for there were no wolves nor riders, nor Koris-beasts troubling the land as they did in the outside. The keep frowned over the fair land like some great stern grandfather over a favored daughter, his head bearing a crown of crenelated walls and jagged towers.

He loved it still. Tears could still swell in his throat at the sight of this place that had been so much of misery to him. For an instant he thought of his boyhood, of spring, and of fat, white-maned Mai, the first Mai—and both his brothers racing with him on one of those days when there was such warmth in the air that not even they could find hate for each other, when blooms were on the orchards and the whole of the great valley lay studded with pink and white clouds of trees.

Before him now there was the light of a dying winter sun upon the walls, and the clatter of armed riders about him, and Morgaine's weight in his arms. She slept now, and his arms were numb and his back a column of fire. She knew little of the ride, exceedingly weak, though the bleeding had ceased and the wound already showed signs of healing. He thought that she might have fought against the weakness, but she did not know that things were amiss, and the men of Nhi were kindly with her. They did whatever it was possible to do for her, short of touching her or her medicines; and their fear of her seemed to have much abated.

She was very fair, and young-seeming, and capable of innocence when her gray eyes were closed. Even with women of quality men of low-clan made coarse jokes, well-meant; with women of the countryside even high-clan men were far more direct. There was none of that where Morgaine was involved —because she had lord-right, perhaps, and because there attended her an *ilin* who must defend her, and that, weaponless as he was, there was no honor in that; but most probably it was because she was reputed to be *qujal*, and men did not make light with anything *qujal*.

Only sometimes Nhi Paren would ask how she fared, and some of the others would ask the same, and wonder that she slept so.

And of one, Nhi Ryn, son of Paren, there were looks of awe. He was very young; his head was full of poets and of legends, and he had a skill with the harp that was beyond what most high-clan men learned. That which resided in his eyes was purely astonishment at first, and then worship, which boded ill for the welfare of his soul.

Nhi Paren had seemed to see it developing, and had sharply ordered the youth to the rear guard, far back along the line.

Now there was an end of such care of them: the horses' hooves rang upon paving as they approached the gates. Nhi Rej had built the channeling and the paving fifty years ago, restoring the work of Yla En—no luxury, for otherwise the whole of the hill would begin to wash down with the spring rains.

The Red Gate admitted them, and red it was, bravely fluttering with the Nhi standards with their black writing. There was no sound but the snap of the flags in the wind and the clatter of hooves on stone as they entered the courtyard. One servant ran out and bowed to Nhi Paren. Orders and information passed back and forth.

Vanye sat the saddle, patient until some decision was reached, and at last the youth Ryn and another man came to help him lift Morgaine down from the saddle. He had expected arrest, violence— something. There was only quiet discussion as if they had been any ordinary travelers. It was decided to put Morgaine in the sunny west tower, and they carried her there, the three of them, and the guards following. There they gave her into the hands of frightened serving women, who clearly did not relish their service.

"Let me stay with her," Vanye pleaded. "They do not know how to care care for her as needs be. . . . At least leave her own medicines."

"The medicines we will leave," said Paren. "But we have other orders with you."

And they took him down the stairs and to a lower hall, into a hall that was home: for there upon the left was Erij's room, and there the stairs that had led up to the middle tower room that had been his. But they took him instead to that which had belonged to Kandrys: the door bolt resisted with the obstinacy of a lock long undisturbed.

Vanye glanced frightened protest at Paren. This was insane, this prison they meant for him. Paren looked intensely uncomfortable, as if he did not relish his orders in the least, but he ordered him inside. Must and mildew and age came out at them. It was cold, and the floor was covered with dust, for dust sifted constantly through Ra-morij, through barred windows and through cracks and crevices.

One servant brought in rush lights. Others brought wood, and a bucket of coals to start the fire. He scanned the room by the dim light, finding it as he had remembered. Nothing must have been disturbed since the morning of Kandrys's death. He saw his doting father's hand in that morbid tenderness.

There were the clothes across the back of the chair, the muddy boots left by the fireside for cleaning, the impression still in the dusty bedclothes where Kandrys had last lain.

He swore and rebelled at that, but firm hands kept him from the door, and men with weapons were outside. There was no resisting the insanity.

Men brought in water for washing, and a plate of food, and wine. All these things they sat on the long table by the door. There was an extra armload of wood, and this they unloaded beside the fireplace, that now blazed up quite comfortably.

"Who ordered this?" Vanye asked finally. "Erij?"

"Yes," said Paren, and his tone said clearly that he did not approve of the business. There was a touch of pity in his eyes, for all that none was owed an outlaw. "We must not leave you your armor, either, nor any weapon."

That was clearly the way things would be. Vanye unlaced and slipped off both leather tunic and mail and undertunic, surrendering them to one of the men, as they had taken his helm earlier, and endured in silence their searching him for concealed weapons. He had besides his boots and leather breeches only a thin shirt, and that was no protection against the chill that still clung to the room. When they left him alone he was glad to crouch down upon the hearth and warm himself; and eventually he found appetite enough to take the food and wine they had offered, and to wash, heating the water in the little kettle that was by the hearth.

And at last the weariness that was upon him overcame the rest of his scruples. He thought that he was probably meant to spend the night guilty and miserable, crouching at the hearth rather than sleep in that ghastly bed.

But he was Nhi enough to be contrary, and determined that he would not let himself be prey to the ghost that hovered about this room, angry at its murder. He drew back the covers and settled himself in, stripped only of boots, though it was the custom of men that slept in hall to sleep naked. He did not trust the hospitality of Morija that far. It was a weary time since he had had relief of the weight of the mail even at night, and that alone was enough to make him comfortable. He slept as soon as he had warmed the cold bedclothes with his body, as soon as the tension had passed from his muscles, and if he dreamed, he did not remember it.

CHAPTER VII

THERE WAS THE scrape of a step on stone, something hovering over him. Vanye in sudden panic turned onto his back, flinging his arm and the covers aside, seeking to rise.

Then a man in black and silver stepped back from him and Vanye stopped, one bare foot on the floor. The fire had almost died. Daylight poured wanly through the narrow slit of a window, accompanied by a cold draft.

It was Erij—older, harder of face, the black hair twisted into the different braid that was for hall-lord. The eyes were the same—insolent and mocking.

Vanye thrust himself to his feet, seeing at once that they were alone in the room and that the door was shut. There would be men outside. He had no illusions of safety. He put up a brave face against Erij and ignored him for the moment, going about the necessary business of getting his boots on. Then he went over to the leavings of last night's wine and had a sip of the wretched stuff, returning to the fireside to drink it, for the chill crept quickly into his bones. All this Erij let him do without troubling him.

And then while he knelt feeding the fire to life he heard Erij's tread behind him, and felt the gentle touch of Erij's long fingers gather back his hair, which hung loose about his shoulders. It was long enough to gather in the hand, not yet long enough to resume the braid that marked a warrior. Erij tugged at it gently, as a man might a child's.

He lifted his head perforce. He did not try to turn, but braced himself for the cruel wrench he was sure would come. It did not.

"I would have thought," said Erij, "that the honors bestowed on you at your leaving would have counseled you against coming back."

Erij let go his hair. Vanye seized the chance to turn and rise. Erij was taller than he: he could not help looking up at his elder brother, close as he stood to him. His back was to the hearth. The heat was unpleasant. Erij did not back a pace to let him away from it.

And then he saw that Erij had no right hand: the member that he kept thrust within the breast of his tunic was a stump. He stared, horrified, and Erij held it up the better for him to see.

"Your doing," said Erij. "Like much else."

He did not offer his sorrow for it; he could not say at the moment that he felt it, or anything else save shock. Erij had been the vain one, the skilled one, his hands clever with the sword, with the harp, with the bow.

The pain of the fire in his legs was intense. He pushed free of Erij. The wine cup spilled on the floor and rolled a trail of red droplets darkly across the thirsty dust.

"You come in strange company," said Erij. "Is she real?"

"Yes," said Vanye.

Erij considered that. He was Myya and coldly practical; Myya doubted much and believed little: they were not notoriously religious. It was doubtful which side in him would win, god-fearing Nhi or cynical Myya. "I have had a look at some of the things she carried," he said. "And that would seem to support it. But she bleeds like any mortal."

"There are enemies on her trail and mine," he said hoarsely, "that will be no boon to Morija. Let us be on our way as soon as she can ride, and we will be no trouble to you and neither will they. Hjemur will be far too busy with the both of us to trouble with Morija. If you try to hold her here, it may well be otherwise."

"And if she dies here?"

He stared at Erij, gauging him, and began to reckon with the two years and what they had wrought: the boy was dead, and the man would kill, cold-bloodedly. Erij had been a creature of tempers, of vanities, of sometime kindness—different than Kandrys. Erij's features now seemed those of a man who never smiled. A new scar marred one cheek. There had come to be lines about the eyes.

"Let her pass," said Vanye. "They will want her and all that ever was hers; you cannot deal with Hjemur. There is no dealing with them at all, and you know it."

"Is that where she is going?" he asked.

"The less Morija has to do with her the better. She has bloodfeud with them, and she is more danger to them than to you. I am telling you the truth."

Erij thought upon that a moment, leaned upon the fireplace and thrust the maimed limb within his tunic once more. His dark eyes rested upon Vanye, hard and calculating. "The last I heard of you was through Myya Gervaine, the matter of a killing and a horse-theft in Erd."

"It took the better part of two years to pass the land of your cousins of Myya," Vance acknowledged. "I lived off them; and took the horse in trade for mine."

Erij's lips tightened in grim mirth at the insolence. "Before you acquired a service, I take it?"

"Before that, yes."

"And how was it that you acquired that service?"

Vanye shrugged. He was cold. He returned to the fire, folding his arms against the chill. "Carelessness," he said. "I sheltered where I ought not—too intent on the woman to remember that she had lord-right. It was fair Claiming."

"Do you sleep with her?"

He looked up at his brother in shock. "*Ilin* with *liyo,* and the like of her? No, I do not. Did not."

"She is beautiful. She is also *qujal.* I do not like having her under roof. She claims no hearth-right here, and I do not intend she should obtain it."

"She does not wish it," said Vanye. "Only send us on our way."

"What is the term of your service to her? What does she claim of you?"

"I do not think I am at liberty to say that. But it has nothing to do with Morija. We only turned here after we were harried in this direction by Hjemur."

"And if released, she will go—where?"

"Out of your lands, by the quickest means." He looked his brother in the face, dropping all arrogance: Erij was due his revenge, had had it in the hospitality he gave them. "I swear it, Erij; and I hold nothing against you for this welcome of yours. If you let us go I will take every care that it brings no trouble on the land—on my life, Erij."

"What do you ask of me, what help?"

"Only return to us the gear you took from us. Give us provisions, if you would. We are scant of everything. And we will go as soon as she can ride."

Erij stared into the fire, sidelong; his eyes flicked back again, frowning. "There is a charge on that charity."

"What charge?"

"You." And when Vanye only stared at him, blank and

hardly comprehending: "I will release her," said Erij, "today, with provisions, with horses, with all your gear; and she may go where she will. But you I will not release. That is the charge on my hospitality."

Bargain us a refuge, she had ordered him before she sank into delirium, *however you can.* He knew that it dishonored her, to abandon him, but he knew the compulsion there was in Morgaine: she lived for that, and for nothing else, her face set toward Hjemur. She would gladly spend his life if it would set her safe at Hjemur's border: she had said that in her own words.

"When I have fulfilled my service with her," he offered, trying that, "I will come back to Morija."

"No," said Erij.

"Then," he said at last, "for such a bargain you owe me fair payment: swear that she will go from here with all that is ours, horses and weapons and provisions adequate to see her to any of our borders she chooses: and let her ride free away from the very gate—no double-dealing."

"And for your part?" asked Erij. "If I grant this, I will have no curse from you or from her?"

"None," said Vanye; and Erij named his oath and swore: it was one that even a half-Myya ought to respect.

And Erij left. Vanye was overcome with cold thereafter and knelt on the hearth, feeding the wood in slowly, until the blaze grew intense. The room was still. He looked into the shadows beyond the light and saw only Kandrys's things. He had never much credited the beliefs that the unhappy dead hovered close about the living, though he served one who should have been dead a century ago; but there remained a chill about the room, a biding discomfort that might be guilt, or fear, or some power of Kandrys's soul that lingered here.

Eventually there was a clatter in the courtyard. He went to the slit of a window and looked out, and saw the black and Siptah saddled, saw men about them.

And, aided by two men, Morgaine was brought down and set upon her horse. She scarcely had the strength to stay the saddle, and caught the reins with an awkward gesture that showed she had almost dropped them.

Anger churned in him, that she was being turned out in such condition. Erij meant for her to die.

He forced his shoulder through the narrow opening, shouted down at her. *"Liyo!"* he cried, his voice carried away on the biting wind. But she looked up, her eyes scanning the high walls. *"Liyo!"*

She lifted her hand. She saw him. She turned to those about her, and the attitude of her body was one of anger, and theirs that of embarrassment. They turned from her, all save those that must hold the horses.

Then he grew afraid for her, that she would take arms and be killed, not knowing the case of things.

"The matter of a bargain," he shouted down at her. "You are free on his oath, but do not trust him, *liyo!"*

It seemed then she understood. She suddenly turned Siptah's head and laid heels to him, putting him to a pace headed for the gate, such that he feared she would fall at the turning. The black that had been Liell's followed, jerked along by the rein made fast to Siptah's saddle. There was a pack on the black's saddle—his own gear.

And one other followed, before the gate swung shut again.

Ryn the singer, harp slung to his back, spurred his pony after her. Tears sprang to Vanye's eyes, though he could not say why; he thought afterward that it was anger, seeing her take another innocent as she had taken him to ruin.

He sank down by the fireside again, bowed his head upon his arms and tried not to think of what lay in store for him.

"Father died," said Erij, "six months ago." He stretched his legs out before the fire in his own clean and carpeted apartments, which had been their father's, and looked down where Vanye sat cross-legged upon the hearthstones, unwilling guest for the evening. The air reeked of wine. Erij manipulated cup, then pitcher, upon the table at his left hand, by gesture offered more to Vanye. He refused.

"And you killed him," Erij added then, as if they had been discussing some distant acquaintance, "in the sense that you killed Kandrys: Father grew morbid over Kandrys. Kept the room as you see it. Everything the same. Harness down in the stable—the same. Turned his horse out. Good animal, gone wild now. Or maybe gone to the wolves, who knows? But Father made a great mound down there by the west woods, and there he buried Kandrys. Mother could not reason with him. She fell ill, what with his moods—and she died in a fall down the stairs. Or he pushed her. He was terrible when he was in one of his moods. After she died he took to sitting long hours out in the open, out on the edge of the mound. Mother was buried out there too. And that was the way he

died. It rained. We rode out to bring him in perforce. And
he took ill and died."

Vanye did not look at him, only listened, finding his
brother's voice unpleasantly like that of Leth Kasedre. The
manner was there, the casual cruelty. It had been terrible
enough when they were children: now that a man who ruled
Nhi sat playing these same games of pointless cruelty, it had
a yet more unwholesome flavor.

Erij nudged him with his foot. "He never did forgive you,
you know."

"I did not expect that he would," Vanye said without turning around.

"He never forgave me either," said Erij after a moment,
"for being the one of us two legitimate sons that lived. And
for being less than perfect afterward. Father loved perfection
—in women, in horses—in his sons. You disappointed him
first. And scarred me. He hated leaving Nhi to a cripple."

Vanye could bear it no longer. He turned upon his knees
and made the bow he had never paid his brother, that of
respect due his head-of-clan, pressing his brow to the stones.
Then he straightened, looked up in desperate appeal. "Let me
ride out of here, brother. I have duty to her. She was not
well, and I have an oath to her that I have to keep. If I
survive that, then I will come back, and we will settle
matters."

Erij only looked at him. He thought that perhaps this was
what Erij was seeking after all, that he lose his pride. Erij
smiled gently.

"Go to your room," he said.

Vanye swore, angry and miserable, and rose up and did as
he was bidden, back to the wretchedness of Kandrys's room,
back to dust and ghosts and filth, forced to sleep in Kandrys's
bed, and wear Kandrys's clothes, and pace the floor in lone-
liness.

It rained that night. Water splashed in through the crack
in the unpainted and rotting shutters, and thunder crashed
alarmingly as it always did off the side of the mountains. He
squinted against the lightning flashes and stared out into the
relief of hills against the clouds, wondering how Morgaine
fared, whether she lived or had succumbed to her wound, and
whether she had managed to find shelter. In time, the rain
turned to sleet, and the thunder continued to roll.

By morning a little crust of snow lay on everything, and

Ra-morij's ancient stones were clean. But traffic back and forth in the courtyard soon began, and tracked the ground into brown. Snow never stayed long in Morija, except in Alis Kaje, or the cap of Proeth.

It would, he thought, make things easier for any that followed a trail, and that thought made him doubly uneasy.

All that day, as the day before, no one came, not even to supply him with food. And in the evening came the summons that he expected, and he must again sit with Erij at table, he at one side and Erij at the other.

This evening there was a Cyha longbow in the middle of the table amid the dishes and the wine.

"Am I supposed to ask the meaning of it?" Vanye said finally.

"Chya tried our border in the night. Your prediction was true: Morgaine does have unusual followers."

"I am sure," said Vanye, "that she did not summon them."

"We killed five of them," said Erij, self-pleased.

"I met a man in Ra-leth," said Vanye, thin-lipped, the while he poured himself wine, "whose image you have grown to be, legitimate brother, heir of Rijan. Who kept rooms as you keep them, and guests as you keep them, and honor as you keep it."

Erij seemed amused by that, but the cover was thin. "Bastard brother, your humor is sharp this evening. You are growing over-confident in my hospitality."

"Brother-killing will be no better for you than it was to me," Vanye said, keeping his voice quiet and calm, far more so than he felt inside. "Even if you are able to keep your half well filled with Myya, like those fine servants of yours the other side of the door—it is Nhi that you rule. You ought to remember that. Cut my throat and there are Nhi who will not forget it."

"Do you think so?" Erij returned, leaning back. "You have no direct kin in Nhi, bastard brother: only me. And I do not think Chya will be able to do anything—if they cared, which I much doubt they do. And *she* was quick enough to leave you. I would that I knew what there was in the witch that could turn the likes of you into the faithful servant, Vanye the self-serving, Vanye the coward. And no bed-sharing, either. That is a great sorcery, that you would give that loyal a service to anyone. You were always much better at ambushes."

Some that Erij said of him he owned for the truth: younger brother against the older, bastard against the heir-sons, he had not always stayed by the terms of honor. And they had laid ambushes of their own, the more so after his nurse died and he came to take up residence in the fortress of Ra-morij.

That was, he recalled, the time when they had ceased to be brothers: when he came to live in the fortress, and they perceived him not as poor relation, but as rival. He had not understood clearly how it was at the time. He had been nine. Erij was twelve, Kandrys thirteen: it was at that age that boys could be most mindfully, mindlessly cruel.

"We were children," Vanye said. "Things were different."

"When you killed Kandrys," said Erij, "you were plain enough."

"I did not want to kill him," Vanye protested. "Father said he never struck to kill, but I did not know that. Erij, he drove at me: you saw, you saw it. And I never would have struck for you."

Erij stared at him, cold and void. "Except that my hand chanced to be shielding him after he had got his death-wound. He was down, bastard brother."

"I was too pressed to think. I was wrong. I am guilty. I do penance for it."

"Actually," said Erij, "Kandrys meant to mar you somewhat: he never liked you, not at all. He did not find it to his liking that you were given a place among the warriors: he said that he would see you own that you had no right there. Myself, it was neither here nor there with me; but that was how it was: Kandrys was my brother. If he had decided to cut your throat, he was heir to the Nhi and I would have considered that too. Pity we aimed at so little. You were better with that blade than we thought you were, else Kandrys would not have baited you in the casual way he did. I have to give you due credit, bastard brother: you were good."

Vanye reached for the cup, swallowed the last, the wine souring in his mouth. "Father had a fine choice of heirs, did he not? Three would-be murderers."

"Father was the best of all," said Erij. "He killed our mother: I am sure of it. He pushed Kandrys to his death, favoring you as much as he did once. No wonder he saw ghosts."

"Then purify this hall of them. Let me ride out of here. Our father was no better to you than he was to me. Let me go from here."

"You keep asking; I refuse. Why do you not try to escape?"

"I thought that you expected me to keep my given word," he said. "Besides, I would never reach the ground floor of Ra-morij."

"You might be sorry later that you missed the chance."

"You want to frighten me. I know the game, Erij. You were always expert at that. I always believed the things you told me, and I always trusted you more than I did Kandrys. I always wanted to think that there was some sense of honor in you—whatever it was that he was lacking."

"You hated the both of us."

"I was sorry about you; I was even sorry about Kandrys."

Erij smiled and rose from the table, walked near the fire, where it was warm. Vanye joined him there. Erij still had his cup in hand, and took his accustomed chair, while Vanye settled on the warm stones. There was silence between them for a long time, almost peace. Two more cups of wine passed from Erij's cup, and his tanned face grew flushed and his breathing heavy.

"You drink too much," said Vanye at last. "This evening and last—you drink too much."

Erij lifted the stump of his arm. "This—pains me of cold evenings. For a long time I drank to ease my sleep at night. Probably I shall have to stop it, or come to what Father did. It was the wine that helped ruin him, I well know that. When he drank, which was constantly after Kandrys died, he grew unreasonable. When he would get drunk he would go out and sit by his tomb and see ghosts. I should hate to die like that."

It was the rationality in Erij that made him seem most mad; at times Vanye almost thought him amenable to reason, to forgiveness. A man could not speak so with an enemy. At such times they were more brothers than they had ever been. At such times he almost understood Erij, through the moods and the hates and the lines that began to be graven into his face, making him look several years older than was the truth.

"Your lady," said Erij then, "has not quitted Morija as you said she would."

Vayne looked up sharply. "Where is she?"

"You might know," said Erij, "since I think you know full well what she is about."

"That is her business."

"Shall I recall her and ask her or shall I ask you again?"

Vanye stared at him, beginning suddenly to see purpose within the madness, the sickly, fragile humors. He liked it no less. "Her business is with Hjemur, and she is no friend of Thiye. Let that suffice."

"Truly?"

"It is truth, Erij."

"All the same," said Erij, "she had not quitted Morija. And all my promises were conditional on that."

"So were mine," said Vanye, "conditional."

Erij looked down at him. There was no mirth there at all. Of a sudden it was Nhi Rijan in that look, young and hard and full of malice. "You are dismissed."

"Do nothing against her," Vanye warned him.

"You are dismissed," said Erij.

Vanye gathered himself up and took his leave with a scant bow, maintaining the slender thread of courtesy between them. There were the guards outside to take him—there always were: Myya; Erij trusted no Nhi to do this duty, walking him to and from his quarters.

But they had doubled since he had come into the room. There had been two. Now four waited.

Suddenly he tried to retreat back within the room, heard the whisper of steel and saw Erij drawing his longsword from its sheath. In that instant of hesitation they hauled him back and tried to hold him.

He had nothing to lose. He knew it, and flung himself at his brother, intent on cracking his skull at least: there should no Myya whelp lord it in Ra-morij, that benefit for the unfortunate Nhi if nothing else.

But they overhauled him, stumbling over each other and overturning furniture in their haste to seize him; and Erij's fist, guarded by the pommel, came hard against the side of his head, dropping him to his knees.

He knew these nether portions of the fortress, those carved deep into the hill for the holding of supplies in the event of siege, a veritable warren of tunnels and rooms of dripping ceilings, frozen in winter. It was this which made the whole east wing unsafe, so that no one lived there: collapse had been reckoned imminent as long as anyone could remember, though the tunnels were shored up and the storerooms braced with pillars and some filled with dirt. As children they had been forbidden these places: as children they had used the upper storerooms on the safe west for their amusements in the bitter days of winter and the heat of summer.

And one time after he came to live in Ra-morij, his brothers had dared him to come with them down to the nethermost depths: they had taken a single lamp and ventured into this place of damp and cold and moldering beams and crumbling masonry.

Here they had left him, where his screams could in nowise be heard above.

And it was into this place that the Myya sealed him, without light and without water, with only his thin shirt against the numbing cold. He fought against them, dazed as he yet was, panicked by the fear that they would bind him here as Kandrys had: fled their grasp and meant to fight them.

They closed the door on him, plunged him into utter dark; the bolt outside crashed across and echoed.

He tried his strength against it until he was exhausted, his shoulder bruised and his hands torn. Then he sank down against it, the only sure point in this absolute dark, the only place that was not cold earth and stone. He caught his breath and heard for a time only the slow and distant drip of water.

Then the rats began to stir again, timid at first, stopping when he would make a sound. Gradually they grew bolder. He heard their small feet, both along the walls and overhead, in the maze of unseen beams.

He loathed them, since that nightmare in the basement of Ra-morij; he hated even seeing them in light, despising them there: the very sight of them brought back the memory, reminding him of dark places where they thrived in numbers, a realm within the walls, under foundations, where they were the terror and he small and helpless.

He no longer dared lie there. They generally avoided a man who was awake: he knew this sensibly, in spite of his fear; but he had heard too much of what they might do to a man asleep. He paced to keep himself awake, and once, when he did lie down to rest, and felt something light skitter over his leg, he came up with a shuddering cry that echoed madly through the dark, and gathered himself to his feet.

The sound made a pause in all the scurryings—only a moment. Then they proceeded fearlessly about their business.

Sometime, eventually, he would have to sleep. There had to be a time that he would fall down exhausted. Already his knees were shaking. He paced until he had to take his rest by leaning against the walls, until he had long moments of knowing nothing, and woke again in the midst of a fall to the ground, to scramble up again, dusting his hands and shuddering, holding himself on his shaking legs with difficulty.

Then, at last, came a clatter in the hall, a light under the door, and it opened, blazing torchlight into his face, dark figures of men. He went to them as to dear friends, flung himself into their arms as into a place of refuge.

They brought him back upstairs, back to the fine hall that was Erij's apartment. It was night outside the window, so that he knew it had been a night and a day since he had slept; and now his knees were shaking and his hands almost incapable of handling the utensils as he seated himself at the accustomed table opposite his brother.

He reached for the wine first, that began to take the chill from his belly, but he could not eat. He picked at a few bites, and ate some of the bread, and a bit of cheese.

The knife clattered from his hand and he had had enough. He shoved his chair back without Erij's leave, withdrew to the warm hearth and lay down there while Erij finished his dinner. His senses dimmed, exhaustion taking him, and he wakened to Erij's boot in his ribs, gently applied.

He gathered himself up, willing to stave off a return to that place by conversation, by applying himself most earnestly to Erij's humors, but the Myya guards were there. They set hands on him to take him back to that place of darkness and rats, and he fought them and cried aloud, sobbing, clawing free of them: he found the table, snatched a knife and laid a man's arm open with it before they wrested it away from him and pulled him down in a clatter of spilling dishes. A booted foot slammed into his head; when he went down his only thought was that they would take him back unconscious, and that the rats would have him. For that reason he fought them; and then a second blow to the stomach drove the wind from him and he ceased to know anything.

He still lay upon the floor. He knew light and heat and felt carpet with his fingers. Then he felt a cold edge prison one wrist against the floor, and opened his eyes upon Erij, who sat against the arm of the chair; upon the bright length of a longsword that rested over him.

"You have more staying power than you used to have,

bastard brother," said Erij. "A few years ago you would have
seen reason two days ago. Is it so much you owe her that
you will not even say why she has come?"

"I will tell you," he said, "though I myself do not understand it. She says that she came to destroy the Witchfires. I
do not know why. Perhaps it is some matter of her honor.
But they never were anything but harm to Andur-Kursh; so
she is no harm to Morija."

"And you do not know what gain that would be to her."

"No. She only says—somehow—she means to kill Thiye,
and that is not . . ." He moved his arm. The blade sliced
skin and he decided against it. "Erij, she is not the enemy."

Erij's mouth twisted into a sour smile. "There have been
more than Thiye that aspired to what Thiye holds. And none
of those have meant us good."

"Not to possess what he holds. To destroy it."

The blade lifted. Vanye struggled to his knees, aching in
head and belly, where he had been kicked. He met Erij's
cynicism with absolute earnestness.

"Little brother," said Erij, "I think you actually believe the
witch. And you have gone soft in the wits if that is so. Look
at me. Look at me. I swear to you—and you know that I
keep my word—that if you forsake that allegiance in truth,
I will not collect the price you owe me." The longsword
flicked at his wrist. Vanye snatched it back, horrified. The
blade instead leveled at his eyes, holding him like the eyes
of a serpent.

"Bastard brother," said Erij, "it has taken me these two
years to learn some skill with my left hand. All for a careless,
useless gesture. Romen's efforts notwithstanding, I lost the
fingers. They went before the hand. Need I tell you how I
have sworn I would do if ever I had you in reach, bastard
brother? Kandrys may have deserved what he had of you;
but I only tried to shield him at that moment—only to keep
you from striking him again, I not even in armor. There was
no honor for you in what you did, little brother. And I have
not forgiven you."

"That is a lie," said Vanye. "You would as gladly have
killed me, and I was less skilled than either of you: I always
was."

Erij laughed. "There is the Vanye I know. Kandrys would
have cursed me to my face and gone for my throat if I
threatened him. But you know I will do it, and you are

afraid. You think too much, Chya bastard. You always had too keen an imagination. It made you coward, because you never learned to put that wit of yours to good advantage. But I will own you were outmatched then. The years have put weight on you, and half a hand to your stature. I am not sure I should like to take you on now, left-handed as I am."

"Erij." He cast everything upon an appeal to reason, put utmost heart into his tone. "Erij, will you have this hall reputed like that of Leth? Let me pass from here. I am outlawed. I admit I deserve it, and I was mad to come here asking charity of Father. I would never have dared come if I had known I would have to ask any grace of you. That was my mistake. But Nhi will lose honor for you. You know that Nhi will have no part of it, or else you would not have to use Myya guards with me."

"For what are you asking me?"

"To treat me as Nhi, as your brother."

Erij smiled faintly, drew from his belt the shortsword, the Honor blade, and cast it ringing onto the stones of the hearth. Then he walked out.

Vanye stared after him, shuddered as the door slammed and the heavy bolt went across. Fear settled into him like an old friend, close and familiar. He did not even look at the sword for a moment. He had not asked for this, but for his release; and yet it honorably answered, more than honorably answered, all that he had asked of Erij.

At last he turned upon his knees and sought the hilt of the blade, picked it up and could not find it comfortable in his hand, even less could find the courage to do with it what was required of him to do.

It was, perhaps, safe refuge from Erij, and Erij's last mercy was this offering: there were pains far worse than the honorable one of this blade.

But it required an act of will, of courage, toward which Erij challenged him—knowing, thoroughly knowing, that his Chya brother would not be able to do it.

And Vanye knew well enough that Erij, in his place, could. So might Kandrys, or their father. There was the bloodiness in them; they would do it if only to spite their enemy and rob him of revenge.

He set it against the floor, at the length of his arms, shut his eyes and stayed there. All that it took from this point was one forward impulse. His arms, his whole body, shook with the strain.

And after a time he ceased to be afraid, for he knew that
he was not going to do it. He let fall the blade and crept over
to the fireside and lay down, shivering in every muscle, his
stomach heaving, his jaws clamped against the further shame
of sickness.

The daylight found him exhausted and placid in his exhaustion, though he did not truly sleep, save one time in the
thickest darkness of the night. He heard steps returning now
in the hall and had only one fleeting impulse toward doing
belatedly what should have been done in dignity.

He did not even meditate killing Erij with the blade. It
would be in the one case futile, for he would die for it,
shamefully; and in the other, the act would be void of any
honor or vindication for himself.

There were several of them that came in. Erij sent the other
men away to wait outside, crossed the carpets and gathered
up the abandoned blade, returned it to its sheath at his belt.

"I did not think you would," he said. "But you cannot
complain of me that *I* disgraced you." And he set his one
hand upon Vanye's shoulder and dropped to his knee, took
him by the arm and pulled at him, to have him up.

Vanye wept: he did not wish to, but like other battles with
Erij, this one was futile and he recognized it. Then to his
further shame he found Erij's arm about him, offering him
shelter, and it was good simply to fall against that and be
nothing. His brother's arms were about him after so long
without sight of home or kin, and his about Erij, and after
a time he realized that Erij also wept. His brother cuffed him
to self-control and to sense with a rough blow and held him
at arm's length: there was the moisture of tears on Erij's
hard face.

"I am breaking oath," said Erij, "because I swore that I
would kill you."

"I wish that you had," Vanye answered him, and Erij embraced him in his hard grip and treated him like the little
brother he had always felt himself to be with Erij, roughed
his hair, which was boy's length, and set him back again.

"You could never have done it," Erij said. "Because you
love life too much to die. That is a gift, brother. It makes
you a bad enemy."

Like Morgaine, he thought. Had that come from her? But
he had had in the beginning of his wandering the broken
halves of his own Honor blade, that his father had shattered;

his weakness was not Morgaine's doing, but that he truly did not deserve the honor of an *uyo* of the Nhi. There were prices of such things, that sometimes had to be paid at the end of possessing them; and he would never be fit to pay such a price.

And he wept again, knowing that. Erij cuffed his ear gently, made him look at him. "You robbed me," Erij said hoarsely, "of brother, mother, father, and a piece of myself. Do you not owe me some recompense? Do you not at least owe me something for it?"

"What do you want from me?"

"We made you an enemy. Kandrys hated you and set out to be rid of you, and Father always found you inconvenient. Myself, I had a brother to be loyal to then. I owed things to him. How do you feel toward me? Hate?"

"No."

"Will you come home? Your *liyo* has left you of her own choice. You are deserted. Your service is at an end if I pardon you so that you do not have to be *ilin* and go out to risk another Claiming. I can do that: I can pardon you. I need you, Vanye. There is only myself left of the family, and I—I have trouble even cutting meat at table. Someday I should need a brother with two good hands, a brother that I could trust, Vanye."

It moved too quickly for him, this quicksilver mood of Erij: he was left amazed, and vaguely troubled, but there had been void so long where there should be family; and the solid pressure of his brother's hand upon his arm and the offer of home and honor where he had none smothered other senses for the moment.

Almost.

He shook his head suddenly. "So long as she lives," he said, "and even beyond that, I have bond to her. That is why she could leave me. I am bound to kill Thiye, to destroy the Witchfires: this she has set on me."

"She has set something else on you," his brother pronounced after a moment, his expression greatly troubled. "Heaven defend a madman. Do you hear your own words, Vanye? Do you realize what she is asking of you? You could not lift your hand against yourself last night; and do you think that what she has set on you is any easier? She has ordered you to kill yourself, that is all."

"It was fair Claiming," he said, "and she was within her right."

"She left you."

"You sent her from me. She was hurt and had no choice."

Erij gripped his arm painfully. "I would give you place with me. Instead of being outlaw, instead of being dead in this impossible thing, you would be in Ra-morij, honored, second to me. Vanye, listen to me. Look at me. This is human flesh. This is human. She is Witchfire herself, that woman—cold company, dangerous company for anything born of human blood. She has killed ten thousand men—all in the name of the same lie, and now you have believed the lie too. I will not see one of my house go to that end. Look at me. See me. Can you even be comfortable to look her in the eyes?"

You do not know how great an evil you are aiding. She lies, she had lied before, to the ruin of Koris. Ilin-*oath says betray family, betray hearth, but not the* liyo; *but does it say betray your own kind?*

Come with me, Chya Vanye.

Liell's words.

"Vanye." His brother's hand slipped from him. "Go. I shall have them set you in your own room, your own proper room, in the tower. Sleep. Tomorrow evening you will know sense when you hear it. Tomorrow evening we will talk again, and you will know that I am right."

He slept. He had not thought it possible for a man who had been deprived of conscience and reason at once, but his body had its own demands to satisfy and after such a time simply closed off other senses. He slept deeply, in his own bed that he had known from childhood, and awoke aching and bruised from the treatment he had had of the Myya.

And awoke to the more painful misery of realizing that he had not dreamed the night in the basement or that in Erij's hall; that he had indeed done the things he remembered, that he had broken and wept like a child, and that the best there was left for him was to assume a face of pride and try to wear it before other men.

Even that seemed useless. He knew that it was a lie. So would everyone else in Morij-keep, most especially Erij, with whom it mattered most. He lay abed until servants brought in water for washing, and this time there was a razor for shaving; he made use of it, gratefully, and put off the clothing he had slept in, and washed his minor hurts before he dressed again in the clean clothing the servants provided him. In a morbid turn of mind he considered doing to himself again what Nhi Rijan had done, cutting off what growth of hair had come in the two years of his exile; and suddenly he gathered it back in his hand and did so, under the shocked eyes of the servants, who did not move to stop him. This a warrior decided, and whether it would please their lord, it was a matter among warriors and the *uyin*. In four uneven handfuls he severed the locks, and cast the razor on the table, for the servants to bear away.

In that attitude he went to his nightly meeting with his brother.

Erij did not appreciate the bitter humor of it.

"What nonsense is this?" Erij snapped at him. "Vanye, you disgrace the house."

"I have already done that," Vanye said quietly. Erij stared at him then, displeased, but he had the sense to let him alone upon the matter. Vanye set himself at table and ate without looking up from his plate or saying many words, and Erij ate also, but pushed away his own plate half-eaten.

"Brother," said Erij, "you are trying to shame me."

Vanye left the table and went over to stand by the hearth, the only truly warm place in all the room. After a moment Erij followed him and set his hand on his shoulder, making him look at him.

"Am I free to go?" Vanye asked, and Erij swore.

"No, you are not free to go. You are family and you have an obligation here."

"To what? To you, after this?" Vanye looked up at him and found it impossible to be angry: there was truly misery on Erij's face at the moment, and he had never known prolonged repentence in his brother. He did not know how to judge it. He walked back to the table and cast himself down there. Erij followed him back and sat down again.

"If I gave you weapons and a horse," Erij asked him, "what would you? Follow her?"

"I am bound by an oath," he said, "still." And then, to see if he could wring it from Erij: "Where is she?"

"Camped near Baien-ei."

"Will you give me the weapons and the horse?"

"No, I will not. Brother, you are Nhi. I pardon your other offenses. I hold nothing against you."

"I thank you for that," said Vanye quietly. "So do I yours against me."

Erij bit his lip; almost the old temper flared in him, but he restrained it. He bowed his head and nodded. "They have been considerable," he acknowledged, "of which this latest has been one of the lesser. But I swear to you, you will be my brother, heir next my own children. And it would be a greater Morija than either I or our father ruled, if you came to your senses."

Vanye reached for the wine cup. Something of the words jarred within him. He set it down again. "What is it you want of me?"

"You know the witch. You are intimate with her. You know what she seeks and I would wager that you know how it is to be had: that is implicit in the commission she gave you. I will warrant you have seen her use whatever powers she holds in those weapons of hers; you have passed together through Koriswood. I would even suspect that you know *how* they are used. I am not a man that believes in magic, Vanye, and neither, I suspect, are you, for all your Chya heritage. Things happen through the hands of men, not by wishes upon wands and out of thin air. Is that not so?"

"What has this to do with me and you?"

"Show me how these things are done. Keep your oath to kill Thiye if you will: but with my help. Remember that you are of human blood; and remember what loyalties you owe to your own kind.—Listen to me! Listen. Not since Irien has there been a power in Andur-Kursh save that of Hjemur, and this was of her making, out of her lies and her leading. Our father's kingdom once ranked high in the Middle Realms. The old High Kings are gone now and so is that power we once held, thanks to her. And it is within our hands to win it back again, yours and mine. Look at me, little brother! I swear to you—I swear to you that you will be second only to me."

"I am still *ilin*," he protested, "and I am safe from all your promises. Morgaine's power is in what she wields, and unless you are a liar, she still holds it. Do not challenge her, Erij, or she will be the death of you: she will kill. And I do not want to see that happen."

"Listen to me. Whatever she means to do with the Witch-fires, whatever she means to do with Thiye's power once she had possessed it—she is no friend of ours. We exchange one Thiye for another, she holding what he held, and she more unhuman than ever he was. Look at what Thiye has done with it, and he is at least in some part man. But she . . . the use of such powers is like the breath of air to her, the element in which she moves; and she is ambitious, for revenge, for power, for what else we do not know. What were you to her against the ambition that moves her? Think on that, brother."

"You said that she is camped near Baien-ei," Vanye answered. "That does not sound to me like what she would do if she had utterly deserted me. She is waiting. She expects me to come if I can."

Erij laughed, and the grin slowly died in Vanye's cold, unhappy stare. "You are naive," said Erij then. "What she is waiting for is not you, not so small a thing as that to her."

"What, then, would that be?"

"Will you show me the manner of the power she uses?" Erij asked him. "I do not ask you to break oath. If she seeks the death of Thiye and the fall of Hjemur, I have no quarrel with that; but if she seeks power for herself, then has she not used you shamefully, Vanye? Is that the oath you swore to her, that you would help set her in power over your own people? If that were so, it was a shameful oath."

"She means to break the power of Thiye," he said, "there was nothing said of creating any other power."

"Oh, come," said Erij. "And having ruined him . . . what? To live in poverty, to retreat to obscurity? Or to risk being overtaken by the bloodfeuds of so many enemies? Having taken power—she will hold it. You are nothing to her; I offered her to have you back, at the exchange of her word to go south again. She refused."

Vanye shrugged, for he had known of her that he had no importance when he ceased to serve her purposes: she had never deluded him in that.

"She simply threw you aside," said Erij. "And what might a heart like that do once in power in Hjemur, when she needs nothing? She will grow the more cold, and the more dangerous. I had rather an enemy with tempers and honest hates. I had rather a human enemy. Thiye is old and half-mad; he muddles about with his beasts and his self-indulgence, and seldom stirs. He has never made war on us, neither he nor his ancestors. But can you see the like of Morgaine being content with things as they are for long?"

"And what would you create of it, Erij?" he asked harshly. "The like of what I have seen in Ra-morij?"

"Look about you at Morija," said Erij. "Look at its people.

It does not fare too badly. Did you see anything amiss, anything in the land or the villages that would be better changed? We have our law, the blessing of church, the peace of our fields and our enemies in Chya fear us. That is my work. I am not ashamed of what I have done here."

"It is true that Morija is faring well now," Vanye said. "But you, yourself, you cannot handle the things that Morgaine does; and she will not yield them. Seek her for an ally if you will. That is the best thing you can do for yourself and Morija."

"Like the ten thousand at Irien that she and her allies helped?"

"She did not kill them. That much is a lie."

"But that is what came of her help, all the same. And I would not lay Morija and Nhi open to the same kind of thing. I would not trust her. But this—*this*—I would trust, that she values powerfully." Excitedly he rose from his place and from the cabinet near the table he drew out a cloth-wrapped bundle. When he took it in his hand the cloth fell away at the top and Vanye saw to his dismay the dragon-hilt of *Changeling*. "This is what holds her encamped at Baien-ei, her desire for this. And I would wager, brother, that you know something of it."

"I know that she bids me keep my hands from it," said Vanye. "Which you had better heed, Erij. She says there is danger in it and that it is a cursed blade, and I believe it."

"I know that she values this above your life," said Erij, "and more than all else she possessed. That was plain." He jerked it back as Vanye tentatively extended his hand toward it. "No, brother. But I will hear your explanation what value it bears to her. And if you are my brother, you will tell me this willingly."

"I will tell you honestly that I do not know," he said, "and that if you are wise you will let me return this thing to her before it does harm. Of all things she possesses, this is one she herself fears."

A second time he reached for it, beginning to be frightened for what Erij purposed with the blade: for it was a thing of power; he knew it by the way Morgaine treated it, who never let it leave her. Of a sudden Erij raised his voice in a shout. The door crashed back: the four Myya were with them.

And Erij shook the sheath from the blade one-handed, and held it naked in his hand. The blade went from translucent ice to a shimmer of opalescent fire, and all the air sang in their ears, a horrid shimmer of air at its tip that of a sudden Vanye knew.

"No!" he cried, flung himself aside. The air roared into a darkness and a wind that sucked at them, and the Myya were gone, whipped away into some vast expanse that had opened between them and the door.

Erij flung the blade away, sent it slithering sideways across the floor, ripping ruin after it, and of a sudden Vanye caught the sheath and scrambled for the abandoned blade, caught it up in his hand as other men poured through the door. The same starry dark caught them up, and his arm went numb.

He knew then the sensation that had prompted Erij to drop the blade, gut-deep loathing for such power, and suddenly he heard his brother's voice shout and felt a hand claw at his arm.

He ran, wiser than to turn and destroy . . . free down the hall and free upon the stairs downward once the *uyin* there saw the unworldly shimmer of the witchblade in his hand.

He knew his way. There was the outer door. He heaved back the bolt and ran for the stable court, feverishly cursed the weeping stableboy into saddling a good horse for him; and all the while from Ra-morij there was a silence. He kept himself clear from the arrow-slits of the windows, knowing that for his greatest peril, and bade the boy creep down in the shadows and open the gate for him.

Then he sprang to horse, keeping reins and sheath in one hand, holding the shimmering blade in the other, and rode. Arrows hissed about him. One plunged within the well of darkness at *Changeling*'s tip and was lost. Another scraped his horse's rump and stung the beast to a near stumble. But he was through. Frightened warders unbarred the gates under the menace of that blade and he was free of the outer gate, clattering down the height of the paved road and onto the soft earth of the slopes.

There was no rush to follow him. He imagined Erij cursing his men to order, trying to find some who would dare it— and that Erij himself would follow he did not doubt. He knew his brother too well to think that he would cease what he had decided to do.

And Erij would well know what road he would ride. If he were not Morij-bred, he would have no chance to evade them, to ride the shorter trails and the quick ones, but he had as

fine a knowledge of the web of unmarked roads in the country
as did Erij.

If was a matter of reaching Baien-ei and Morgaine, if it
were possible, before the Myya and their arrows.

CHAPTER VIII

THE PURSUIT WAS behind him again. When he looked back against some patch of unmelted snow in the starlight, he could see a dark knot atop a hill or along the road; but the laboring bay kept the same distance between them.

They had not delayed long. There were most of all the arrows to fear. If they had him once within arrow range, he could not survive it; and he did not doubt that they were Myya, and keen on killing him—it was the only way to safely wrest away the thing he carried.

It was the stopping that was the most dangerous. At times he had to stop and rest the horse; and he chose such times as he did not see them behind him and reckoned that they were doing the same, well knowing that at some time he might make an error, or fail to run again in time. They had come a day across the plain of Morija, and the signal fires were still lit: he could see their glow on hilltops, warning the whole land that there was an enemy abroad, a stranger that meant no good to Morija. That net of signals was the countryside's defense. All good men would turn out to patrol the roads, to challenge any comer near the vital passes, and he had no wish to kill—or whatever it was the witchblade did to them that fell within its power; besides, some of the countrymen, of clans San and Torin, were no mean archers themselves, and he feared any meeting with them.

At their first stopping he had contrived to sheathe the horrid blade, fearing to expose his own flesh to the danger of that fire, which was that about the Gates themselves. He laid the sheath on the ground and eased the point within, fearful that even that could not contain it. But the light ceased the moment the point had gone within, and then it was possible to lift and bear it like any normal sword.

It was the look of the four men of Myya that he could not get from his mind, that awful lostness as they whirled away

into that vast and tiny darkness, men who could not understand how they were dying.

If it were possible he would gladly have hurled *Changeling*
from him, have rid himself of that dread weight and let it
lie for some other unfortunate master. But it was his in
charge, and it was for Morgaine, who had sense enough to
keep it sheathed. He himself dreaded the thought of drawing
it again, almost more than he dreaded the arrows behind
him. There was sinister power about it that was far more
lingering than the ugliness of Morgaine's older—lesser—
weapons. His arm still hurt from wielding it.

In the hours' passing he tried at last just to keep the bay
moving, stopping dead only when he must; he knew that the
animal was going to fade long before he could make Baien-ei
and Morgaine's camp. There were villages: the Myya could
have remounts; they would run him to the bay's death. His
insides hurt from the constant jolting, already bruised from
the beating he had had of them. He began to have the taste
of blood in his mouth and he did not know if this was from
his bruised jaw or from somewhere inside.

And when he looked back of a sudden the Myya were no
longer with him.

There was no hope left but to go off the main road, to try to
confuse pursuit and hope that he could fight through ambush
at the end, at Baien-ei. The next time that he saw the chance
of another lane, one already well marred with tracks since
the melting of the snow, he took that road and coaxed the
poor horse to what pace he could maintain.

He knew the road. A little village lay a distance past the
second winding, the hamlet of San-morij, a clan that possessed
a score of smaller villages hereabouts—common and unpre-
tentious as the earth they held, kindly folk, but fierce to
enemies. There was a farmhouse that he well remembered,
that of the old chief armorer of Ra-morij, San Romen; he
owed a great debt to that old tutor of his, who alone of men
in Ra-morij had shown some sympathy for a lord's bastard,
who had soothed his hurts and treated the hidden wounds
with drafts of rough affection.

It was a debt that deserved better payment than he was
about to give; but desperation smothered any impulses to
honor. He knew where the stable was, around at the back of
the little house, a place where he and Erij had watered their
mounts once upon a better time. He left the bay tied to a

branch by the side of the road, and took *Changeling* upon his shoulder, and slipped down the ditch by the roadside until he was within sight of the stable.

Then he ran across the yard, skidded into the shadows and flung open the door, already hearing the livestock astir: the men of Romen's house would be waking, seeking arms at any moment, and running out to see what was among them. He chose the likeliest pony he could in the dark, already haltered in its stall: he put a length of rope in the halter ring, the only thing there was to hand, flung open the stall door and backed the pony out.

Running footsteps pelted up to the door. He expected its opening, swung up to the pony's bare back with the halter rope for a rein, and as the door was flung open, he rammed his heels into the pony's flanks and the frightened animal bolted out into the yard—an honest horse and unused to such treatment. It ran for the road, scrambled up the side of the ditch, and he wrapped his legs about its fat ribs and clung, unshakable. He wrenched its head over in the direction he wanted it to go, and when he reached the crossroads over by San-hei, he turned there, heading for Baien-ei by a slightly longer road, but a lonelier one.

There was a rider on the road ahead, *sai-uyo,* Vanye thought, *uyo* of the lesser clans, but *uyo,* and armored: he rode like a warrior. There was no hope that the little beast he rode could match a proper horse. There was no avoiding the meeting. Vanye rode along at leisure, legs dangling, like any herder-boy returning at evening. Only upon the heights the warning-fires still gleamed, and the roads were watched; and he for his part could not look to be a herdsman, for boots and breeches were of weathered leather such as was proper to an *uyo,* not a countryman, he carried a great sword, and his shirt of white lawn marked him for a man untimely rushed from some great hall, high-clan: *dai-uyo,* Nhi.

This man, he thought unhappily, he might have to kill. He reached to the belt, unhooked the sheath, and gripped the sheath of *Changeling* in one hand and the hilt in the other, and the *sai-uyo* on his fine dappled charger came closer.

And perhaps he already recognized what quarry he had started, for he moved his leg and lifted his blade from its place on his saddle, and rode also with his sheathed blade in hand.

It was one of Torin Athan's sons: he did not know the man, but the look of the sons of Athan was almost that of a clan apart: long-faced, almost mournful men, with a dour attitude at variance with most of the flamboyant men of Torin. Athan was also a prolific family: there were a score of sons, nearly all legitimate.

"*Uyo*," Vanye hailed him, "I have no wish to draw on you: I am Nhi Vanye, outlawed, but I have no quarrel with you."

The man—he was surely one of the breed of Athan—relaxed somewhat. He let Vanye ride nearer, though he himself had stopped. He looked at him curiously, wondering, no doubt, what sort of madman he faced, so dressed, and upon such a homely pony. Even fleeing, a man might do better than this.

"Nhi Vanye," he said, "we had thought you were down in Erd."

"I am bound now for Baien. I borrowed this horse last night, and it is spent."

"If you look to borrow another, *uyo*, look to your head. You are not armored, and I have no wish to commit murder. You are Rijan's son, and killing you even outlawed as you are would not be a lucky thing for the likes of a *sai-uyo*."

Vanye bowed slightly in acknowledgment of that reasoning, then lifted up the sword he carried. "And this, *uyo*, is a blade I do not want to draw. It is a named-blade, and cursed, and I carry it for someone else, in whose service I am *ilin* and immune to other law. Ask in Ra-morij and they will tell you what thing you narrowly escaped."

And he drew *Changeling* part of the way from its sheath, so that the blade remained transparent, save only the symbols on it. The man's eyes grew wide and his face pale, and his hands stayed still upon his own blade.

"To whom are you *ilin*," he asked, "that you bear a thing like that? It is *qujalin* work."

"Ask in Ra-morij," he said again. "But under *ilin*-law I have passage, since my *liyo* is in Morija, and you may not lawfully execute Rijan's decree on me. I beg you, get down. Strip your horse of gear and I will exchange with you: I am a desperate man, but no thief, and I will not ride your beast to the death if I have any choice about it. This pony is of San. If yours knows the way home, I will set him loose again as soon as I can find a chance."

The man considered the prospects of battle and then wisely

capitulated, slid down and busily stripped off saddle and belongings.

"This horse is of Torin," he said, "and if loosed anywhere in this district can find his way; but I beg you, I am fond of him."

Vanye bowed, then gripped the dapple's mane in his hands and vaulted up, turned the animal and headed off at a gallop, for there was a bow among the *sai-uyo*'s gear, which he reckoned would be shortly strung, and he had no wish for a red-feathered Torin arrow in his back.

And from place to place across the face of Morija, his pursuers would have found ready replacements for their mounts, fine horses, with saddles and all their equipment.

The night was falling again, coming on apace, and the signal fires glowed brighter upon the hilltops, one blaze upon each of the greater hills, from edge to edge of Morija.

And when that *uyo* managed to reach San-morij with the little pony—Vanye intensely imagined the man's mortification, his fine gear borne by that shaggy little beast—then there would be two signals ablaze on the hill by San-morij and upon that by San-hei, and no doubt which fork of the road he had gone. There would be the whole of San and now the clan of Torin riding after him, and the Nhi and the Myya upon the other road, to meet him at Baien-ei.

To have stripped the man of weapons and armor which he so desperately needed would likely have meant killing him: but *Changeling* was not the kind of blade that left a corpse to be robbed. To have killed the man would have been well too, but he had not, would not: it was his nature not to kill unless cornered; it was the only honor he still possessed, to know there was a moral limit to what he would do, and he would not surrender it.

It would not be paid with gratitude when Torin caught him, and least of all when they brought him to Nhi and Myya.

Now he and the whole of Ra-morij—and if messengers had sped in the wake of his pursuers, the whole of the midlands villages by now—knew where he must run. There was a little pass at Baien-ei, and hard by it a ruined fort where every lad in Morija probably went at some time or another in their farings about the countryside. The best pasturage in all of Morija was in those hills, where ran the best horses; and the ruined fort was often explored by boys that herded for their fathers; and sometimes it served as rendezvous for fugitive lovers. It had had its share of tragedies, both military and private, that heap of stones.

And Morgaine's guide was a Nhi harper with the imagination of a callow boy on lovers' tryst, who would surely know no better than to lead her there for shelter, into a place that had but one way out.

There were men guarding the hillside. He had known there must be even before he set out toward it. Any break from Baien-ei by riders had to be through this narrow pass, and with archers placed there, that ride would be a short one.

He left the dapple tethered against the chance he might have to return; the branch he used was not stout, and should mischance take him or he find what he sought, the animal would grow restless and eventually pull free, seeking his own distant home. He took the sheathed sword in hand and entered the hills afoot.

All the paths of the hills of Baien-ei could not be guarded: there were too many goat-tracks, too much hillside, too many streams and folds of rock: for this reason Baien-ei had been an unreliable defense even in the purpose for which it was built. Against a massive assault, it was strong enough, but when the *jein*, the peasant bowman, had come into his own, and wars were no longer clashes between *dai-uyin* who preferred open plain and fought even wars by accepted tradition, Baien-ei had become untenable—a trap for its holders more than a refuge.

He moved silently, with great patience, and now he could see the tower again, the ruined wall that he remembered from years ago. Sometimes running, sometimes inching forward on his belly and pausing to listen, he made himself part of the shadows as he drew near the place: skills acquired in two years evading Myya, in stealing food, in hunting to keep from starvation in the snowy heights of the Alis Kaje, no less wary than the wolves, and more solitary.

He came up against the wall and his fingers sought the crevices in the stonework, affording him the means to pull himself up the old defensework at its lowest point. He slipped over the crest, dropped, landed in wet grass and slid to the bottom of the little enclosure on the slope inside. He gathered himself up slowly, shaken, feeling in every bone the misery of the long ride, the weakness of hunger. He feared as he had feared all along, that it was nothing other than a trap laid for him by Erij: Myya deviousness, not to have told him the truth. That his brother should have committed a mistake in telling him the truth and in trusting him was distressing. Erij's mistakes were few. His shoulders itched. He had the feeling that there might be an arrow centered there from some watcher's post.

He yielded to the fear, judging it sensible, and darted into shadows, rounded the corner of the building where it was tucked most securely against the hill. There was a crack in the wall there that he well remembered, wide as a door, and yet one that ought to be safest to use, sheltered as it was.

He crept along the wall to that position, caught the stable-scent of horses. Large bodies moved within.

"*Liyo!*" he hissed into the dark. Nothing responded. He eased his way inside, the pale glimmer of Siptah to his left, to his right, blackness.

"Do not move," came Morgaine's whisper. "Vanye, thee knows I mean it."

He froze, utterly still. Her voice was from before him. Someone—he judged it to be Ryn—moved from behind him, put his hands at his waist and searched him cursorily for some hidden weapon before taking hold of the sword belt. He moved his head so that the strap could pass it the more easily: he was unaccountably relieved at the passing of that weight, as if he had been in the grip of something vile and were gently disentangled from it and set free.

Ryn carried it to her: he saw the shadow pass a place of dim starlight. For his own part his knees were trembling. "Let me sit," he asked of her. "I am done, *liyo*. I have been night and day in the saddle reaching this place."

"Sit," she said, and he dropped gratefully to his knees, would gladly have collapsed on his face and slept, but it was neither the place nor the moment for it. "Ryn," she said, "keep an eye to the approaches. I have somewhat to ask of him."

"Do not trust him," Ryn said, which stung him with rage. "The Nhi would not have made him a gift of the sword and set him free for love of you, lady."

Fury rose in him, hate of the youth, so smooth, so unscarred, so sure of matters with Morgaine. He found words strangled in his throat, and simply shook his head. But Ryn left. He heard the rustle of Morgaine's cloak as she settled kneeling a little distance from him.

"Well it was thee spoke out," she said softly. "A dozen or so have tried that way these past two days, to their grief."

"Lady." He bowed and pressed his forehead briefly to earth, pushed himself wearily upright again. "There is a large force, either on its way or here already. Erij covets Thiye's power, thinking he can have it for himself."

"You cried at me not to trust him,"—she said, "and that I did believe. But how do I trust you now? Was the sword gift or stolen?"

What she said frightened him, so much as anything had power to frighten him, tired as he was: he knew how little mercy there was in her for what she did not trust, and he had no proof. "The sword itself is all that I can give you to show you," he said. "Erij drew it: it killed, and he feared to hold it. When it fell, I took it and ran—it is a powerful key, lady, to gates and doors."

She was silent for a moment. He heard the whisper of the blade drawn partway, the soft click as it slipped back to rest. "Did thee hold it, drawn?"

She asked that in such a tone as if she wished otherwise.

"Yes," he said in a faint voice. "I do not covet it, *liyo*, and I do not wish to carry it, not if I go weaponless." He wished to tell her of the men of Myya, what had happened: he had no name for it, and saw in his mind those lost faces. In some deeper part of him, he did not want to know what had become of them.

"It taps the Gates themselves," she said, and moved in the dark. "Ryn, do you see anything?"

"Nothing, lady."

She settled back again, this time in the dim starlight that fell through the crack, so that he could see her face, half in shadow as it was, the light falling on it sideways. "We must move. Tonight. Does thee think otherwise, Vanye?"

"There are archers on the height out there. But I will do what you decide to do."

"Do not trust him," Ryn's voice hissed from above. "Nhi Erij hated him too well to be careless with him or the blade."

"What does thee say, Vanye?" Morgaine asked him.

"I say nothing," he answered. Of a sudden the weariness settled upon him, and it was too much to argue with a boy. His eyes stayed upon Morgaine, waiting her decision.

"The Nhi gave me back all but *Changeling*," she said, "not knowing, I suspect, that some of the things they returned were weapons: they recognized the sword as what is was, but not these others. They also gave me back your belongings, your armor and your horse, your sword and your saddle. Go and make yourself ready. All the gear is in the corner together. I do not doubt but what you are right about the archers; but we have to move: all this coming and going of yours cannot have gone entirely unmarked."

He felt his way, found the corner and the things she described, the familiar roughness of the mail that had been his other skin for years. The weight as he settled it upon him was greater than he remembered: his hands shook upon the buckles.

He considered the prospect of the ride they would make, down that throat of a pass, and began to reckon with growing fear that there was not enough left in him to make such a ride. He had spent and spent, and there was little more left in him.

It was not likely, he thought, that they would escape from this unscathed: Myya arrows were a sound that had come to strike a response in his flesh. He had escaped too many of them, in Erd and in Morija. The odds were in favor of the arrows.

Morgaine came upon him, sought his hand, took it and turned his wrist upward. The thing that hit was like a weapon, unexpected, and he flinched. "Thee does not approve," she said. "But I will have it so. I have little of that to spend: unlike my other things, the sun does not renew it, and when it is gone, it is gone. But I will not lose thee, *ilin*."

He rubbed at the sore place, expecting a wound, finding none, and beginning to feel something amiss with himself, the tiredness melting, his blood moving more strongly. It was *qujalin*, or whatever race she named as her origin, and once the thing she had done would have terrified him: once she had promised him she would not do such things with him.

I will not lose thee, ilin.

She had lingered in this snare in Morija because of *Changeling*. He knew that in his heart and did not blame her. But there was in that word a small bit of concern for the *ilin* who served her, and that, from Morgaine, was much.

He set to work about his preparations with the determination that he would not be lost, that so long as he had a horse under him he would make it down the pass and into Baien's hills.

They had three horses: Siptah; the ungrateful black, who tried to bite and desisted sullenly with a rap of the quirt along his jaw; and Ryn's dun horse, hardly fine-blooded, but long in the legs and deep in the chest. Vanye estimated that the beast might hold the course they set, at least as long as need be; and the youth could ride: he was Morij, and Nhi.

"Leave the harp," Vanye protested when he saw the thing slung on the youth's back, as they led their horses out into the starlight. "The rattle of it will kill us all."

"No," said the youth flatly, which was what one might expect of Nhi Ryn Paren's-son. And rather than snatch it from him and delay for argument, Vanye cast a stern look at Morgaine, for he knew that the boy would heed her word.

But she forbore to do anything, and, effectively set in his place, Vanye led the black after Siptah's tail, until they were at the corner. There was a gate to be opened: he led the black to that point and heaved back the rusty bolt, shouldered it wide; and Morgaine and Ryn thundered through, Vanye only an instant slower, springing to the saddle and laying heels to the animal. Siptah's white tail flipped gay insolence as the big gray took the retaining wall, warning Vanye what he had forgotten over the years: that there was a jump there. Ryn took it; his own black gathered and jolted down to a landing, skidding downslope, haunches down like a bird in landing, for the grass was wet.

And arrows flew. Vanye tucked down to the black's opposite side, making himself as inconspicuous as possible. He hoped the others had the same sense. But through the black's flying mane he saw a streak of red fire, Morgaine's hand-weapon; and there was silence from that quarter then, no more arrows. Whether she had hit anything firing blind, he did not know, but they were Morij, those men, and in his heart he hoped that the archers had simply lost heart and run.

Bruising force hit his side. He gasped and nearly lost his grip for the pain of it, and he knew that he had been hit: but no arrow at that range could pierce the mail. His worst fears were for the vulnerable horse. It went against Morij honor to hit a man's horse, but here was no chivalry. These men must face Erij if they let them through, and that was no pleasant prospect for them.

They were near the end of the pass. He laid heels to the black and drove him harder, and the panicked beast gathered himself, saliva spattering back against Vanye's leg as the horse took the rein he wanted. He passed even Siptah, answered to main force as Vanye hauled his head round toward the north again, toward the cleft of Baien's pass through the hills, and

leaped forward under the brutal impact of Vanye's heels. In
that instant he almost loved the vile beast: there was heart
in him.

Morgaine, low in the saddle, was by him again: Siptah's
head, nostrils wide, was alongside with the starlight in his
white mane. Unaccountably Morgaine laughed, reached out
a hand to him that did not touch, and clung again to the
saddle.

And they were through. Beyond all range of archers, safe
on Baien's level plain, they were through, and Vanye reined
down the snorting black and brought him to a stop, only then
remembering the youth who rode in their wake. He came,
a good bowshot behind them, and they both waited—silent,
Vanye reckoned, in the same concern, that the boy might have
been hit, for he rode low in the saddle.

But he was well enough, pale-faced in the dim light when
he rode in among them, but unscathed. The dun horse was
spent, his rump sinking on one side as if he favored that leg,
and Vanye dismounted to see to it: an arrow had ripped the
hide and perhaps hung for a time. He explored the wound
with his fingers, found it not dangerously deep.

"He will last," Vanye pronounced. "There will be time
later."

"Then let us be off," Morgaine said, rising in the stirrups
to look behind them, even while he climbed back into the
saddle. "The surprise of the matter will not last long. They
had not seen me fire before; now they have, and they will
accustom themselves to the idea and recover their courage
about it."

"Where will you?" Vanye asked.

"To Ivrel," she answered.

"Lady, Baien's hold lies almost athwart our path. They
were hearth-friends to you once. It may be we could shelter
there a time if we reached them before Erij."

"I do not trust hold or hall this near Ivrel," she said. "No."

They rode, an easy pace now, for the horses were spent
and might be called on again to run; and soon the fire of
whatever thing had entered his veins was spent as well, and
he felt his senses going. His side hurt miserably. He felt of
the place and found broken links in the mesh, but little hurt
beneath. Assured then that was not bleeding his life away,
he hooked one leg over the high bow of the saddle, and
wrapped his arms tightly about him for support, and so gave
himself to sleep.

Bells woke him.

He looked up and eased cramped muscles out of their long-held position, and saw to his shame that Ryn led his horse, and that it was well into morning. They filed along a peaceful pine-shaded lane by the side of a stone wall.

He leaned forward and took the reins, beginning to realize where they were, for he had visited this place in his youth. It was the Monastery of Baien-an, the largest in all Andur-Kursh that still remained safe and occupied by the Gray Fathers. He rode forward to join Morgaine, wondering whether she knew what this place was, or if she had been led to it on Ryn's advice, for here was an abundance of witnesses to her passing, and a place that could not be friendly to her.

Brothers tending their wall paused at their work in wonder. A few started forward as they might to welcome travelers, and then hesitated, and seemed to abandon the idea altogether, their faces bewildered. They were gentle men. Vanye had no fear of them.

And there was a terrible weariness upon Morgaine's face, pain, as if her wound troubled her. He saw that, and bit his lip in reckoning. "Do you think to stay here?" he asked of her.

"I do not think that the Abbot would abide that," she said.

"I do not think that you are fit for much further riding," he said. And he saw also the youth Ryn, who was shadow-eyed, and miserable; and he reckoned that pursuit would not look to find them here.

He reined the black in by the gate, for he remembered a guesthouse that was kept by the abbey, probably little used in winter, but it was there for such persons as were not acceptable within the holy walls.

He brought them there, asking no permission, taking them past the wondering eyes of the Brothers in the yard, and into the privacy of the house beyond its evergreen hedge. There he dismounted, and held up his hands to help Morgaine down as he might a lady: she tried awkwardly to accept his help, better suited to dismounting on her own, but her leg gave with her when she touched the ground, and she leaned upon his arm, thanking him with a weary nod and a look of her gray eyes.

"There is sanctuary here," he said. "It is the law. There will none touch us here, and if the place is surrounded . . . well, we will reckon with that when it happens."

She nodded again, plainly at the end of her strength, and a

sorry three they were, she and the youth and a warrior so stiff
with bruises and wounds that he could scarcely manage to
climb the steps himself.

There were no other guests. He was thankful for that, and
helped Morgaine to the first of the several cots, before he went
out to tend the horses and bring Morgaine's gear into the
room: she was concerned with that above all else, he knew,
and she gave him a grateful look before she tucked the dreadful sword into her arms and sank down upon the bare mat-
tress.

Ryn helped him with the horses, and carried all their gear
and their saddles into the guesthouse; and afterward Ryn
joined him in the stables and stood by with concern in his eyes
as Vanye applied some of their cooking oil to the wound in the
dun's rump.

"He will not go lame," Vanye judged. "It was an arrow
mostly spent, and it is not the season for pests to infest the
wound. Oil will ease it, but it will scar, I think."

Ryn walked with him back to the guesthouse, a short distance hence, among the tall pines and the hedge. The bells
had fallen silent now, the Brothers filing in to their prayers.

There was a difference in Ryn. He did not quickly decide
what it was, but that a boy had slung harp on his back and ridden after Morgaine from Ra-morij; it was a tired, older youth
that walked beside him in the daylight and observed things in
silence. Ryn carried himself differently. He walked with a
bearing as out of place in these pine-rimmed lanes as Vanye's
own. They had ridden out of Baien-ei and he had ridden hind-
most; there was a new hardness to his eye that had learned to
reckon more than to wonder.

Vanye took account of that new silence in him, estimated
it, clapped a weary hand upon his shoulder when they had
come into the guesthouse. He lowered his voice, for Morgaine
seemed asleep.

"I shall watch," Vanye said. "I am not good for long; yours
is next, then hers."

The youth Ryn might have found some silly protest; he had
been sullen at his father's orders when they first rode together
into Morija. Now he nodded assent to that justice of things,
and sought a bare cot himself, while Vanye took his sword
and set himself on the front steps of the guesthouse, point set
between his feet, hands gripping the quillons, head leaned
against its hilt. In such position he could stay awake enough.

In such a manner he had watched many a night on the road.

And considering himself then, he reflected wryly that he had seen such occupations of Morija's lower guesthall only when there was some marginally honorable hill-clan passing through, bound for other pastures and asking road-right. Some bandit chief asleep in the guesthouse, his men lounging about swilling cheap wine and scarring the furniture with their feet, while as seal upon the door, some man more villainous looking than the rest sat the steps as door-warden, sword in arms and a sour expression on his face, terrifying the boys who lurked to see what visitors had come among them.

It was a warning to other would-be guests that they would be mad to seek that shelter, and must look elsewhere. Villainy had possessed the only beds, and unless the lords in the hall would take arms and dispossess them, so it would remain until the morning.

So the Brothers found him.

He came fully awake at the first tread upon the flagstone walk, and sat there with his sword between his knees while the gray-robed Brothers came cautiously up to the steps with earthen jars of food.

They bowed, hands tucked in robes. Vanye recognized innocent courtesy when it was offered and made as profound a bow as he could from his seated posture.

"May we ask?" It was the traditional question. It could be refused. Vanye bowed again, full courtesy to the honest Brothers.

"We are outlaws," he said, "and I have stolen, and we have killed no few men in the direction from which we come: but none in Baien. We will not touch flock nor herd, nor field of yours, nor do violence to any of the house. We ask sanctuary."

"Are—" There was hesitance in the question, which was always asked, if questions were asked at the granting of sanctuary. "Are all among you true and human blood?"

Morgaine had not worn the hood when she rode in; and she was, in the white furs and with her coloring, very like the legends, one survivor of which had come to die a holy man at Baien-an.

"One of us may not be," he acknowledged, "but she avows at least she is not *qujal.*" Their gentle eyes were much troubled at that answer; and perhaps through the legends they know who and what she was, if sanity would let them believe it.

"We give shelter," they said, "to all that enter here under

peace, even to those of tainted blood and those that company with them, if they should need it. We thank you for telling us. We will purify the house after you have gone. This was courtesy on your part, and we will respect your privacy. Are you a human man?"

"I am human born," he said, and returned their bows of farewell. "Brothers," he added when they began to turn away. They looked back, suntanned faces and gentle eyes and patient manner all one, as if one heart animated them. "Pray for me," he said; and then because some charity on his part was usually granted for that: "I have no alms to give you."

They bowed together. "That is of no account. We will pray for you," said one. And they went away.

The sunshine felt cold when they had done so. He could not sleep, and watched far beyond the time that he should have called Ryn to take his place. As last, when he was very weary, he went down the steps and gathered up the earthen jars and took them inside, letting Ryn replace him on the step.

Morgaine wakened. There was black bread and honey and salted butter, a crock of broth and another of boiled beans, which both were cooling, but wonderful to Morgaine, whose fare had been less delicate than his the last many days, he suspected; and he took Ryn his portion out upon the step, and the youth ate as if he were famished.

The Brothers brought down great armloads of hay and buckets of grain for their horses, which Vanye saw to, storing the grain in saddlebags against future need; and in the peace of the evening, with the sun headed toward the western mountains, Ryn sat in the little doorway and took his harp and played quiet songs, his sensitive fingers tuning and meddling with the strings in such a way that even that seemed pleasant. Some of the Brothers came down from the hill to stand by the gate and listen to the harper. Ryn smiled at them in an absent way. But they grew grave and sober-eyed when Morgaine appeared in the door; some blessed themselves in dread of her, and this seemed greatly to sadden her. She bowed them courtesy all the same, which most returned, and retired to the inner hearth, and the warmth of the fire.

"We must be out of this place tonight," she said when Vanye knelt there beside her.

He was surprised. "*Liyo,* there is no safer place for us to be."

"I am not looking for a refuge: my aim is Ivrel, and that is all. This is my order, Vanye."

"Aye," he said, and bowed. She looked at him when he straightened again and frowned.

"What is this?" she asked of him, and gestured toward the back of her own neck, and his hand lifted, encountered the ragged edge of his hair, and his face went hot.

"Do not ask me," he said.

"Thee is *ilin*," she said, a tone that reproved such a shameful thing. And then: "Was it done, or did thee—?"

"It was my choice."

"What chanced in Ra-morij, between you and your brother?"

"Do you bid me straightly tell you?"

Her lips tightened, her gray eyes bore into him, perhaps reading misery. "No," she said.

It was not like her to leave things unknown, where it might touch her safety. He acknowledged her trust, grateful for it, and settled against the warm stones of the hearth, listening to the harp, watching Ryn's rapt face silhouetted against the dying light, the pine-dotted hill beyond, the monastery and church with the bell-tower. This was beauty, earthly and not, the boy with the harp. The song paused briefly: a lock of hair fell across Ryn's face and he brushed it back, anchored it behind an ear. Not yet of the warriors, this youth, but about to be, when he made choice. His honor, his pride, were both untouched.

The hands resumed their rippling play over the strings, quiet, pleasant songs, in tribute to the place, and to the Brothers, who listened.

Then the vesper bell sounded, drawing the gray lines of monks back into their holiness on the hill, and the light began to leave them quickly.

They finished the food the Brothers gave them, and gave themselves by turns to sleep for most of the night.

Then Morgaine, whose watch it was, shook them and bade them up and make ready.

The red line of dawn was appearing on the horizon.

They were quickly armed and the horses saddled, and Morgaine warmed herself a last time by the fire and looked about the room, seeming distressed. "I do not think that they would have any parting-gift of me," she said at last. "And there is nothing I have anyway."

"They bade us be free of the matter," Vanye assured her, and it was certain that his own gear was innocent of anything valuable to the Brothers.

Ryn searched his own things, took out a few coins and left them on the bed, a few pennies—it was all.

It was upon the road with the morning light still barely bringing color to things that Vanye remembered the harp, and did not find it about the person of Ryn.

There was instead only the bow slung from his shoulders, and he was strangely sorry for that. Later he saw Morgaine realize the same thing, and open her lips to speak; but she did not. It was Ryn's choice.

It was said by men of Baien that Baien-an was a fragment left from the making of Heaven. However that was, it was true that this place surpassed even Morija for fairness. Winter though it was, the golden grass and green cedar gave it grace, and the mighty range of Kath Vrej and Kath Svejur embraced the valley with great ridges crowned with snow. There was a straight road, with hedges beside it—one did not see hedges kept so anywhere else but in Baien—and twice they saw villages off the road, golden-thatched and somnolent in the wintry sun, with white flocks of sheep grazing near like errant clouds.

And once they must pass through a village, where children huddled wide-eyed at their mothers' skirts and men paused with their work in hand, as if they were held between rushing to arms or bidding them good day. Morgaine kept her hood upon her at that time, but if there was not the strangeness of her, riding astride and with a sword-sheath under her knee, there was Siptah himself, who had been foaled in this land, before all the great herd of king Tiffwy had been taken by Hjemur's bandits. Mischance had befallen them, and they had been seen no more: Baienen said that it was because they were the horses of kings, and would not carry the likes of their Hjemurn masters.

But perhaps the villagers blinked again in the sunlight, and persuaded themselves that they had no proper business with travelers going east: it was only those who came from it, out of Hjemur, that need trouble them to take arms; and there were gray horses foaled who were not of the old blood. Siptah had grown leaner; he was muddy about legs and belly; and he spent none of his strength on high-blooded skittishness, although his ears pricked up toward any chance move and his nostrils drank in every smell.

"*Liyo*," said Vanye when they were quit of the town, "they will hear of us in Ra-baien by evening."

"By evening," she said, "surely we will be in those hills."

"If we had turned aside there, and sought welcome at Ra-baien," he insisted, "they might have taken you in."

"As they did in Ra-morij?" she answered him. "No. And I will accept no more delays."

"What is our haste?" he protested. "Lady, we are all tired, you not least of all. After a hundred years of delay, what is a day to rest? We should have stayed at the Monastery."

"Are you fit to ride?"

"I am fit," he acknowledged, which was, under less compulsion, a lie. He ached, his bones ached, but he was well sure that she was in no better case, and shame kept him from pleading his own. She had that fever in her again, that burning compulsion toward Ivrel; he knew how it was to stand in the way of that, and if she would not be reasoned into delay, it was sure that there was little else would stop her.

Then, when the sun was at their backs, reddening into evening upon the snows of Kath Svejur before them, Vanye looked back along the road they had come as he did from time to time.

This time the thing he had constantly dreaded was there.

They were pursued.

"*Liyo,*" he said quietly. Both she and Ryn looked. Ryn's face was pale.

"They will surely have changed horses in Ra-baien," Ryn said.

"That is what I have feared," she said, "that there is no war nor feud between Morija and Baien."

And she put Siptah to a slightly quicker pace, but not to a run. Vanye looked back again. The riders were coming steadily, not killing their horses either, but at a better pace than they.

"We will make the hills and choose a place for them to overtake us as far as we can toward the border," said Morgaine. "This is a fight I do not want, but we may have it all the same."

Vanye looked back yet again. He began to be sure who it was, and there was a leaden feeling in his belly. He had already committed one fratricide. To fight and to kill a *liyo*'s order was the duty of an *ilin,* even if he were ordered against family. That was cruel, but it was also the law.

"They will be Nhi," he said to Ryn. "This fight is not lawful for you. You are not *ilin,* and until you lift hand against Erij and your kinsmen, you are not an outlaw. Go apart from us. Go home."

Ryn's young face held doubt. But it was a man's look too, not the petulance of a boy, which was not going to yield to his reason.

"Do as he tells you," Morgaine said.

"I take oath," he said, "that I will not."

That was the end of it. He was a free man, was Ryn; he rode what way he chose, and it was with them. It pained Vanye that Ryn had no more than the Honor blade at his belt, no longsword; but then, boys had no business to attempt the longsword in a battle; he was safest with the bow.

"Do you know this road?" Morgaine asked.

"Yes," said Vanye. "So do they. Follow."

He put himself in the lead, minded of a place within the hills, past the entry into Koris, where Erij might be less rash to follow, near as it was to Irien. The horses might be able to hold the pace, though it was climbing for some part. He cast a look over his shoulder, to know how things were with those behind.

The Morijen had fresh mounts surely, to press them so, grace of the lord of Ra-baien, and how much Baien knew of them or how Baien felt toward them was yet uncertain.

There was the matter of Baien's outpost of Kath Svejur, manned by a score of archers and no small number of cavalry. There was that to pass beneath.

He chose pace for them and held it, not leaving the highroad despite Mogaine's expressed preference for the open country.

They had speed to take them through, unless there were some connivance already arranged between Baien's lord and Erij—some courier passed at breakneck speed during the night, to cut off their retreat. He hoped that had not happened, that the pass was not sealed: otherwise there would be a hail of arrows, to match what rode behind them.

Those behind were willing enough to kill their mounts, that became certain; but there was the pass ahead of them, the little stone fort of Irn-Svejur high upon its crag.

"We cannot pass under that," Ryn protested, thinking, no doubt, of arrows. But Vanye whipped up his horse and tucked low, Morgaine likewise.

They were within arrowshot both from above and from behind. Doubtless in their fortress the guards looked down and saw the mad party on the road and wondered which was friend and which was foe: yet there was in both Morija and Baien that simple instruction that what rode east was friend, and what rode west was enemy; and here rode two bands madly eastward.

Vanye cast a look back as they won through. A rider left pursuing them to mount the trail to the fort. He breathed an oath into the wind, for there would be men of Irn-Svejur after them shortly, and Ryn's dun was faltering, dropping behind him.

Here, upon the open road and with precious scant cover, the cursed dun spelled end to their flight. Vanye began to pull in, where a bend of rock gave a little shelter before the brush began. Here he leaped down, bow and sword in hand, and let the black take what way he would down the road. Morgaine alighted into cover also, bearing *Changeling* in the one hand, and the black weapon at her belt, he doubted not. And breathlessly last came Ryn; he stayed to strike the dun and make it move, and the poor beast took an arrow then, reared up and crashed down, flailing with its hooves.

"Ryn!" Vanye roared, his voice cracked and hoarse, and Ryn came, stumbled in, his arm all bloody with the black stump of an arrow broken in the flesh. He could not flex to string the bow he carried, and it was useless. The riders pressed them, came in, close quarters—men of Nhi and Myya, and Erij with them.

Vanye ripped his longsword from its sheath, too late for other defenses; and he saw Morgaine do the same, but what she drew, he would not attempt to flank to protect her. The opal blade came to life, sucked arrows amiss, bent them up and otherwhere, and sent a man after them, screaming.

The winds howled within that vortex, the sword sure, a hand that knew it upon its hilt; and nothing touched them, nothing passed the web of shimmer that it wove. Through watery rippling he saw Erij's black and furious form. Erij pulled up, but some did not, and rushed toward nothingness.

And one was Nhi Paren, and another Nhi Eln, and Nhi Bren, spurring after.

"No!" Vanye cried, snatched at Ryn, who cried the same, and flung himself from cover, between blade and riders.

And ceased to be.

One instant Morgaine flung the blade aside, a saving reaction too late: her face bore horror—a rider thundered past, struck down at her, drove her stumbling aside.

Vanye cut at horse, dishonorable and desperate, tumbled beast, tumbled rider, and killed Nhi Bren, who had never done him harm. He whirled about then to see the red beam dropping beast and man indiscriminately, corpses and dying, writhing wounded. The mass of them that came reined back into better cover, still pursued by lancing fire that started conflagrations in the brush and in the grass—full twenty beasts and men lay stretched upon the road, the visible dead, and tongues of flame leaped up in the dry trees, whipped by the wind, *Changeling* still unsheathed in her right hand.

They fled, these others. Vanye saw with relief that Erij was among those that fled: though he knew that his brother had never run from anything, Erij fled now.

Vanye fell to his knees, leaned upon his sword's hilt, and gazed about at what they had wrought. Morgaine too stood still, the glimmer of *Changleing* dim in her hand now, still opal. She sought its sheath and it became like fine glass again, slipping into its natural home.

And so she rested, one hand upon the rock, until at last with a gesture like one grown old she felt her way back from that place and turned to look at him.

"Let us find the horses before they gather courage for another attack," she said. "Come, Vanye."

She did not weep. He gathered himself up, caught her, fearing that she would fall, for she walked like one that would; and he thought then that she would have tears, but she leaned against him only a moment, shivering.

"Liyo," he pleaded with her, "they will not come back. Stay, let me go find the horses."

"No." She freed herself of him, returned the black weapon to her belt, tried to lift the strap of *Changeling* to her shoulder, and her hands trembled too much. He helped her with it. She accepted its weight, eased it on her shoulder, and cast one backward look, before she began with him to seek the way the horses had gone.

And, brush rustling, there were with them brown men, gray men, men in green and mottled; men of Chya, who placed themselves across their path. With the men was Taomen, and another and another that they had seen before: they were Chya of Ra-koris, and leading them, last to appear, was Roh.

The eyes of the master of Chya swept the road behind them, gazed with horror on the thing that they had done.

Then with a quiet gesture he called Taomen, and gave orders to him, and Taomen led the others away, back into the wood.

"Come," said Roh. "One of my men is holding your horses a little distance down the road. We knew them. It was they that brought us to help you, when we saw them bolt from this direction."

Morgaine looked at him, as if doubtful whether she would trust this man, though she had slept lately in his hall. Then she nodded and set out, unneedful now of Vanye's arm. He paused to clean his sword upon the grass before he overtook her: her blade needed no such attention.

It was indeed some distance. Men other than Roh walked with them all the same: there were rustlings in the forest about them, shadows whose nature they could not determine in the gathering dusk, but it was sure that they were Chya, or Roh would have been alarmed.

And there stood the horses, being tended and rubbed with dry grasses: the Chya were not riders, but they took tender care of the beasts, and Vanye for his part thanked the men when they took their animals back in hand. Then Morgaine thanked them too. He had thought her in such a mood she would not.

"May we camp with you?" Vanye asked of Roh, for the night was gathering fast about them and he was himself so weary he felt like to die.

"No," Morgaine interrupted him with finality. She slipped the strap of *Changeling*, and hung the weapon on her saddle, then gathered the reins about Siptah's neck.

"Liyo." Vanye seldom laid hands on her. Now he caught her arm and tried to plead with her, but the coldness in her eyes froze the words in his throat.

"I will come," he said quietly.

"Vanye."

"Liyo?"

"Why did Ryn choose to die?"

Vanye's lips trembled. "I do not think he knew he would. He thought he could stop you. He was not *ilin*, not under *ilin* law. One of the men was his lord, my brother. Another was Paren, his own father. Ryn was not *ilin*. He should have gone from us."

He thought then that Morgaine would show some sign of grief, of remorse, if it was in her. She did not. Her face stayed hard, and he turned from her lest he shame himself—

from anger, no less than grief. Half-blind, he sought his horse's rein and flung himself to its back. Morgaine had mounted: she laid heels to Siptah and sped him down the road.

Roh held his rein a moment, looked up at him. "Chya Vanye, where does she go?"

"That is her concern, Chya Roh."

"We of Chya have both eyes and ears in Morija, well-placed. We knew how you must come if you came from Kursh into Andur. We waited. expected a fight. Not—*that*."

"I am falling behind, Roh. Let go my rein."

"*Ilin*-oath is more than blood," said Roh. "But, Chya Vanye, they were kin to you."

"Let go, I say."

Roh's face drew taut with some weight of thought. Then he held the rein yet tightly, a hand within the bridle. "Take me up," he said. "I will see you to the edge of my lands, and I know you will not stay for a man afoot. I want no more mischances with Morgaine. You stirred us up Leth, and they are still aprowl; you brought us Nhi and Myya, and Hjemur at once; and now all Baien is astir. This woman brings wars like winter brings storms. I will see you safely through. My presence with you will be enough for any men of Chya you meet, and I will not have their lives taken as she took those of Nhi."

"Up, then," said Vanye, moving his foot from the stirrup. Roh was a slender man; his weight was still cruelty to the hard-ridden horse, but it was all that could be done. He feared to lose Morgaine if he were delayed more.

Roh landed behind him, caught hold, and Vanye set heels to the black. The horse tried a quick gait, could not hold it, settled at once to a slower pace when Vanye reined back in mercy.

Morgaine would not kill Siptah. He knew that when her fury had passed, she would slow. And after a time of riding he saw her, where the road became a mere trail through an arch of trees, a pale glimmering of Siptah's rump and her white cloak in the dark .

Then he put the black to a quicker pace, and she paused and waited when she heard his coming. The black weapon was in her hand as they rode up, but she put it away.

"Roh," she said.

There was moisture on her cheeks. Vanye saw it and was

glad. He nodded courtesy to her, which she returned, and then
she bit her lip and leaned both hands upon the saddlebow.

"We will camp," she said, sensible and calm, the manner
Vanye knew in her, "in whatever place you can find secure."

CHAPTER IX

IVREL WAS ALL the horizon now, snow-crowned and perfect amid the jagged rubble of the Kath Vrej range, anomaly among mountains. The sky was blue and still stained with sunrise in the east, as much as they could see of the sky in that direction. A single star still remained high and to the left of Ivrel's cone.

It was beautiful, this place upon the north rim of Irien. It was hard to remember the evil of it.

"Another day," said Morgaine, "perhaps yet one more camp, will set us there." And when Vanye looked at her he saw no yearning in her eyes such as he had thought to see, only weariness and misery.

"Is it then Ivrel you seek?" Roh asked.

"Yes," she said. "As it always was." And she looked at him. "Chya Roh, this is the limit of Koris. We will bid you good-bye here. There is no need that you take us farther."

Roh frowned, looking up at her. "What is there that you have to gain at Ivrel?" he said. "What is it you are looking for?"

"I do not think that is here or there with us, Roh. Goodbye."

"No," he said harshly, and when she would have urged Siptah past, ignoring him: "I ask you, Morgaine kri Chya, by the welcome we gave you, I ask you. And if you ride past me I will follow you until I know what manner of thing I have helped, whether good or evil."

"I cannot tell you," she said. "Except that I will do no harm to Koris. I will close a Gate, and you will have seen the last of me. I have told you everything in that, but you still do not understand. If I wished to leave you the means to raise another Thiye, I might pause to explain, but it would take too long and I should hate to leave that knowledge behind me."

Roh gazed up at her, no better comforted than before, and

154

then turned his face toward Vanye. "Kinsman," he said, "will you take me up behind?"

"No," said Morgaine.

"I do not have her leave," Vanye said.

"You will slow us, Roh," said Morgaine, "and that could be trouble for us."

Roh thrust his hands into the back of his belt and scowled up at her. "Then I will follow," he said.

Morgaine turned Siptah for the northeast, and Vanye with heavy heart laid heels to his own horse, Roh trudging behind. Though they would go easily, wanting to spare the horses, they were passing beyond the bounds of Koris and of Chya, and there was no longer safety for Roh or for any man afoot. He could follow, until such time that they came under attack of beasts or men of Hjemur. Morgaine would let him die before she would let him delay her.

So must he. In a fight he dared not have his horse encumbered. In flight, his oath insisted he must keep to Morgaine's side, and he could not do that carrying double, nor risk tiring the horse before the hour of her need.

"Roh," he pleaded with his cousin, "it will be the end of you."

Roh did not answer him, but hitched his gear to a more comfortable position on his shoulder, and walked. Being Chya-reared, Roh would be able to walk for considerable distances and at considerable pace, but Roh must know also that he stood almost certainly to lose his life.

Had it been his own decision, Vanye thought, he would have ridden far ahead at full gallop, so that Roh must realize that he could not keep up and abandon this madness; but it was not his to decide. Morgaine walked her horse. That was the pace she set; and at noon rest Roh was able to overtake them and share food with them—this grace she granted without stinting; but he fell behind again when they set out.

But for knowing where they were, the land was still fair for some considerable distance; but when pines began to take the place of lowland trees, and they climbed into snowy ground, then Vanye suffered for Roh and looked back often to see how he fared.

"*Liyo*," he said then, "let me get off and walk a time, and he will ride. That can tire the horse no more."

"His choice to come was his affair," she said. "If trouble comes on us unexpectedly, I want you, not him, beside me. No. Thee will not."

"Do you not trust him, *liyo*? We slept in Ra-koris in his keeping, and there was chance enough for him to do us harm."

"That is so," she said, "and of men in Andur-Kursh, I trust Roh next to you; but thee knows how little trust I have to extend; and I have less of charity."

And then he fell to thinking of the night and day ahead, which he had yet to serve, and that she had said that she would die. That saddened him, so that for a time he did not think of Roh, but reckoned that there was something weighing on her mind.

She spoke of the same matter, late in the afternoon, when the horses had struck easier going along a ridge. Crusted snow cracked under them, and their breath hung in frosty puffs even in sunlight, but it was an easy place after the rocks and ice that they had passed.

"Vanye," she said, "thee will find it difficult to pass from Hjemur after I am gone. It would be best if thee had a place to go to. What will thee do? Nhi Erij will not forgive thee for what I have done."

"I do not know what I will do," he said miserably. "There is Chya, there is still Chya, if only Roh and I both come through this alive."

"I wish thee well," she said softly.

"Must you die?" he asked her.

Her gray eyes went strangely gentle. "If I have the choice," she said, "I shall not. But if I do, then thee is not free. Thee knows what thee has to do: kill Thiye. And perhaps then Roh might serve thee well: so I let him follow. But if I live, all the same, I shall pass the Gate of Ivrel, and in passing, close it. Then there will be an end of Thiye all the same. When Ivrel closes, all the Gates in this world must die. And without the Gates, Thiye cannot sustain his unnatural life: he will live until this body fails him, and be unable to take another. So also with Liell, and with every evil thing that survives by means of the Gates."

"And what of you?"

She lifted her shoulders and let them fall. "I do not know where I shall be. Another place. Or scattered, as the men were at Kath Svejur. I shall not know until I pass the Gate where I can make it take me. That is my task, to seal Gates. I shall go until there are no more—and I shall not know that, I fear, until I step out the last one and find nothing there."

He tried to grasp the thing she told him, could not imagine, and shivered. He did not know what to say to her, because he did not know what it meant.

"Vanye," she said, "you have drawn *Changeling*. You have a proper fear of it."

"Aye," he acknowledged. Loathing was in his voice. Her gray eyes reckoned him up and down, and she cast a quick look over her shoulder at Roh's distant figure.

"I will tell thee," she said softly, "if something befall me, it could be that thee would need to know. Thee does not need to read what is written on the blade. But it is the key. Chan wrote it upon the blade for fear that all of us would die, or that it would come to another generation of us—hoping that with that, Ivrel still might be sealed. It is to be used at Rahjemur, if thee must: its field directed at its own source of power would effect the ruin of all the Gates here. Or cast back within the Gate itself, the true Gate, it would be the same: unsheath it and hurl it through. Either way would be sufficient."

"What are the writings on it?"

"Enough that could give any able to read them more knowledge of Gates than I would wish to have known. That is why I carry it so close. It is indestructible save by Gates. I dare not leave it. I dare not destroy it. Chan was mad to have made such a thing. It was too great a chance. We all warned him that *qujalin* knowledge was not for us to use. But it is made, and it cannot be unmade."

"Save by the Witchfires themselves."

"Save by that."

And after they had ridden a distance: "Vanye. Thee is a brave man. I owe it to thee to tell thee plainly: if thee uses *Changeling*, as I have told thee to do, thee will die."

The cold seeped inward, self-knowledge. "I am not a brave man, *liyo*."

"I think otherwise. Can thee hold the oath?"

He gathered the threads of his thoughts, scattered and snarled for a moment with the knowledge she had given him. He was strangely calm then, what he had known from the beginning settling into place as it ought to be.

"I will hold to it," he said.

"He is coming," said Vanye with relief. Snow crunched underfoot beyond the place where they had stopped to wait, around the bend of the trees and the hillside. It was dark. Snow lit by the stars was all about them, bright save in the shadow of the pines. They had lost sight of Roh for a time. "Let me ride back to him."

"Hold where you are," she said. "If it is Roh, he will arrive all the same."

And eventually, a mere shadow among the barred shadows of the pines on the lower slope, there trudged Roh, stumbling with weariness.

"Ride down to him," said Morgaine then, the only grace she had shown the bowman for his efforts.

Vanye did so gladly, met Roh halfway down the hill and drew his horse to a halt, offering stirrup and hand.

Roh's face was drawn, his lips parted and the frosted air coming in great raw gasps. For a moment Vanye did not think that Roh would accept any kindness of him now: there was anger there. But he dismounted and helped his cousin up, and rose into the saddle after. Roh slumped against him. He urged the horse uphill at a walk, for the air grew thin here, and hurt the lungs.

"This is a proper place for a camp," said Morgaine when they joined her. "It is defensible." She indicated a place of rocks and brush, and it was true: however acquired, Morgaine had an eye to such things.

"Surely," said Vanye, "we had better do without the fire tonight."

"I think it would be wise," she agreed. She slid down, shouldered the strap of *Changeling*, and began to undo her saddle. Siptah pawed disconsolately at the frozen earth. There was still grain left from the supply the Brothers had given them; there was food left too. It would not be a bitter camp, compared to others they had spent near Aenor-Pyvvn.

Vanye let Roh slide to the ground, and slid down after. The bowman fell, began at once to try to gather himself up, but Vanye knelt beside him and offered him drink, unfrozen, the flask carried next the horse's warmth. Then he began to chafe warmth into the man. There was danger of freezing in his extremities, particularly in his feet. Roh was not dressed for this.

Morgaine silently bent and exchanged her cloak for Roh's, and the bowman nodded gratitude, his eyes fixed on her with thanks and anger so mingled in him that it was hard to know which prevailed.

They fed the horses and ate, which warmed them. There was little spoken. Perhaps there would have been, had Roh not been there; but Morgaine was not in the mood for speech.

"Why?" Roh asked, his voice almost inaudible from cold. "Why do you insist to go to this place?"

"That is the same question you asked before," she said.

"I have not yet had it answered."

"Then I cannot answer it to your satisfaction," she said.

And she held out Roh's cloak to him, and took her own again, and went over to a rock where there was shelter from the wind. There she slept, *Changeling* in her arms as always.

"Sleep," said Vanye then to Roh.

"I am too cold," said Roh; which complaint Vanye felt with a pang of conscience, and looked at him apologetically. Roh was silent a time, his face drawn in misery and fatigue, his limbs huddled within his thin cloak. "I think"—Roh's voice was hoarse, hardly audible—"I think that I shall die on this road."

"It is only another day more," Vanye tried to encourage him. "Only one day, Roh. You can last that.

"It may be." Roh let his arms fall forward on his knees and and bowed his head upon them, lifting his head after a moment, his eyes sunk in shadow. "Cousin. Vanye, for kinship's sake answer me. What is it she is after, so terrible she cannot have me know it?"

"It is nothing that threatens Chya or Koris."

"Are you sure enough to take oath on that?"

"Roh," Vanye pleaded, "do not keep pressing me. I cannot keep answering question and question and question. I know what you would do, to have me defend my way step by step into answering you as you wish, and I will not, Roh. Enough. Leave the matter."

"I think that you yourself do not know," said Roh.

"Enough. Roh, if things go amiss at Ivrel, then I will tell you all that I do know. But until that time, I am bound to remain silent. Go to sleep, Roh. Go to sleep."

Roh sat a time with his arms folded again about him and his knees drawn up, plunged in thought, and at last shook his head. "I cannot sleep. My bones are still frozen through. I will stay awake a little while. Go and sleep yourself. My oath I will see you take no harm."

"I have an oath of my own," said Vanye, though he was bone-weary and his eyes were heavy. "She did not give me leave to trade my watch to you."

"Must she give you leave in everything, kinsman?" Roh's eyes were kind, his voice gentle as a brother's ought to be. It recalled a night in Ra-koris, when they had sat together at the hearth, and Roh had bidden him return someday to Chya.

"That is the way of the thing I swore to her."

But after an hour or more, the forest still, the weight of the long ride and days of riding and sleeplessness before began to settle heavily upon him. He had a dark moment, jerked awake to find a shadow by him, Roh's hand on his shoulder. He almost cried out, stifled that outcry as he realized in the same instant that it was only Roh, waking him.

"Cousin, you are spent. I tell you that I will take your watch."

It was reasonable. It was sensible.

He heard in his mind what Morgaine would say to such a thing. "No," he said wearily. "It is her time to watch. Rest. I will move about a while. If that will not wake me, then she will wake and take the watch. I have no leave to do otherwise."

He rose, stumbled a little in the action, his legs that numb with exhaustion and cold. He thought Roh meant to help him.

Then pain crashed through his skull. He reached out hands to keep himself from falling, hit, lost most senses; then the weight hit his skull a second and third time, and he went down into dark.

Cords bound him. He was chilled and numb along his body, where he had been lying on his face. It was almost all that he could do to struggle to his knees, and he did so blindly, fearing another assault upon the instant. He turned upon one knee, saw a heap of white that was Morgaine—Roh, standing over her with *Changeling*, sheathed, in his hands.

"Roh!" Vanye called aloud, breaking the stillness. Morgaine did not stir at the sound, which sent a chill of fear through him, sent him stumbling to his feet. Roh held the sword as if he would draw it, threatening him.

"Roh," Vanye pleaded hoarsely. "Roh, what have you done?"

"She?" Roh looked down, standing as he was above Morgaine's prostrate form. "She is well enough, the same as you. An aching head when she wakes. But you will not treat me as you have, Chya Vanye—as she has. I have the right to know what I sheltered in my hall, and this time you will give me answer. If I am satisfied, I will let you both go and cast myself on your forgiveness, and if I am not, I do swear it, cousin, I will take these cursed things and cast them where they cannot be found, and leave you for Hjemur and the wolves to deal with."

"Roh, you are vain and a madman. And honorless to do this thing."

"If you are honest," said Roh, "and if she is, then you have your right to outrage. I will admit it. But this is not for pride's sake. Thiye is enough. I want no more Irien, no more wars of *qujal,* no more of the like of Hjemur. And I do think that we are safer with Thiye alone than with Thiye and an enemy let loose to our north. *We* are the ones who die in their wars. I gave her help, would have defended her at Kath Svejur had she needed it. I would have helped her, kinsman. But she has treated me as an enemy, as a cast-off servant. I think that is all we in Koris will ever be in her mind. She treats free men as she treats you, who have to be content; and maybe you are content with that, maybe you enjoy your station with her, but I do not."

"You are mad," Vanye said, came forward a step nearer than Roh wished: Roh's hands drew *Changeling* partway from the sheath.

"Put it down!" Vanye hissed urgently. "No, do not draw that thing."

Then Roh saw the nature of the thing he held, and looked apt to drop it upon the instant: but he rammed it safely into its sheath again, and cast it in abhorrence across the snow.

"*Qujalin* weapons and *qujalin* wars," Roh exclaimed in disgust. "Koris has suffered enough of them, kinsman."

Morgaine was stirring to wakefulness. She came up of a sudden, hands bound, nearly fell. Roh caught her, and had he been rough with her, Vanye would have hurled himself on Roh as he was. But Roh adjusted her cloak about her and helped her sit, albeit he looked far from glad to touch her.

Morgaine for her part looked dazed, cast a glance at Vanye that did not even accuse: she seemed bewildered, and no little frightened. That struck him to the heart, that he had served her no better than this.

"*Liyo,*" Vanye said to her, "this kinsman of mine took me from behind; and I do not think he is an evil man, but he is a great idiot."

"Get apart," said Roh to him. "I have had what words I will have with you. Now I will ask her."

"Let me go," said Morgaine, "and I will not remember this against you."

But there was a sound intruding upon them, soft at first,

under the limit of hearing, then from all sides, the soft crunch of snow underfoot. It came with increasing frequency about them.

"Roh!" Vanye cried in anguish, hurled himself across the snow toward the place where *Changeling* lay.

Then dark bodies were upon them, men that snarled like beasts, and Roh went down beneath them, mauled under a black flood of them, and the tide rushed over Vanye, hands closed upon his legs. He twisted over onto his back, kicked one of them into writhing pain, and was pinned, held about his knees. Cord bit into his ankles, ending all hope of struggle.

They let him alone then, to try to wrench himself up to his knees, laughing when he failed twice and fell. On his third effort he succeeded, gasping for air, and glowered into their bearded faces.

They were not Hjemurn, or of Chya.

Men of Leth, the bandits from the back of the hall: he recognized the roughest of them.

There was quiet for a moment. He had had most of the wind knocked from him, and bent over a little to try to breathe, lifted his head again to keep a wary eye upon their captors.

They were prodding at Roh, trying to force him to consciousness. Morgaine they let alone, she with ankles bound the same as he, and now with her back to a rock, glaring at them with the warmth of a she-wolf.

One of the bandits had *Changeling* in hand, drew it partway, Morgaine watching with interest, as if in her heart she urged the man on in ignorance.

But riders were coming up the hill. The sword slammed into its sheath, in guilty hands. The bandits stood and waited, while men on horses came into the clearing, horses blowing frost in the starlight.

"Well done," said Chya Liell.

He dismounted and looked about the clearing, and one presented to him the things that had been taken, all of Morgaine's gear; and *Changeling*, which Liell received into respectful and eager hands.

"Chan's," he said, and to Morgaine paid an ironic bow. He considered Roh, half-conscious now, laughed in pleasure, for he and the young lord of Chya were old enemies.

And then he came to Vanye, and while Vanye shuddered with disgust knelt down by him and smiled a faithless smile, lordly-wise, placed a hand upon his shoulder like some old friend, and all too possessively. "*Ilin* Nhi Vanye i Chya," he said softly. "Are you well, Nhi Vanye?"

Vanye would have spit at him: it was the only recourse he had left; but his mouth was too dry. He had a Lethen's hand in his collar behind, holding him so that he was half-choking; he could not even flinch, and Liell's gentle fingers touched and brushed at a sore place on his temple.

"Be careful with him," said Liell then to the Lethen. "Any damage or discomfort he suffers will be mine shortly, and I will repay it."

And to those about them:

"Set them on horses. We have a ride to make."

The day sank toward dark again, reddening the snows that stretched unmarred in front of them. They moved slowly, because of those on foot, and because of the thinner air. Liell rode first. He had taken back his own black horse and his gear. *Changeling* hung from his saddle, beneath his knee. Several Lethen riders were between him and Morgaine, and two men afoot led Siptah, as two led also the horse they had borrowed for Roh, who had no strength to walk; and the black mare that Vanye rode was Liell's grace, personal, offered with cynical courtesy—exchange of the mare for the one he had stolen.

And bound as he was, hands behind, even feet bound securely by ropes under the mare's ribs, he could not even stretch his legs against the torment of the long ride, much less be aid to Morgaine. She and Roh were in no better case. Roh hung in the saddle much of the time, giving the appearance of a man who would as likely collapse and fall if the cords let him. Morgaine at least seemed unhurt, though he could guess the torment there was in her mind.

Liell was *qujal* and knew the ancient science. Perhaps he could even read the runes of *Changeling*, and then Thiye, whom Morgaine had called ignorant, a meddler in sciences, would have a rival he could not withstand.

They came among trees again, pines, rough brush, sometime outcroppings of black rock. And the trees began to be twisted and stunted things, writhing out of all true shape for their kind. Bare limbs held tufts of sickly needles, bare trunks described horrid, frozen evolutions.

And in the snow they saw a dead dragon.

At least so it seemed to be—an object leathery and twisted, and the horses shied from it. It was monstrous, frozen in its

death throes so that it was yet less lovely. One membraneous
wing was half unfolded, stiff and stark. The other side was
bare bone, taken by other beasts.

The Lethen described a wide path about that corpse. Vanye
stared back at the thing as they passed and the bile rose in
his throat.

Other things they saw dead too. Most were small. One
resembled a man, but the wolves had had it.

The light faded in this place of evil. They moved among
the twisted pines in twilight, and went carefully. Men had
bows ready, eyes constantly scanning the forest.

Then the trees thinned out, quite abruptly. Upon the great
shoulder of the mountain was a lesser rise, and upon that were
broken pillars, fair-colored, rune-graven, out of place among
the black rocks of Ivrel's cone.

And the Gate.

It was vast, unlike that of Aenor-Pyvvn or Leth at Domen:
metal uncorroded by the years, casting a web of shimmer that
had depth, stars winking in a black arch against the twilit
white side of Ivrel. The air here worked at the nerves. The
horses fought to shy off,—men that rode dismounted, and
prepared to wait.

Morgaine was helped down first, her ankles freed, and she
was made fast against one of the few twisted pines that grew
this near the Gate. Next Roh was similarly treated, though
he strove to fight them. Finally Vanye was lifted down, and
he thought that they would do the same with him, but instead
Liell ordered him brought forward in the line.

He kicked a man, threw him to the ground writhing in
pain, and a Lethen hit him, kicked him down and laid a quirt
to him: Vanye tucked down against the blows, unhurt by
reason of the mail, save where the quirt hit neck or hands.

And of a sudden Liell was by him, cursing the man, other
Lethen hauling Vanye up, and the man that had struck him
cringed away.

"No hand on him!" Liell said. "No harm to him. I will kill
the man that puts a mark on him." And carefully he unlaced
the cloak from Vanye, and gave it to a man, walked all about
him, full circle. Then he made to lay hands on him and Vanye
flinched back, constrained to bear it in patience while Liell
gently probed bones, as if to see whether they were sound or
no. In bitter humor he cherished the ache in his skull, the
worse pain in his legs and joints where the ride bound to
the saddle had bruised him—his only revenge on Liell. It

was a sorry, sad thing, he thought of a sudden, that he had
been taken so easily, and it was no comfort at all that Roh
was about to pay dearly for his idiocy.

And by that time, there would be nothing left of Nhi
Vanye, though his body would continue to move and live,
housing for Liell-Zri, which would take revenge upon Roh,
upon Morgaine.

That image struck him as Liell began to climb that last
distance, and they began to force him up the long barren
slope. It took from him what courage he had left, such that
he would have fallen if not for the men on either side of
him. He stumbled on the loose rocks, Liell striding sure-
footedly beside him, up in that clear place where air cut at
the lungs like the edge of ice. There was only the Gate above
them, and the stars within, and wind that gently sucked at
them, aiming into that gulf.

It grew as they walked, until there was no more sky. The
Lethen with them balked, and Vanye thought for one wild
soaring moment that they would lose their courage and fail to
hold him. But Liell cursed them and threatened them, and
they drew him up and up, until they stood swaying in that
awesome wind, poised upon a level place near the Gate.

There Liell bade them unbind his hands and hold him fast:
"I will not enter an impaired shelter," he said. And this
they did, but held his numb arms and strengthless wrists still
wrenched behind him with such cruel force that he could not
struggle free. He stared up into that great gulf, dizzied,
faltered and lost his balance even standing still.

"How is it done?" he asked of Liell. He did not want to
know, but his courage was never proof against the unknown:
he feared that he would shame himself at the last, crying out,
if he did not know. He knew Morgaine's things, that there
were laws and realities that governed them; he insisted to
believe so even in this.

"It is less pleasant for me than for you," said Liell. "I must
ruin this present body of mine, enough to die; but you—you
will only seem to fall for a moment. You will never reach
bottom. Do not fear; you will not suffer."

Liell knew his fear and mocked him with it. Vanye set his
lips and forbore to say anything, head bowed.

"Those companions of yours," Liell said. "Have you fond-
ness for them?"

"Yes," he said.

Liell's lips made a slight smile, which his eyes did not

share. "As for Chya Roh, that is an old and personal matter, which I shall enjoy settling. That which you are about to bequeath me is well capable of handling the lord of Chya, of claiming what he rules, by the blood you share; and claiming Morija too. You never appreciated your heredity as I do. And do not fear so much for Morgaine. Without her weapons she is harmless, and she has knowledge that will be of great interest to me. And in other ways, with your youth, she is of interest. Flis is tiresome."

Vanye made a sound like spitting, at which Liell was neither amused nor troubled, and they began to climb again. He balked, had his arms painfully wrenched, and gave up resistance, lost in what loomed over them.

Dark was all their vision now, stars more numerous than shone in the sky, clouds upon clouds of stars. The air was dead. It numbed. The vision seemed about to drink them into that shimmering nothing—though they climbed, it seemed a pit, a downward plunge into which one could fall and fall, and that they leaned impossibly above it. The mountain on which they walked seemed out of proper alignment with earth. The wind skirled about them, maleficent and voiced, humming with power, blurring senses.

Liell reached the Gate and touched its arch; his fingers moved upon it, and all at once there was utter dark within the Gate. The wind ceased. The humming altered its tone, higher pitched. The opalescent of *Changeling* itself burst and coruscated within the arch, flung light at them.

The Lethen faltered. Vanye spun, flung himself downslope, lost footing and slid, brought up against a level place and staggered to his feet, dazed, blinded, aware of shouting ahead and behind in the gathering dark.

Out, was the only thing his senses grasped at the moment; and hard upon that single light of reason: *Morgaine*.

He could not help her. They would have a dozen men upon him before he could free her.

Changeling.

He ran, sliding, mail-protected, but leaving skin of his hands on rocks, battering himself in one spill and another. Men tried to head him off at the bottom. He gasped air, spun left, veering off from Morgaine and Roh, scattering horses as he fled. Then there was the familiar black before him: he vaulted for the saddle, shied the beast and clung, clawed his way firmly into the saddle and caught the flying reins. The beast knew him, gathered himself and sprang forward under his guidance.

Riders were already starting after him. Tumult and shouting were in his wake, though no arrows flew. He did not even seek the hill, to brave that weight of air, that awful climb, not with pursuit and enemies and a frightened horse to confound matters. He headed back along their trail.

If the Gate were barred to him, there was still Ra-hjemur, where Thiye ruled. There was *Changeling* under his knee, its dragon-hilt familiar to his anxious fingers. With that in hand and the power of the Gate to feed it, he could force his way to the heart of Thiye's power, destroy its source, whatever it was, destroy the Gate—destroy himself and Morgaine too, he knew.

And Liell.

The world had not yet seen what Liell could do with the power of Morgaine added to his own. Thiye was small compared to that evil.

He rode the horse without mercy, whipped the poor beast down snowy slopes and across trails and down, doing all he could to clear Ivrel.

Even Liell must have care of him now. Even Morgaine's other weapons were nothing to the power of the opal blade, that drank attack and cast it elsewhere, that drank lives and cast them into nothing. And armed as he was, with that power in his hands, it was madness to kill the horse that was his best hope of reaching Hjemur: he came to his senses when he had cleared the steepest portion of the road, and come to the main trail. There he slowed his pace at last, let the horse breathe.

Around the limb of the lower slope the main road led, bending toward Ra-hjemur. It must be. There was no other place in Hjemur that could even boast a road.

He kept the horse to a holding pace. Lethen might be reluctant to follow, but Liell would drive them to it—timid as Morgaine avowed herself to be, able to spend others' lives before her own, she was capable of fearful risks when it became necessary; and Liell surely would prove no different: when caution would not serve, then there would be nothing reserved, nothing. When Liell knew finally that the Gates themselves were at stake, he would surely follow. The only hope was that he had yet to understand what *Changeling* was, or that a Morij *ilin* might understand what had to be done with the blade.

A shadow thundered out at him. The black screamed shrilly and shied, and an impact hit his shoulder, tumbling him inexorably over the black's rump, head over heels, and into snow and hard ice.

Joints moved, bones unbroken, but shaken; he tried to gain command of his battered limbs and move, but a shortsword pressed under his chin, forcing his head down again into the numbing snow. A body hovered over him, the arm that rested across the figure's knee ending abruptly.

"Brother," said Erij, whispering.

CHAPTER X

"ERIJ." VANYE TRIED a second time to rise, and in a sudden move Erij moved back and let him. Then he snapped the Honor blade back into his belt and stalked up the road a space where his horse stood, along with Vanye's black.

Vanye stumbled up from the ditch, limping, trying vainly to overtake him and prevent him, saw to his dismay that Erij had already found what the black horse bore on its saddle.

A fierce grin spread over Erij's face as he took the sheathed blade in hand, and with the sheath in the crook of his arm and his hand upon its hilt, he waited Vanye's coming.

Vanye stopped short of the threat he posed him, still shaking in all his limbs, trying to gather his breath and his wits and frame some reasonable argument.

"There is a *qujal* out of Leth," he began, his voice hardly audible. "Erij, Erij, there are Lethen and the devil himself behind me. We are both in danger. I will go with you clear of this road—not try at escape, at least that far. I swear, I swear it, Erij."

Erij considered, his dark eyes fluid in the dark. Then he nodded abrupt decision, hooked the sheath of *Changeling* to his own belt—one-handed as he was, he wore it at his hip, not his back—and swung up to mount.

Vanye hauled his aching body into the saddle on a second effort, sent the black galloping down the road in Erij's company, down side trails into forest, though at every turn the forest looked more ominous in itself. The horses went at a careful pace now, wending their way down into rocky ground. Here was still patches of snow in which to leave prints, but brush and woods were so thick that pursuit of them could not be easy for any group of men, and their trail was somewhat obscured. It held no feeling of safety, this place—rather, the same kind of queasiness that all of Erij's ambushes had held, from boyhood up, screaming alarm, such that he

169

thought, like another dream by Aenor-Pyvvn, that he might have ridden this place in some bad dream, wherein he had died. The trees, the rocks etched themselves into his sight, his senses clinging to them as strongly as fingers might cling to some last handhold on solidity. *I am losing these,* he thought, and: *I am mad to go with him like this.* But he had no strength left, and Erij held *Changeling,* held his duty as *ilin* to hostage: Erij could reason, could be reasoned with—his hope insisted so.

Then, in a clear place among the trees, Erij reined in and ordered him down.

Panic struck him. Almost he did lay heels to the horse. But he found himself climbing down, careful of strained knees as he caught his balance on the ground. He moved out uncertainly as Erij motioned him to the center of the clearing.

"Where is she?" Erij asked then, and as he asked, climbed down, and unhooked the sheath of *Changeling.*

Then he knew of a certainty that Erij meant to kill him when he had answered; and *Changeling* slipped inexorably from its sheath, Erij knowing the nature of the blade now, well able to wield it.

Vanye hurled himself at Erij waist-high, grappled and came down with him, *Changeling* falling still sheathed.

Erij's elbow crashed into his face, blinding him. Vanye was suddenly underneath again, losing, as he had always lost, as it had always been with his brothers. He could not see, could not breathe, could not feel for a moment. With his last effort he heaved over and clung, fighting only for leverage. Then his hands were slamming Erij's head into the snowy ground, again and again, until Erij's limbs weakened and ceased to struggle. He scrambled up to find *Changeling,* his mind next clearing as he reached his horse, holding the sword-sheath, groping blindly for the reins.

The horse shied. Erij's rush carried into his lower back, hurling him, stunned, almost under the hooves. *Changeling* flew from his nerveless fingers, beyond reach, and when he struggled after it, Erij kicked him over by the shoulder. He came halfway up, staggered, and met Erij's fist, which laid him backward into the snow. Then Erij fell upon him with a knee upon his chest and his maimed arm still strong enough to strike his arm aside: Erij ripped the Honor blade from his belt and slipped it within the throat-laces of his armor, cutting down the thongs like so much rotten thread.

"A third of Nhi died at Irn-Svejur," Erij gasped at him,

hoarse and out of breath. "Your doing—and hers. Where is she?"

Vanye swallowed against the blade's pressure, unable to answer. He fought instinctively to breathe and froze, trembling with the effort, when he felt moisture trickling down the sides of his neck. Raw pain rode on the edge of the blade as it eased slightly.

"Answer me," Erij hissed.

"Leth." He moved an arm as heavy as his whole body ought to be, ceased. "*Qujal*—men from Leth caught her—to make her give them what she knows. Erij—Erij, no, do not kill me. They will have her knowledge—theirs—Thiye's—together—against us."

The pressure eased altogether, but it was there. The faint hope there was of Erij's interest sent the sweat coursing over him. Erij's knee hampered his breathing: he felt himself losing touch with his senses again, dizzied and numb. "And you, bastard?" Erij asked him. "What are you doing loose and alone?"

"Hjemur—the source. That can stop them. I am to kill Thiye —take Ra-hjemur. Erij, let me go."

"Bastard, I have chased you from Irn-Svejur. The others had no stomach for Hjemur's territory and Morgaine's weapons, but I swore to them that I would go where I had to go to bring back your head. I would bring back the whole of you alive, but one-handed as I am, I know I cannot manage that. For Nhi and for Myya, for San and Torin—most especially for Nhi and its dead, I will do this thing, and then find how to put this gift you have given me to best use. I have no enemies I need fear so long as I wield that. If it would bring you safely to Ra-hjemur, then it could bring me there too."

"Go with me there, then."

"I offered you the chance of sharing power once, bastard, and I meant it; but you loved the witch more than you loved Morija, enough to kill Nhi for her."

"Erij, you know at least that I will not break an oath. Help me—to Ra-hjemur. Now. Before our enemy takes it. Let me have my revenge on Thiye—for Morgaine; on the *qujal* too if I can. I am speaking sense, Erij. Listen to me. There are weapons in Ra-hjemur, surely—and if our enemy lays hands on them, even holding *Changeling* might not be enough to take the citadel. Do this. Come with me. That is my oath to her—to deal with Thiye. After that, anything that is between us will be between us, and I will not cry foul at anything."

Erij's shadowed eyes took on a narrow, reckoning look. "You were condemned to be *ilin* by our father's law, for Kandrys; and you will be clean of that if I listen to you. But you have me yet to satisfy. Suppose I were to sentence you to another year."

"I would think that was too slight a thing to satisfy you."

"Swear," said Erij, "by that oath you regard with her, that you will stay for Claiming by me, no treachery, no aid from her if she should somehow live. And that will not be a year that you will thank me for, Chya bastard, and it will not stop me from turning you over to the kinsmen of Paren and Bren when it is finished. But if it is worth the price to you, I will refrain from cutting your throat here and now. I will even go with you to Ra-hjemur. Is that the way you want it, bastard? Will you pay that?"

"Yes," Vanye said without hesitating; but Erij's blade still rested under his chin.

"And I will wager," said Erij, "that you know the use of the sword and that you know the witch herself better than any now living. If taking Hjemur purges you of her—that being the service she named for you, and not merely a year—then let us agree, my brother, that when Hjemur falls, it is mine, and you are mine—from that moment. And you will not speak of this oath of ours—not to her, not to Thiye, not to anyone."

He saw the trap then, which Erij wove for Morgaine, treachery suspecting treachery in everyone, and admired the cunning of the man: Myya to the heart, thinking of all possibilities save one—that neither of them would survive the taking of Hjemur.

He did not like the oath: it was woven too tightly.

"I will agree," he said.

"And upon your soul you will not betray me," Erij said. "You will hand me Hjemur and hand me Thiye and the witch and this *qujal* himself."

"As many as live," Vanye agreed.

"That you will not desert me or raise hand against me before then."

"I agree."

"Your hand," said Erij.

It was not right to do: by *ilin*-law he ought not to yield another oath, and any crossing of the two obligations was on his soul, his own fault; but Erij insisted, and he yielded up his hand and clenched his teeth as Erij drew the blade across the palm. Then Erij touched it with his mouth, and Vanye likewise, spat blood into the snow. It was not Claiming, for there was no signing with it, but it was an oath and a binding one, and when Erij released him to get to his feet, he knelt clenching numbing snow in his fist as he had knelt once in a cave in Aenor-Pyvvn, shaking this time in utter misery, such that his senses threatened to leave him.

The *liyo* he served could by rights curse his soul to perdition; he had yielded his brother the same right. And yet he knew that he would have mercy of Morgaine, and none at all of Erij. He knew his *liyo,* that though she was cruel in other ways, she would not curse him; and that knowledge of her perversely made him sure which oath he would follow.

And kill his brother, as he had killed a third of Nhi.

He had done this for his *liyo,* serving her: *ilin*-oath had bound him, and he had killed kinsmen. There had seemed no worse act that he could be drawn to commit.

Until this, that he oath-broke, and murdered his brother by his silence.

I owe it to thee to tell thee plainly; if thee uses Changeling *as I have told thee to do—thee will die.*

Changeling was not selective in its destructions.

"Come, on your feet," said Erij. He hooked the blade to his saddle-harness, displacing his own to the useless right-hand fastenings. Then he gathered reins and climbed up, waiting for him.

Vanye gathered himself up and sought the black, who stood, reins dangling, some distance away across the clearing. He set foot in the stirrup and rose into the saddle with a wince of strained muscles.

"You are guide," said Erij. "Lead. And be mindful of your oath."

He retraced the way that they had come, then cut north, aiming to come out upon the highroad at a different place than they had left it. When they had it in sight among the trees he was relieved to see that there were as yet no tracks marring the snow.

Only as they came out into the open road, something fluttered through the trees, alarmed by their passing—a rapid clap of wings in the dark. Erij stared after it with hate in his face, the honest loathing of a human man for things that frequented these woods.

Vanye had even ceased to shudder at such things. He set a good pace, reckoning that they were laying a clear trail for Liell and his men if they would follow; but it could not be helped. There was one quick way to Hjemur's heart, and they were on it.

The black was laboring. It was impossible to drive the horse farther, hard-put as he had been on the road to Ivrel. And at last Vanye reined in, looked back and considered stopping. It was an uncomfortable place. Forest was on one side, high rocks upon the other.

"Let us be moving," Erij said.

"I am not going to kill this horse," Vanye protested, but he kept the animal at a walk all the same, and did not stop.

Then Erij spurred his own horse and the black dutifully matched the pace. Vanye smothered his temper and hoped that the horse would last to the gates of Ra-hjemur.

And they came upon tracked snow, where an unexpected road intersected theirs at an angle from the direction of Ivrel. Men afoot—horses—the short-footed sign of the smallish northerners, Hjemurn mixed with the larger prints of men: Andurin.

And blood upon the snow, and bodies lying in the road, abandoned.

Vanye swung down, Erij ordering him otherwise: he ignored his brother, went quickly from one body to the other, turning them to see the faces. Two were Lethen. The other three were the small, dark men of Hjemur, and one fair, like *qujal.* Relief flooded over him.

Erij hissed, drawing his attention: suddenly there was a stirring, a crunch of snow and a rattling of rocks, and he pulled himself out of his thoughts, looked up to see a dark shadow crouched upon the ledge overhanging the road.

He ran, sprang for the horse, hauled himself into the saddle as the startled animal began to run: he gathered reins awkwardly and tucked low as Erij did.

"Erij," he gasped when he could, "Hjemurn have come in behind, but Chya Liell and the Lethen are on the road ahead of us—the Hjemurn could not hold them. Ease off, ease off, or we will be riding into them."

"Then," said Erij, "we will be one enemy the less."

Morgaine too, and Roh, if they still lived: Erij, who held the sword, would as gladly kill them both as Chya Liell and Lethen: Nhi's bloodfeud with Chya was old and well-exercised, and that with Morgaine was as fresh as Irn-Svejur, and still painful.

"Give me a sword," Vanye asked of him then, for he had not so much as a dagger. "If not hers, then at least some / weapon."

"Not at my back," said Erij, insulting the oath there was between them. But that was Erij's privilege: it did not lessen the oath.

Vanye pressed his lips tightly in anger and kept with him, counting Erij for a madman, to press both horses so, to ride unshielded after any company containing Morgaine after his bitter lesson at Irn-Svejur. He regretted his oath for a new reason: that Erij would kill the both of them and hand *Changeling* to the enemy, madder than Chya Roh and almost as great an idiot.

The road was winding, the turns blind, woods and rocks cutting off their view upon the right, trees almost taking the road in places upon the left.

And they met it, inevitably: the rear of Liell's column, men warned by their noise and braced to receive them with a hedge of spears, a bristling shadow in the dark.

Erij ripped *Changeling* loose and let its sheath slide, lost, nothing hesitating. He spurred his uncertain horse and drove the beast at the spears, while the blade flared into opal and a peculiar starry dark hovered at its tip. The Lethen that touched it were quickly nothing: others fled aside, closed in, in renewed determination as Vanye tried to ride through, but few, few of them. Instead came dark, fur-clad bodies off the ridge, dropping thick upon his path— Hjemurn, howling their blood-chilling cries. In his last clear sight of the column ahead he saw a glimmer of white—Siptah among those horses: and the Lethen riders began to run, abandoning those on foot, perhaps knowing what pursued them.

Dark bodies poured between. Vanye kicked his faltering horse, himself and the beast being pulled down together. A spear rammed at his ribs and rocked him badly. Weaponless, he seized the shaft with both hands and tried to wrench it free from its owner.

Then the horse collapsed, and arms encircled him, pulling him to the ground at the same moment. A blade flashed down and rebounded off his mail, surprising the would-be killer. Others hacked at him, with the same result, bruising, driving the wind from him. He was smothered in bodies and sinking into dark.

And as suddenly released.

He scrambled for his feet, still dazed, and sprawled in the stained snow. Screams were in his ears, then silence, a howl of wind, hollow and abruptly silenced too.

He struggled to one knee as steps crunched up to him, looked dazedly upon Erij, who held the sword in the sheath. There were no bodies, and there were no Hjemurn to be seen, only themselves, and the horses standing side by side.

Quickly, he twisted about to look in the direction the riders had taken. There was nothing to be seen there either.

"The riders," Vanye said. "Killed or fled?"

"Fled," said Erij. "If you had not fallen—but that must be the Chya blood in you. Get up."

He rose, steadied unexpectedly by Erij's hand, and he was surprised into a closer look at his brother, that same dark expression he had known in Ra-morij—anger compounded by something else violent; but the hand that still held him was solidly gentle.

"Why stay for me?" Vanye taunted him, for he truly suspected some brotherly sentiment in the man. "Did you want revenge that badly?"

Erij's lips trembled in anger. "Bastard that you are, I will not leave even Nhi refuse for the Hjemurn. Get mounted."

And out of the contradictions that were Erij, he pushed him and hit him at once, no cuff, but a blow that brought him to one knee, dizzy as he was. Vanye gathered himself to rise, went after Erij, and halted as Erij's own longsword hit the snow between them. He seized it up without hesitating.

And there was Erij by his horse, glaring at him with hate and fear staring naked out of his eyes.

If he had not known Erij he would have thought him mad as Kasedre himself; but of a sudden he knew the feeling himself, an old one, and familiar. Erij did fear him. Maimed by him, his former skill cut away by him, Erij feared, and likely wakened in the night in such dreams as Vanye himself knew, dreams of Rijan, of Kandrys, and a morning in the armory court.

Father loved perfection, Erij had told him once. *He hated leaving Nhi to a cripple.*

He never forgave me either, for being the one of us two legitimate sons that lived. And for being less than perfect afterward.

But Erij had sense enough finally to arm him, in spite of all instincts otherwise. A one-handed man coming alone into

Hjemur . . . he perhaps feared to die less than he feared to be proved weak.

Vanye bowed an awkward respect to his brother. "Likely we will die," he said, that sure knowledge a weight of guilt at his heart. "Erij, lend me *Changeling* instead. I do swear to you, I will go through with it—myself. Whatever can be done by a man carrying that thing, I will do. I will hand you Ra-hjemur if I live, and if I do not, then it was impossible anyway. Erij, I mean it. I owe you to do that."

Erij gave a short and uneasy laugh, tucked his handless arm behind him. "Your gratitude is unnecessary, bastard brother. The fact is, I dropped the sword-sheath and came back after it."

"You came back in time," Vanye insisted doggedly. "Erij, do not make it nothing. I know what you did; and I say I would do this."

"You are expert in treachery, and I am not about to trust you, especially where *she* is concerned. You are trying to delay me now, and there is an end of it. Get mounted."

He could not hold the course Erij set. He came near to falling as they took a slippery downslope, hung on grimly, but dropped a rein. The horse stopped at the bottom as a consequence, well-trained, stood with its own sides heaving between his knees, and Vanye slowly bent over the saddle, trying to clear his vision and making no effort to recover the lost rein.

Erij rode close to him, hit his horse and started it forward. He clung, but the horse stopped again, and he disregarded Erij and used his remaining strength to climb down and walk, leading his horse, toward a place where a flat rock promised a place to sit. He walked like a drunken man, and ached so that he more fell down than sat down when he reached it. He lay over on his side, tucked his limbs up against the cold and simply ignored Erij's attempts to rouse him: a time to let the pain leave his gut—it was all he asked.

Erij pulled at him roughly, and Vanye realized finally that Erij was attempting to lift his head upon his maimed arm; and himself took the wine flask and drank.

"You are chilled," Erij said distantly. "Sit, sit up."

He understood then that Erij was trying to put his cloak about him, and leaned against his brother, warmed against him so that finally he began to shiver and abused muscles began to knot up in reaction to cold.

"Drink," said Erij again. He drank. Then, briefly, he slept.

He meant it to be brief, only a closing of his eyes. But he awoke with the sun warming him, and Erij sitting nearby with *Changeling* tucked within his arms as Morgaine was wont to rest. Erij did not sleep: Vanye's first move brought him alert and sharp-eyed with suspicion.

"There is food," said Erij after a moment. "Get to horse and we will eat in the saddle. We have wasted enough time."

He did not contest the order, but dragged his aching limbs up and obeyed. There was an edge to the wind when they were out of the fold of the hill; he was glad of the little bit of wine Erij shared with him, and the coarse, crumbling bread and strong cheese. Food put strength into him. He looked at his brother in the daylight and saw a man equally haggard, shadow-eyed, hollow-cheeked, unshaven; but at a sane pace and with provisions to last them, he reckoned their chances of reaching Ra-hjemur better, at least, than he had reckoned them last night.

"They are surely making little better time than we," he said to Erij. "Ahead of us that they are . . . still, there is a limit to their horses, and their strength."

"It is possible that we can overtake them," said Erij. "It is at least possible."

Erij seemed soberly sane after the impulses of the night had run themselves out: for a moment there seemed even implied apology in his tone. Vanye snatched at it instantly.

"I am stronger," Vanye said. "I could go on. Listen to me. You have made a kind of Claiming; and once I am quit of my oath to her, then I serve your interests at that point, and I will hold Ra-hjemur for you."

"And of course the witch would let you."

"She has no ambitions for Ra-hjemur: only to settle with Thiye and then to go her own way. She will not come back. She is no threat to you, none. Erij, I beg you, I earnestly beg you, do not seek to kill her."

"You have to ask that, of course, being *ilin* to her; I respect that. But knowing that—of course I have to go with you into Ra-hjemur and above all I will not put this blade into your loyal hands, bastard brother. You had me willing to believe you once, and that cost me, that cost me bitterly in lives and in honor. Do not expect me to make the same mistake twice."

Then, Vanye concluded, he must obtain the blade from Erij by force or by theft, or somehow deceive Erij so that Erij himself would do what had to be done—oath-breaking and murder at once.

And ever since he had known of Morgaine what must be done, he had begun to suspect what manner of death there would be for him when he had obeyed her orders.

Its field directed at its own source of power would effect the ruin of all the Gates, she had said. And: *Cast back within the Gate itself, it would be the same: unsheathe it and hurl it through. Either way should be sufficient.*

Changeling fed upon the Witchfires of Ivrel. The black void beyond the Gate was that tiny nothingness that glimmered at *Changeling*'s tip, to seize whole men and whirl them through, winds howling into skies where men could not survive, as the dragon had perished in the snow . . . other skies where there was never day. *Changeling* aimed at the Gate would be void aimed at void. wind sucking into wind, ripping at its own substance and drawing all things in.

And perhaps even Ra-hjemur itself would follow it, and all within it. The force that had taken ten thousand men upon the winds at Irien and left no trace behind could not be so delicate as to take one man, if rent wide open, destroying itself.

He thought with a shudder of the retreating faces of those he had seen drawn into the field, the horror, the bewilderment, like men new arrived in Hell.

This would be theirs, this ending for the surviving sons of Nhi Rijan, for all their hate and striving against each other.

He kept his face turned from Erij until the wind had dried the tears upon his face, and gave himself up finally to do what he had given oath to do.

There lay before them the greatest valley in the north, and of Hjemur's hold, a grassy land ringed about by snow-capped peaks, fair to be seen save in one place, and that bare and blighted, even from such a distance.

"That," said Vanye, pointing to the ugliness, and thinking of the waste the Gates made about them, "that would be Ra-hjemur." And when he strained his eyes he could see the imagining of a rise there, a hill such as might be Ra-hjemur, hazy in distance.

They had not, after all, overtaken Liell. There lay the road. Nothing moved upon it. They seemed alone in all the land.

"It is too fair," said Erij, "too open. I should feel naked upon that road, by daylight."

"By night?"

"That seems the only good sense."

"I can tell you better," Vanye said, persistent to the last. "That you let me do this."

Erij stared at him and seemed to estimate him, so fearful in his own expression that fear of discovery wound itself through Vanye's belly. Almost he expected some harsh words, some flaring suspicion.

"What is it?" Erij asked, his tone curiously earnest. "What is it you expect down there? Has she warned you?"

"Brother," said Vanye, "the both of you have me by oath; and if my proper *liyo* is alive and with them . . . I have one responsibility to Morgaine, another to you. Between the two of you, you will be the death of me, and I could think more clearly if there were not the two of you in one place, about to go for each other's throats."

"I will give you this much," said Erij, "that if she does not seem to need killing, I will not. I have never killed a woman. I do not like the idea."

"Thank you for that," Vanye said earnestly.

And then, thinking of Liell: "Erij. If it comes to being captured—die. Those tales of Thiye's long life are true. If they took you, your body would go on ruling either in Ra-hjemur or Morija, but it would not be your soul in it."

Erij swore softly. "Truth?"

"For my sake, you have an ally if Morgaine is alive. Help me set her free and our chances of living become a thousand-fold better."

Erij merely stared at him, hard-eyed.

"I am almost as ignorant as you are," Vanye protested. "I do not know the half of what is contained down there. I think she does. And for her own sake she would take our side. It is sure that no one else would. If you are going to start by killing our only possible ally in this business, or in keeping her helpless, well, then, you might as well tie me hand and foot before we go, since I am hers for a time yet . . . the hands, of which her science is the mind in this matter: and you would be wiser if you make use of both."

Erij gave him no answer, yet it seemed he thought seriously about his words, and they rode down together into a wooded place where they could no longer see the valley.

"We will rest here a time." said Erij, "and come in by night. Will Thiye resist Liell's entry?"

"I do not know," answered Vanye. "I think Morgaine thinks Thiye once was master and Liell his servant, at least

at Irien; and that they had some falling-out. But if Liell brings
Morgaine to Thiye, she may be the key that opens doors for
him. And then, I think, if the same ambitions move *qujal*
as move human men—which I do not know—then there may
be treachery, and we may have either Thiye or Liell to deal
with, whichever one wins the throw. I think perhaps Liell has
waited a very long time to find some key that would admit
him to Ra-hjemur. But this is my estimation: Morgaine said
nothing of her own reckoning of their plans." He added, as
Erij sat still upon his horse, listening, "I am not sure that
Thiye is *qujal* or whether he is not simply some human man
who employed a *qujal* for a servant and is now about to reap
his reward for meddling; meddler is what Morgaine called
him, and ignorant, and the Witchfires have no healthful effect
on anything living. For some reason, if rumor is true, at least,
he has let himself grow old. So Thiye may not be *qujal* at all,
and I know that Morgaine is not, whatever you believe—but
Liell is. That is the sum of it, Erij. Thiye is the matter of my
oath, but I extend that oath to Liell most of all: and in good
sense, you will let me do that."

"You wish to free the witch, that is what."

"Yes. But in doing that, I will kill Liell, who is a threat to
both our causes, and I want your help in it, Erij. I want you
to understand that I have business in Ra-hjemur beyond
Thiye, and that freeing Morgaine would not be treachery
against you."

Erij slid down. Vanye did not, and Erij looked up at him,
face drawn against the winter sun. "There is one clear point
in all of this: you will guard my life and help me take
Ra-hjemur for myself. That is the sum of matters."

"You have taken my oath," Vanye said, miserable at heart.
"I know that that is the sum of matters."

There was no moon, and clouds had moved in. There was
that help, at least.

Ra-hjemur sat upon a low, barren hill, a citadel surely of
the *qujal*, for it was simply a vast cube, unadorned, un-
towered, without protecting ring-walls or any defense evident
to the eye. A stony path ran up to its gate; no grass grew
upon it, but then, no grass grew anywhere on the hill.

They crouched a time by the bend of the knoll where they
had left their horses, merely surveying the place. There was no
stir of life.

Erij looked at him as if seeking his opinion.

"The sword can breach the door," Vanye said. "But beware of traps, brother, and mind that I am behind you: I do not care to die by the same chance that Ryn did.

Erij nodded understanding, then slipped from cover, seeking other shadows, Vanye quick to follow. They came not directly up the road to the gate, but up under the walls, and in their shadow, to the gate itself.

It was graven with runes upon its metal pillars, but the gate was iron and wood, like the door of many an ordinary fortress; and when Erij drew *Changeling* and touched its black field to the joining of the doors the air sang with the groan of metals. The doors parted their joinings, and the pillars too, and stone rumbled, loosed from its supports. Dust choked them, and when it cleared a mass of rubble partly blocked the entry.

Erij gazed but a moment at the destruction he had wrought, then clambered over the rubble and sought the echoing inside of the place, which burned with light no fires supplied.

Vanye hurried through, asweat with dread, snatched up a sizable rock in the process, and as Erij started to look back at him, smashed it to Erij's helmeted skull. It was not enough. Erij fell, but still retained half-senses and heaved up with the blade.

Vanye saw it coming, twisted to evade the shimmer, kicked Erij's arm so that it wrung from him a cry of pain, and the sword fell.

He snatched it up then, gazed down on his brother, whose face was contorted with fury and fear. Erij cursed him, deliberately and with thought, such that it chilled his blood.

He took the sheath from Erij, who did not resist him; and upon an impulse to pity for Erij, he cast down Erij's own longsword.

Arrows flew.

He heard their loosing even before he whirled and knew they had come from the stairs, but *Changeling* in his warding hand made an easy path to elsewhere for the arrows, and they both remained unharmed. He knew the sword's properties, had seen Morgaine wield it, and knew its uses in ways Erij did not. Erij would as likely have taken an arrow as not.

And perhaps Erij understood that fact, or understood at the least that continuing their private dispute could be fatal to them both: Erij gathered up the longsword with but a glowering promise in his eyes, and rose, following as Vanye began to lead the way.

Killing a man from behind was an easy matter, even were he in mail; but Erij needed more hands than one: he risked everything on it.

And quickly he dismissed the threat of Erij from his mind, overwhelmed by the alien place. Breath almost failed him when he considered the size of the hall, the multitude of doors and stairs. Morgaine had sent him here ignorant, and there was nothing to do but probe every hall, every hiding place, until he either found what he was seeking or his enemies found his back.

Save that, held straight before them, *Changeling* gave forth a brighter glow, and when lifted, sent a coursing of impulses through the dragon-hilt, such that it seemed to live.

Carefully, Erij treading in his wake, he took the stairs to the level above.

They found a hall very like the one below, save that at its end there was a metal door, of that shining metal very like the pillars of the Witchfires. *Changeling* began to emit a sound, a bone-piercing hum that made his fingers ache; it grew stronger as he neared it. He ran toward that gate, figuring speed their best defense against a rally from Hjemurn: and froze, startled, as that vast door lightly parted to welcome him.

And startled more by the sight of gleaming metal and light that stretched away into distance, glowing with colors and humming with the power of the fires themselves. *Changeling* throbbed, his arm growing numb from holding it.

The field directed at its own source of power would effect the ruin of all the Gates.

The pulsing of conflicting powers reached up his arm into his brain, and he did not know whether the blade's wailing was in the air or in his own outraged senses.

He lifted it, expecting death, found instead that it did not much worsen, save when he angled it right. Then the pain increased.

"Vanye," Erij shouted at him, catching his shoulder. He saw stark fear on his brother's face.

"This is the way," Vanye said to him. "Stay here, guard my back." But Erij did not. He knew his brother's presence close behind him as he entered that hall.

He understood now: it greatly disagreed with Morgaine's careful nature, to have expected him to carry out so important a thing with so few instructions. There had been no need: the sword itself guided them, by its impulses of sound and pain. After a time of walking down that glowing corridor of *qujalin* works, the sound wiped out other senses until nothing but vision was left.

And in that vision stood an old man, hairless and wrinkled and robed in gray, who held out hands to them and mouthed silent words, pleading. Blood marred his aged face.

Vanye lifted the sword, threatening with that dreadful point, but the vision would not yield, barring their path with his very life.

Thiye, some sense told him: Thiye Thiye's-son, lord of Hjemur.

All at once the old man fell, clawing at the air, and there was an arrow in the robes at his back, and the red blood spreading.

A figure stood clear of the hall behind, gray and green, the young lord of Chya, lowering his bow. With sudden, breathless haste, Roh started toward them, slinging his strung bow to his back.

Vanye sought *Changeling*'s sheath at once, hope surging in him. The sudden silence in the air as that point found its proper haven was overwhelming: his abused ears could hardly hear Roh's voice. He felt Roh's eager hands grasp his arms, distant even from that sensation.

"Vanye, cousin," Roh cried, ignoring the threat of his blood-enemy Erij who stood beside, sword in hand. "Cousin, Thiye—Liell—they are at odds. Morgaine escaped them both, but—".

"Is she alive?" Vanye demanded.

"Alive, aye, well alive. She had the hold, Vanye. She means to destroy it. Come, come, clear this place. It will tumble down stone from stone. Hurry."

"Where is she?"

Roh's eyes gestured up, toward the stairs. "Barricaded up there, with her weapons in her possession again, and willing to kill anyone who comes within range. Vanye, do not try to reach her. She is mad. She will kill you too. You cannot reason with her."

"Liell?"

"Dead. They are all dead, and most of Thiye's servants are fled. You are free of your oath, Vanye. You are free. Escape this place. There is no need of your dying."

Roh's fingers tugged at him, his dark eyes full of agony; but of a sudden Vanye broke the hold and began to run toward the stairs upward. Then he looked back. Roh hesitated, then began to run in the other direction, vanishing quickly toward the safety of the downward stairs, a wraith in green. Erij cast a look in either direction, as if torn between, then raced toward the ascending stairs, longsword in hand, pointed it at Vanye, his eyes wild.

"Thiye is dead," Erij said. "He is dead. Your oath to the witch is done. Now stop her."

The fact of it hit him like a hammer blow: he stared helplessly at Erij, owning the justice of his claim, trying to think where his obligation truly lay. Then he shook off everything and suspended thought: his duty to either one lay in reaching Morgaine with all possible speed.

He turned and ran, taking the steps two at a time, until he came up, breathless, into yet another hall like the one below.

And confronted Morgaine, as Roh had warned him, hale and well and facing them both with the deadly black weapon secure in her hand.

"*Liyo!*" he cried, flung up his empty hand as if that alone could ward off harm, and with the other cast *Changeling* at her feet.

"No!" Erij cried in fury, but bit off further protest as Morgaine smoothly gathered the sheathed blade up, yet keeping the black weapon trained upon them. Then she lowered it.

"Vanye," said Morgaine. "Well met."

And she joined them, and began to descend the stairs from which they had come, carefully, trusting Vanye at her back; of a sudden he surmised what she sought thus cautiously.

"Thiye is dead," he said.

Her gray eyes cast back an unexpected look of agony. "Your doing?"

"No. Roh's."

"Not Roh's," she said. "Thiye freed me—that being his only hope of defeating Liell and keeping his life. He gave me this slim chance. I would have saved his life if I could. Is Roh down there?"

"He ran," said Vanye, "saying you meant to destroy this place." Horrid suspicion came over him. "It was not Roh, was it?"

"No," said Morgaine. "Roh died at Ivrel, in your place."

And she raced then down the stairs, pausing only to be careful at the turning, and came into that dread hall of *qujalin* design.

It was empty, save for Thiye's sprawled corpse in a widening pool of blood.

Morgaine ran, her footsteps echoing upon the floor, and Vanye followed, knowing that Erij was still with them, and little caring at the time. Anger seethed in him for Liell's mocking treachery with him; and dread was in him too for what Morgaine might intend with these strange powers.

She reached the very end of the hall, where there rose a vast double pillar of lights, and her hand abandoned the sword upon the counter an instant, while she wove a sure, practiced pattern among the lights. Noise thundered from the walls, voices gibbered ghostlike in unknown languages. Lights flared up and down the pillars, and began to pulse in increasing agitation.

She made it all cease, as quick as a move of her hand, and leaned against the counter, head bowed, like one who had suffered some mortal blow.

Then she turned and lifted her head, her eyes fixed earnestly on Vanye's.

"You and your brother must quit this place as quickly as you can," she said. "Liell spoke the truth in one thing: it will be destroyed. The machine is locked in such a way I cannot free it, and Ra-hjemur will be rubble in the time a rider could reach Ivrel. You are free of your oath. You have paid it all. Good-bye."

And with that she brushed past him and walked quickly down the long aisle alone, headed for the stairs.

"*Liyo!*" he cried, stopping her. "Where are you going?"

"He has locked the Gate open on a place of his choosing, and I am going after him. I have not much time: he has a good start on me, and surely he has allowed only what he thinks enough time for himself. But he is timid, this Liell: I am hoping that he has given himself too much grace, too much margin."

And with that she turned again, and began to walk and more quickly, and at last to run.

Vanye started forward a pace. "Brother," Erij reminded him. He stopped. She vanished down the stairs.

When the last sound of her footsteps was gone he turned again, of necessity, to face the anger in his brother's face. He went down upon the chill floor and pressed his forehead to it, making the obeisance his oath made due Erij.

"Your humility is a little late," said Erij. "Get up. I like to see your eyes when you answer questions."

He did so.

"Did she tell the truth?" Erij asked then.

"Yes," said Vanye. "I think it was the truth. Or if you doubt it, at least doubt it from a day's-ride distance from here. If you see it still standing after that, then it was not the truth."

"What is this of Gates?"

"I do not know," he said, "only that sometimes there is another side to the Witchfires and sometimes not, and that once she goes, she will be nowhere we can reach. I am sorry. It was not a thing she explained clearly. But she will not be back. Ivrel is a Gate that will close when this place dies, and after that there will be no more Witchfires, no more Thiyes, no more magics in the world."

He looked around him at the place, for that complexity was like the living inside of some great beast, though its veins were conduits of lights and its heart and pulse glowed and faded slowly.

"If you do not want to die, Erij," he said, "I suggest we take her advice and be as far from here as possible when it happens."

The horses were where they had left them, patiently waiting in the gray dawn, cropping the sparse grass as if there were nothing unusual in the day. Vanye checked the girths and heaved himself up, and Erij did the same. They rode the open and faster road this time, pausing for a view of the great cube of Ra-hjemur, which looked, with its breached gate, like a creature with a mortal wound.

Then they set out together for Morija.

"There is no more lord of Hjemur," said Vanye at last. "You and Baien are all the clan-lords left of any stature at all. It is within your reach to gain the High Kingship without Hjemurn magics after all, and perhaps that will be better for human folk."

"Baien's lord is old," said Erij, "and has a daughter. I do not think that he will want a war to cloud his old age and ruin his land. I will perhaps be able to make an alliance with him. And Chya Roh left no heirs. His people will be less trouble to us. Pyvvn's lady is Chya, and with Chya in Koris in our hands, Pyvvn will submit." Erij sounded almost cheerful, counting his prospects and reckoning lightly of a few wars.

But Vanye gazed to the road ahead, where it wound out of sight and into view again toward the south, hoping earnestly to see her, seeing her in his mind, at least, as she had ridden that evening out of Aenor-Pyvvn's Gate.

"You are not listening," Erij accused him.

"Aye," he said, blinking and breaking the spell, and looking again toward Erij.

And ever and again after that, he saw Erij look curiously at him, and there was a growing sourness on Erij's face, as if whatever alliance there had been to make them brothers this dawn in Ra-hjemur were fast shredding asunder. He held out little hope for his peace as he saw that sullen estimation grow more and more grim.

"There is none of the high-clan blood in Morija left, but us," said Erij that noon, when the sun was almost warm, and they rode still knee to knee.

Oh Heaven, Vanye thought, looking out upon the sunlight and the hills with regret, *now it comes;* for he had long since come to the conclusion he was sure would occur to Erij: that, enemies as they were, Erij was mad to flaunt a high-clan prisoner in Morija. Without Ra-hjemur from which to rule, he had not power enough to bear a taint of dishonor—or a rival. Politics and ambitions would swarm about a bastard Chya like flies to honey. Such conclusions as Erij had no doubt reached were dishonorable, better meditated in the dark of night than in such a fair day.

"Bastard that you are," said Erij, "you could make yourself a threat to me, if you were minded to do so. There is no lord in Chya. It comes to me, bastard brother, that you are heir to Chya, if you were to claim it, and that no lord can be claimed as *ilin.*"

"I have not laid any claim to Chya," said Vanye. "I do not think I could, and I do not intend to."

"They had rather own you than me, I do not doubt it at all," said Erij. "And you are still the most dangerous man to me in all of Andur-Kursh, so long as you live."

"I am not," said Vanye, "because I regard my oath. But you do not regard your own honor enough to trust mine."

"You did not regard your oath in Ra-hjemur."

"You were not in danger from Morgaine. I did not have to."

Erij gazed long at him, then reached across. "Give me your hand," he said, and Vanye, puzzling, yielded it to his left-handed handclasp. His brother pressed it in almost friendly fashion.

"Leave," said Erij. "If I hear of you after this I will hunt you down . . . or if you come to Morija, I will set Claim on you and let you work off that year you owe me. But I do not think you will come to Morija."

And he gestured with a nod to the road ahead.

"If she will have you—go."

Vanye stared at him, then gripped his brother's strong, dry hand the more tightly before he broke the clasp.

Then he set heels to the horse, dismissing from his mind every thought that he was weaponless and that Morgaine would have opened a wide lead on them during the morning.

He would gain that distance back. He would find her. He realized much later to his grief that he had not even looked back once at his brother, that he had severed that tangled tie without half the pain he thought it must have cost Erij to let him go.

In that loosing, he thought, Erij had paid for everything; he wished that he had spoken some word of thanks.

Erij would have sneered at it.

He did not find her on the road. In the second day, he cut off the track the two had used, and took the one on which Liell had come from Ivrel, the one he thought Morgaine would surely choose. Ivrel was close and there was no more time left for stopping, though he was aching from the ride and the horse's breath came in great gasps, such that he must dismount and half pull the beast up the steeper places of the trail. The delay tormented him and he began to fear that he had lost the way, that he would lose her once for all.

And yet finally, finally, when he came out upon the height, there stood Ivrel's great side to be seen, and the barren shoulder of the mountain where the Gate would be. He urged the black to what speed the horse could bear and climbed, sometimes losing sight of his goal, sometimes finding it again, until he entered the forest of twisted pines and lost it altogether.

In the snow were footprints, the old ones of many men, and some of animals, and some of those not good to imagine what had made them; but now and again he could sort out new ones.

Roh-Liell-Zri, upon the black mare, most likely, and Morgaine upon his trail.

Breath hung frozen in the sunlight, and air cut the lungs. He had at last to walk the horse, out of mercy, and scanned the black sickly pines about him, remembering all too keenly that he had no weapons at all, and a horse too weary for headlong flight.

Then through those pines he caught a glimmer of movement, a white movement amid the blaze of sun on snow, and he whipped up his horse and made what speed he could on the trail.

"Wait!" he cried.

She waited for him. He came in beside her breathless with relief, and she leaned from the saddle and reached for his hand.

"Vanye, Vanye, you ought not to have followed me."

"Are you going through?" he asked.

She looked up at the Gate, shimmering dark again, stars and blackness above them in the daylight. "Yes," she said, and then looked down at him. "Do not delay me further. This following me is nonsense. I do not know how the Gate is behaving, whether that will bring me through to the same place that Zri has fled or whether it will fling me out elsewhere. And you do not belong. You were useful for a time. You with your *ilin*-codes and your holds and your kinships . . . this is your world, and I needed a man who could maneuver things as I needed them. You have served your purpose. Now there is an end of the matter. You are free, and be glad of it."

He did not speak. He supposed finally that he merely stared at her, until he felt her hand slip from his arm, and she moved away. He watched her begin the long slope, Siptah refusing it at first. She took firm grip on the reins and began to force the animal against his will, driving him brutally until he decided to go, gathering himself in a long climb into the dark.

And was gone.

We are not brave, we that play this game with Gates; there is too much we can lose, to have the luxury to be virtuous, and to be brave.

He sat still a moment, looked about the slope, and considered the tormented trees and the cold, and the long ride to Morija, cast off by her, begging Erij to bear his presence in Andur-Kursh.

And there was pain in every direction but one: as the sword had known the way to its own source, his senses did.

Of a sudden he laid heels to his horse and began to drive the beast upslope. There was only a token refusing. Siptah had gone: the black understood what was expected of him.

The gulf yawned before him, black and starry, without the wind that had howled there before. There was only enough breeze to let him know it was there.

And dark, utter dark, and falling. The horse heaved and twisted under him, clawing for support.

And found it.

They were running again, on a grassy shore, and the air was warm. The horse snorted in surprise, then extended himself to run.

A pale shape was on the hill before them, under a double moon.

"Liyo!" he shouted. "Wait for me!"

She paused, looking back, then slid off to stand upon the hillside.

He rode in alongside and slid down from his exhausted horse even before the animal had quite stopped moving. Then he hesitated, not knowing whether he would meet joy or rage from her.

But she laughed and flung her arms about him, and he about her, pressing her tightly until she flung back her head and looked at him.

It was the second time he had ever seen her cry.

DAW

PRESENTING C. J. CHERRYH

Two Hugos so far—and more sure to come!

The Morgaine novels
GATE OF IVREL   (#UE1956—$2.50)
WELL OF SHIUAN   (#UE1986—$2.95)
FIRES OF AZEROTH   (#UE1925—$2.50)

The Faded Sun novels
THE FADED SUN: KESRITH   (#UE1960—$3.50)
THE FADED SUN: SHON'JIR   (#UE1889—$2.95)
THE FADED SUN: KUTATH   (#UE1856—$2.75)

DOWNBELOW STATION   (#UE1828—$2.75)
MERCHANTER'S LUCK   (#UE1745—$2.95)
PORT ETERNITY   (#UE1769—$2.50)
WAVE WITHOUT A SHORE   (#UE1957—$2.95)
SUNFALL   (#UE1881—$2.50)
BROTHERS OF EARTH   (#UE1869—$2.95)
THE PRIDE OF CHANUR   (#UE1694—$2.95)
SERPENT'S REACH   (#UE1682—$2.50)
HUNTER OF WORLDS   (#UE1872—$2.95)
HESTIA   (#UE1680—$2.25)
VOYAGER IN NIGHT   (#UE1920—$2.95)
THE DREAMSTONE   (#UE2013—$2.95)
TREE OF SWORDS AND JEWELS   (#UE1850—$2.95)